"I Made a Choice, Jennifer,"

Michael said. "To take a chance on you. On us. I realized something. We're alike, you and I. We both started out with these wild, high hopes of how good things were going to be. I was going to be the healer of messed-up heads, setting lives right. And you were going to bring good news to a nutzo world. Two optimists. Flagrantly out of step with the rest of the universe.

"Oh, Jennifer, Jennifer . . ." He took her hand in his, and his presence wove a magical spell. "Let's try," he said. "I want to do the impossible, make this work between us."

Dear Reader:

There is an electricity between two people in love that makes everything they do magic, larger than life. This is what we bring you in SILHOUETTE INTIMATE MOMENTS.

SILHOUETTE INTIMATE MOMENTS are longer, more sensuous romance novels filled with adventure, suspense, glamor or melodrama. These books have an element no one else has tapped: excitement.

We are proud to present the very best romance has to offer from the very best romance writers. In the coming months look for some of your favorite authors such as Elizabeth Lowell, Nora Roberts, Erin St. Claire and Brooke Hastings.

SILHOUETTE INTIMATE MOMENTS are for the woman who wants more than she has ever had before. These books are for you.

Karen Solem
Editor-in-Chief
Silhouette Books

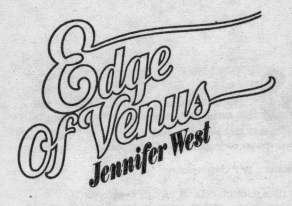

Edge Of Venus

Jennifer West

Silhouette Intimate Moments
Published by Silhouette Books New York
America's Publisher of Contemporary Romance

Silhouette Books by Jennifer West

Star Spangled Days (IM #31)
Edge of Venus (IM #71)

SILHOUETTE BOOKS, a Division of Simon & Schuster, Inc.
1230 Avenue of the Americas, New York, N.Y. 10020

Distributed by Pocket Books

ISBN: 0-671-50720-6

First Silhouette Books printing October, 1984

10 9 8 7 6 5 4 3 2 1

America's Publisher of Contemporary Romance

Printed in the U.S.A.

To my friend, the real "Michael T. Messiah"

Chapter 1

Steam from the Styrofoam cup of coffee rose up, swirling into the white haze of June coastal fog. With her free hand, Jennifer Winters checked the numbers on her digital watch: four a.m., an ungodly hour. It seemed idiotic to have risked getting a speeding ticket in order to be on time to do nothing more than wait.

Shivering, trying to remain alert, she pulled the turtle-neck higher, burying her chin into the folds of the sweater. Physics. She should have studied physics in college. Or computer science. Had she only listened to her father, her mother, her high school counselor, she would be in a nice warm car with a heater that worked, not sitting in the vintage wreck of an MG roadster without a top.

But instead she had chosen to study journalism, and in making that decision had sentenced herself to low pay, strange hours, and long reflective sessions over the meaning of truth in society. In fact, that had been her master's thesis.

The committee assigned to read it had made glowing notations on her insight, commending her on her treatise, "Integrative Perspective on Reality Versus Myth." Her grade had been an A, and the paper was subsequently published in a scholastic journal. Now, five years later, she would write a different paper on the subject of reality. She doubted that it would get an A; the truth, she had learned, was rarely well received.

The air was heavy with moisture, the silence around her acute, straining with anticipation. Or so it seemed.

Los Angeles was not usually a city given to deep silences. The energy of so many manic seeking souls permeated the atmosphere with ceaseless activity. It did not matter where these spiritual refugees had come from, whether from a gray Eastern steel town or an Asiatic city rife with terror; they all had related to the one moment when they could not bear their existences as they were, where they were. So they came to L.A. with suitcases and emotion-charged fantasies of how it was going to be different for them, and then lived out their lives sparring with the realities hiding behind the lure of palm trees and blue skies and leased Mercedes Benzes. It was a city peopled with millions of Don Quixotes. It was a city that Jennifer loved not only because it was home, but also because she, too, found it a fine place to tilt at windmills.

Across the street the studio's main entrance loomed like a massive sentinel in the gloom. An expanse of spiked iron bars guarded the entertainment fortress, its exterior designed during a more quixotic age in Hollywood's history to resemble a fairy-tale castle. A uniformed man moved back and forth inside a guard shack. Lit as it was by a single yellow bulb, the cage took on the image of a glowing, all-seeing eye scanning for intruders.

Jennifer shrank lower into the MG's seat.

Ten minutes passed. There were two false alarms: first, a delivery van; next, a late model Chevrolet let out a young woman who flashed her card at the gate, was admitted, and hurried to her job.

More waiting.

It was twenty minutes later when the low hum of an automobile's engine could be heard through the mist. Jennifer looked up, tensing slightly as her rearview mirror caught the flash of headlights cutting through the dark haze.

She began to hope again.

The dark blue knitted cap she wore ended just above a pair of eyes a shade or two lighter than the wool; eyes that now clung like magnets to the white Biarritz Cadillac passing slowly by on her right. The vehicle stopped across the street.

All right, Jenny whispered, excitement rising in her like a flare. It was *her:* Darla Hart, in person.

Still with her eyes on the Cadillac, Jenny removed her keys from the ignition and wedged them into her jeans pocket. Ready to go, a human rocket about to launch, she felt for the purse on the seat beside her.

The driver's side of the Cadillac swung open.

Jennifer put her hand on the MG's door handle.

Across the street a man emerged from the Biarritz. She studied him in the yellow glow cast from the guard shack. He wore form-fitting jeans and a leather jacket, continental style; expensive, she assessed quickly, storing away the data for future use.

The man walked around to the passenger side. He was facing her now and Jennifer saw that he looked to be in his early thirties. Dark hair cut short, but full, slightly wavy. Would she rate him handsome? No, but attractive; add *very*. Strong, compelling features. She did a fast mental cross-reference to current screen idols . . . De Niro, Pacino.

Power and character. *Ooo-la-la,* she thought, and just as quickly dismissed her random imaginings. *This was business.*

He moved back, his hand held out to assist the woman who took it and stepped onto the sidewalk, into the pool of light.

Jennifer's breath caught.

Darla Hart was magnificent. At four in the morning she was swathed in a full-length white mink, her silver hair shining under the light.

But America's premier advice columnist did not look happy. Jennifer leaned forward and tried unsuccessfully to read more from the expression.

There followed a brief, animated conversation between Darla and her escort before the columnist appeared to move reluctantly to the gate, the white mink flowing behind her like the train of a queen. A fitting image, Jennifer considered, watching the living legend disappear into the studio.

She waited, aggravated, counting off the lost and precious seconds while the man walked back to the car, started the engine, and finally, at long last, steered the Cadillac out from the curb. She couldn't have risked him challenging her story. The red taillights dissolved into the fog.

She threw open her door and started across the street, walking quickly to gain time. Free of the cap, her hair fell to her shoulders in a haphazard mass, its shade that of bleached wheat. The leonine mane was a natural God-assigned attribute, happening to coincide with a current fashion trend. It was the only time in her life that Jennifer could remember having had the right style at the right time.

Once in clear view of the gate she prudently reduced her speed to a studied amble and continued the rest of the way seemingly engrossed in a search through the contents of her purse.

At the glass cage she raised the small plastic-coated card. It bore the magical inscription, Press Pass.

The guard slid open the window.

"Morning," she said, not so cheerily to be suspicious but went heavy on the personal charm, smiling at the guard who scrutinized her without expression or comment.

On impulse she cast an anxious glance past the gate. There was no sign of Darla. *Not to worry. She would ask directions.*

"Name?" the guard was saying.

"Jennifer Winters. Station KZAM. Interview with Miss Hart." No sense in lying about her identity. It was all on her I.D. anyway.

The guard consulted his clipboard. His finger traced down a computer printout. "No Jennifer Winters on the list." His look and the accompanying shrug was a "nice try" dismissal. She could read body language as easily as the morning headlines.

"I definitely have an interview with Darla Hart," Jennifer said, her voice laced with indignation.

No sale. The guard closed the sliding window separating them, the subject of the interview being likewise closed.

Jennifer smiled wanly in defeat. The man knew his business. But why not? In a city filled with an overabundance of frauds, of would-be moguls and stars, and garden-variety wheeler-dealers, anyone with a little experience and a nose could sniff out the pretenders from the genuine articles.

In a way the two of them were in the same business.

She turned, looking down the street, thinking about what she was going to do. The fog was lifting with the on-coming daylight.

Then, suddenly seized with inspiration, she sprinted back across the street to her car.

She wasn't down yet. She had better not be; she liked to eat and her job was on the line.

Being raised in Los Angeles afforded her a certain edge over the others on the news research staff of *Everyday*. When she was young, her family had moved from neighborhood to neighborhood as her father's fortunes steadily improved. Her knowledge of its streets, along with a personal acquaintance with its demographics, was as solid as the knowledge of her own apartment.

It stood to reason that a man in the company of someone like Darla Hart would not be from the surrounding lackluster neighborhood. If she had to, she'd bet on Beverly Hills or Bel Air, possibly the Marina Del Rey. Unless he was a masochist, he'd take the freeway and get home fast before the morning traffic clogged the city's streets.

She was right, and fortunately for her he was slow. The Cadillac was just easing its way onto the freeway when she came speeding up behind it, then dropped back a discreet distance as soon as she was certain it was the correct car.

Darla Hart's fame had begun five years ago when her first personal advice columns were syndicated nationally. Later, newspapers throughout the world carried her sage instructions on how to handle the real and imagined miseries of life. Her appeal was universal, crossing age and sexual boundaries; a Japanese businessman was every bit as likely to find solace in Darla Hart's prescription for psychic peace as a Midwestern housewife.

But no one had ever seen Darla Hart until yesterday morning. The *Today* show had presented an exclusive interview with the columnist, televised live from Los Angeles; the second segment was scheduled to air within two more hours.

Jennifer guessed that half of America had tuned in to get its first glimpse of the woman who had made a career out of saving hearts and souls on the brink of disintegration. What they had seen was a woman of about forty-five, extremely attractive, with silver hair and wide green eyes; a woman whose manner was calm, whose voice soothed, and who gave no clue whatsoever as to what lay behind the public persona that so charmed the world.

Well, the man in the Biarritz knew Darla Hart; and soon he was going to know Jennifer Winters, too. "The Real Darla Hart" would make one hell of a story. And Jennifer would be able to pay her rent.

Chapter 2

THE SUN HAD JUST BEGUN TO BREAK WHEN THE CADILLAC turned right onto the coast highway. The landscape glowed as if covered by a translucent mantle of golden gauze.

To Jennifer's left lay the Pacific. Surfers in wet suits had begun to assemble on the side of the road. Some removed surfboards from the racks of cars, others stood in clusters talking, their boards balanced upright at their sides like tribal shields. Above, an enterprising gull lanced the air with a hunter's cry. From the corner of her eye Jennifer watched as the gull swooped over steep sand cliffs blazing with the vermilion fire of ice plant. A mate joined it and together they headed for the sea.

To her right, high on a promontory and barely visible between palms and pines to those who knew where to look, was a reconstructed Roman villa housing the Getty art collection.

She had forgotten. There was more to life than chasing Cadillacs at dawn. There were such things as beach burgers. There were strolls to be taken through rooms of cool marble where one could commune with armless Grecian statues. There were long lunches filled with idle gossip, one's only obligation being to sip frothy drinks from coconut shells. Reasons to live that had no reason. How could she have forgotten about all of that?

But the vague sense of dissatisfaction dissolved as in front of her the Cadillac swerved suddenly into the right lane. It continued at a reduced speed for twenty or so yards, then veered off the road.

What was this?

Then she saw that he had parked in front of a twenty-four hour convenience store.

She cruised by slowly and noted that he had left his car and was headed for the store's entrance. Doubling back, she found a place for the MG several spaces from his.

The cashier looked up when she entered. He looked middle-aged and tough, possibly an ex-career Marine who could handle the kind of trouble that sometimes came in the small hours of the morning. Her mind went to Sung Ock, the Korean proprietor of the Stop N' Go market near her apartment. Sung, who was small and gentle and kind, who kept an American flag on display in his store, had been the victim of frequent robberies. Dismayed at the violence that seemed to have followed him across the ocean to his new home, he nevertheless refused to keep a gun on hand. But this man, at this counter, would have a gun. It would be loaded and he would use it upon provocation. Jennifer could almost smell the latent violence hovering in the atmosphere. But maybe that was good, she thought; maybe that same sensory perception worked as a deterrent to those who came to take rather than to pay.

She smiled a greeting. He returned a half-nod and continued to read what looked like a racing form for Santa Anita.

A moment of confused panic filled her. The man she had been following was not there. Then, from behind an aisle, he rose up holding a loaf of bread. He was looking straight at her.

Casually, she glanced away, as if she hadn't noticed him. But the intensity of the dark brown eyes had shaken her. The master of surprise had been caught off-guard by her quarry. Could he know she had been tracking him? No, impossible.

Out of desperation, Jennifer found herself moving to the rear of the store near the frozen food section. She felt as if those dark eyes had read into her, had leafed through her mind as if he were turning pages. At the milk section she opened the glass doors, stared at the cardboard cartons. Just as she had dissected the store's manager, she had been evaluated by Darla Hart's companion.

Preposterous, of course. She was merely projecting her own motives onto him.

"Excuse me."

Jennifer started, and swung around and into the man who had come up behind her. Instinctively, his hand shot out to steady her. "Oh, sorry!" she said.

"No problem," he returned lightly, smiling down at her.

She realized then that he wasn't as tall as she first thought. Perhaps he was six feet, no more than that. Embarrassed, she drew away from him. The firm touch of his grip on her shoulder lingered like phantom fingers.

"Milk," he said.

He was looking behind her, over her shoulder. It took her a moment to understand she was in his way. Quickly, she stepped to the side. While he took out a half-gallon of milk, she surveyed the next compartment's display of yogurt.

"Did you get what you needed?" He had turned back to her again. The glass door was held ajar as he waited for her answer.

"Oh, yes, I got it, thanks." Her hands were empty. You jerk, Winters, she thought. "That is, I changed my mind."

With his arm extended he guided the door closed. Another fraction of an inch and he would have grazed her breast. Her senses were filled by his presence, with the smell of his leather jacket, by a hint of musk cologne. An unbidden image of him having just awakened in bed, black hair mussed, the tactile impression of warm skin, taut sinewy limbs stretched over sheets, prompted her to interrupt her wild imaginings with the sound of her own voice.

"I remembered that I've milk at home." The statement came out bald, a beat too late to be part of the natural flow of conversation.

He was looking at her curiously. Behind the dark eyes she sensed amusement. Did he think she was trying to pick him up? For a second she was indignant, then almost laughed herself. That had been her plan, hadn't it? To use herself as bait. Only something had gone wrong.

For an instant she thought he was going to ask her something, but the moment passed uneventfully. He nodded perfunctorily, as if putting a period on the end of an unspoken sentence, and went on to shop.

She crossed through the space he had just vacated; the air felt charged, as if emotions lingered where he had stood.

Head bent, now and then examining a can, she continued through the aisles. Occasionally she would raise her eyes to see where he was. One by one he had placed each of his purchases on the counter. Eggs. Bread. Milk. Now he put down a can of orange juice. Big scoop, huh, Winters? News alert!: Man eats balanced breakfast.

She was trying to think of what to do. But first she had to decide which one of them was the butterfly and which the collector with the net? It was discouraging. Questions and answers were her stock-in-trade. So far, the only thing she knew about him was that breakfast was a part of his destiny.

As he began to pay for his purchases a wave of panic replaced her paranoia with reality. She had blown it. Somehow he had managed to out-finesse her in her own game. The way it was supposed to have happened was routine. They were to meet accidentally, which they had. She was to smile. He was to melt. While she shopped, he would hover in the aisles nearby, watching her. By the time she had paid for her groceries, he would have screwed up his courage enough to insist on carrying her bag to her car. He would close the trunk, then with the two of them standing awkwardly in silence, he would shyly suggest lunch and dinner. He would probably include a disclaimer about how he realized the situation of their meeting was unusual, but his intentions were proper.

That, at least, was the way it was supposed to have happened. Instead, he had smiled and she had melted. It was disorienting. In a flash, to bolster her sagging confidence, she replayed more successful scenarios from the past in her mind.

Her biggest asset in her work had always been her looks. Through a quirk of DNA, she was the living incarnation of the California Girl, the smiling, tanned, wholesome but sexy blond kitten of ten thousand glossy magazine advertisements and as many television soft drink commercials. But to have an appearance that was a cliché was not in all ways wonderful. She had paid a stiff penalty in her personal life for the outer cover that prompted a mistaken identity of the inner contents. And so, out of an ironic sense of cosmic justice, she had turned what other people considered to be a physical advantage (although experienced as an annoyance verging on minor tragedy to her) into a professional asset. An ordinary smile could open an ordinary door. A well-directed smile over a lunch or dinner could open secret compartments. In such instances she would recall the old adage "It takes a thief to catch a thief," transposing it to her own situation. Many, in attempting to capitalize on her apparent innocence, manipulated themselves to disadvantage.

The past was little consolation now. With a kind of forlorn acceptance of defeat, she watched the man leave the store without so much as a backward glance in her direction. So much for fatal charm.

Seconds later she followed him into the parking lot. He was already starting the Cadillac's engine. Giving it one last try, she flashed her best smile as she passed by on the way to the MG. He wasn't paying any attention. That somehow made it worse. What use was artillery if there was no one on the opposing side?

Dejectedly, she opened the door to the MG. Glancing to the Cadillac, she saw the man leave the car. He slammed the door shut, turned, and looked in her direction. A wave of relief flooded through her. She hadn't lost after all.

But instead of coming her way, he went back into the store.

The look on his face hadn't reflected lust; no, he was a man trying to remember if he should get bacon or kippers or butter, something decidedly mundane. She was an inconsequential, if not an invisible entity in the scope of his concerns.

To have begun her enterprise with such confidence and to have seen her energies wasted was disappointment enough.

But to have a spark of hope revive from the ashes all for nothing was downright devastating. She was feeling like a fool when she turned the key in the MG's ignition.

Nothing.

She tried again. More of the same dead nothing. Still, the time had not come to panic yet. The MG was a pure neurotic. During the five years they had shared adventures, she had had no other choice but to learn to treat it gently when it gave in to one of its periodic mechanical sulks. She waited a moment before slowly pumping the gas pedal, then tried the key again. Suddenly the engine caught and turned over. It died a moment later, just as suddenly. The sound of silence was absolute, her dismay similarly total. Her whole Darla Hart scheme was down the tubes. There had been a good chance that she might have made it back to the studio in time to follow Darla to wherever she was staying. Or she might have continued to follow the man, although that would be risky since they had met face-to-face. Now both alternatives to action were impossible.

A dark shadow fell over her. For a moment she imagined it to be a manifestation of her emotional state. She saw she was wrong.

"Sounds like a bad solenoid."

"No," she said, "only a bad mood." Jennifer looked up into the man's sympathetic face. Those eyes again, pulling her to him.

"Do you belong to the Automobile Club?"

"Don't I wish," she answered. If she couldn't afford a top to her car, she could hardly afford such luxuries as road service clubs. "Guess I'll have to get gouged by a tow service." She reached into her purse to pull out her wallet for a dime. "Oh, God . . ." Dropping her hands into her lap, she shook her head. No wallet. No wallet! She had a friend who was an astrologer. The friend had warned her . . . what was it? Something was eclipsing something and something else—a node? a cusp?—was conjunct with Venus. When she hadn't understood the star talk, the friend had finally relented and given her the bottom line. This period was going to be bad. And good. "That's the way life always is," Jennifer had disparaged. "Well, for a while it's going to be more so," her friend assured.

"She was right," Jennifer said aloud.

"Who was right?"

"No one," she answered. "And nothing." Gritting her teeth, she muttered low under her breath and smacked the steering wheel with both palms. "I am such an idiot! No wallet!"

"Oh. Well . . . yeah."

The man had stepped away from the car and was looking thoughtfully down the highway. For almost the first time since she had seen him, Jennifer was not interested in what he was doing or thinking. She was wondering who she could call for a lift.

"I'm Michael Casari," the man said abruptly. He had come back beside the MG. His expression was tentative, as if he had just made a monumental decision and wasn't sure if he wanted to live with it. "This is very awkward," he went on. "I haven't slipped into my white knight armor in a long time. The thing is, provided you don't live on Mars or in Arizona, I'd offer you a ride home and back so you could get your wallet, only I have to be back at my house this morning. So I can't."

"Like you said in there, no problem."

"But," he interrupted, "if you don't mind waiting for me to take care of business, and if you'll trust me not to be an axe murderer, you can come back with me, have some breakfast, and when I'm through I'll drive you home to get your dough."

"Thanks, but—"

"Sure. I understand. For all you know I could be a fiend." He grinned.

Jennifer smiled back politely. She was thinking he would be the most gorgeous fiend L.A. had ever seen.

He dug into his pocket and pulled out some change. "Assuming you have accommodating friends, some other white knight can come to your aid as soon as they get the distress signal."

The only knights Jennifer knew had rusty armor. To ask any of them for a favor was to set off a symphony of groans and clanks as they formed their excuses.

"Thanks," she said, accepting the change.

He pulled out a five dollar bill and dropped it into her lap. "Just in case," he said.

"Do you have a business card? I'll send you a check."

"Not necessary." He began to back off.

It was hard to analyze the disappointment she felt in seeing him leave. She was overcome with a sense of futility. The same sense of dissatisfaction with herself filled her as when she had passed the surfers and the Getty Museum. She felt like one of those furry creatures who spend their days on a treadmill, going fast and going nowhere. The sum total of her existence could be analogized to her present situation. She was broke and tired and alone. She who had chased the truth for the past five years was winded by the ceaseless effort her career entailed. No one wanted the truth, anyway. Everyone, from her station boss on down to the viewing public, wanted hype, bigger-than-life stories that exposed rather than informed. Only an inborn streak of stubborn and blind idealism had allowed her to overlook the reality of the state of her profession. But now, as she watched Michael Casari climb into the white Cadillac, she knew she couldn't kid herself any longer. She was tired of prostituting her ideals. Otherwise, she would have accepted his invitation to breakfast.

The Cadillac's engine purred into service, the sound cutting through her reverie of self-pity.

Suddenly she was opening the MG's door, running across the blacktop. The Cadillac had just started to back away. When he saw her standing there looking at him, he stopped. Her heart thumped in time to the beat of the Cadillac's idle as she crossed the rest of the distance.

Inexplicably shy, feeling foolish, she stood a foot away from the car and fixed her attention on Michael Casari's leather sleeve resting on the open window. She didn't care about the scoop of a decade. What she wanted was some old-fashioned companionship with a sympathetic soul; she needed it, even if only for a morning. "My stomach's overruled me. If the invitation's still—"

A current of understanding passed between them, but all he said was, "Hop in."

Nevertheless, she detected a barely veiled look of amusement in his dark eyes as she crossed in front of the car. When she was seated beside him, he looked over and smiled.

She had to look away.

More cars had taken over the highway as they headed north on the coast road. She pretended intense interest in the scenery, which now mostly consisted of sheared cliffs on her right and the garages of beach-front villas to her left. A thin film of moisture clouded her vision. Sleep, she needed more sleep. Maybe vitamins, too. It was unnatural to be so vulnerable to a smile, to simple kindness. A tear dripped down her cheek. She brushed it away, hoping he hadn't seen.

Only he must have, because a moment later he said, "Busted wheels always make life seem bleak."

"Yeah, kind of," she answered vaguely, glad he didn't suspect the truth, that she was undergoing a minor identity crisis. If he were smart he would just leave things well enough alone or she would show him the true meaning of bleak by probably bursting into a torrent of tears.

"You want to talk about it?"

"About my busted wheels?" She shot him a sarcastic look.

"About what's really bothering you." He looked over to her and with that peculiar, indefinable intimacy, their eyes touched again.

"No," Jennifer said, "not really."

His expression relaxed into what she took as a state of relief. Quickly he chose another topic. "How do you like your eggs? Over easy, hard, scrambled?"

"However they come out."

"Good. That's the way I serve them."

This time they both smiled.

Jennifer knew that to those unfamiliar with Southern California lore, Malibu colony would appear to be no more than a line of garage doors facing the street. The attached homes were packed together, one upon the other, blocking vast expanses of the Pacific. They came in various styles— some of the more popular being California beach modern, rustic beach shack, imitation English estate, and fake Spanish hacienda—all of them in the same price range: astronomical.

Residents of the colony were often movie stars or film producers, directors, or those who slept with same. The neighborhood where Michael Casari lived wasn't noted for being your typical, down-home kind of neighborhood.

He swung the Cadillac across two lanes, guiding it into a double garage whose electronically operated doors had sprung into service. Following him through the garage and up four steps where he opened a door, she found herself in a narrow galley kitchen. An open counter was at one end of the room, and from where she stood she could see straight through into the dining area, and beyond to the living room. Behind a floor-to-ceiling wall of plate glass, the Pacific lay in majestic serenity until it dropped out of view beyond the horizon.

She thought of the apartment complex where she lived. The place she called home was a drab purgatory in comparison to a pad like this which was so clearly, so painfully heaven.

"Take a look around," he said, noting her interest. "If you're into star gazing, you might catch some familiar faces out for their morning constitutionals."

She took him up on his offer to explore, entering the living room as he called after her.

"Do you jog?"

"Not for recreational purposes." She had to smile. In the line of duty she had run many a merry race.

"That sounds intriguing." He came up behind her with two glasses of champagne. "And dangerous."

She accepted hers, and as they went through the ritual of clinking glasses she had to wonder if she was really losing her marbles, bringing up—for crying out loud—what she did for a living. "I'm into research," she said. A little truth was innocent enough.

"Research. A broad spectrum, research. Scientific research?"

She shrugged. "Whatever needs peering into. Freelance stuff." It wasn't an outright lie. In most instances she was free to pick and choose her topics.

His hair had caught the light from the window. It was

luxuriously dark, a thick covering bringing to mind black velvet. He had removed his leather jacket. A cream-colored polo shirt was tucked into his jeans, accentuating his spare frame. His body looked naturally muscular, unlike those that had been honed in a gym as part of the body-beautiful craze sweeping the city. She couldn't help herself. She did what men instinctively did to women; she imagined what making love with him would be like.

When she refocused her attention on his face, she saw that his eyes were again probing hers and that he wore that same quizzical expression so unsettling to her in the store.

"You blush beautifully," he said.

"The champagne. It's the champagne. It does that to me. Sometimes." Turning, she made a big show of looking at the ocean. "Fabulous. You must love living here."

"Most of the time." He took a thoughtful sip of his drink. Staring out at the soft swells placidly rising and falling, he said, "The briny deep has a way of keeping things in perspective, doesn't it? No matter how big your ego gets, all you have to do is look out there to know how unimportant you are."

"Are you important?" she asked.

"No."

He answered a little too quickly—even defensively—for her to believe him.

"Well, you must do something pretty wild to afford this place." She swung around slowly, appraising the surroundings.

It was one of the California beach contemporaries. The outside was framed in redwood siding, starkly angular and utilitarian, weathered dull-gray from the lash of the elements. Masculine, she thought. All the furniture looked simple and expensive: modern sling chairs of chrome and natural brown leather, a low sofa covered in nubby, raw white Haitian cotton, a fluffy white flokati rug from Greece, glass and marble coffee and end tables, extension lamps resembling giant erector sets that swooped down from behind the furniture. On one side of the room was an impressive stone fireplace with logs ready to be burned. A bar with stereo components built into the back wall, took up the opposite side of the room.

Michael had gone back to the kitchen. She heard bacon sizzling. "That depends," he called over his shoulder.

She followed him in, watching as he flipped the bacon over. "On what?" she asked.

"On what constitutes wild in your opinion."

"Oh, race car driving. Being a secret agent. An international jet-setter playboy." She changed positions slightly in order to see his face. Her curiosity was a knee-jerk reaction more than anything else. She considered herself off-duty now. The decision to accept his invitation had been based more upon personal motive, need to get a ride back home, and a sudden sweeping impression of loneliness, rather than any desire to pander to the jaws of yellow journalism.

Anyway, there was no visible reaction to her probes, unless someone could make a case out of dropping two frizzled pieces of bacon on towels to drain. There was certainly nothing there to appeal to the *Enquirer*.

"All sounds good to me," Michael said, putting bread in the toaster.

Maybe it was because she didn't actually care, but it took her a long moment to realize that he had avoided her implied question: What was it that he did for a living?

"But you said you had business to take care of," she said. "Here. You work at home?"

"I try not to call it that. The word has an ominous ring."

He laughed, and handed her a couple of plates and some silverware. She started into the dining area with them, but turned suddenly and caught him unawares. His eyes had been cruising her body. It was a look not entirely innocent, nor was it offensive. More than anything else, it was honestly masculine and somehow she didn't mind the once-over. So far he hadn't exactly been treating her like a sex object.

"You know, you're being very mysterious," she said. "Why's that?"

This time a slight shadow passed over his face. He busied himself again, picking up an egg and taking overt pains to crack it into the pan. Without looking up, Michael said, "It's easier that way."

While she set the table, she kept up the conversation. "What's easier?"

"Work. Life in general."

"Oh, I get it." She had come back to the kitchen again. "Napkins?"

"Where you're standing. Top drawer."

"You're one of the new breed, huh? No involvement, no commitment. Don't you know? The entire population of unmarried American women are skinning your type alive in scathing magazine articles."

He looked quickly to her. "Are you married?"

"Should I tell you?"

"Yeah, you should." Currents of emotions richocheted between them, independent of the dialogue which both knew was only minimally important next to the attraction they felt for each other.

"Why?"

"Because I want to know." He grinned at her, a spatula poised in the air.

"That's not a reason."

"Of course it is. To me it is. I'm single. There, a trade's a trade."

"Yup. I'm unhitched too."

He passed by, bringing the coffee to the table. "I thought so."

"Oh? And what gave you that idea? Not my wanton behavior, I hope." She was joking, but not entirely, needing reassurance that he understood she wasn't in the habit of joining strange men for breakfast. If she had been there on assignment, it would have been different. She couldn't have cared less what he thought. But somehow this was different. This was personal, and at the moment she wasn't feeling particularly sure of herself. More sleep, all you need, Jenny baby, is more shuteye and you'll be your old brittle, hardened career-girl self again.

"I put two and two together. Exceedingly attractive females usually end up with exceedingly wealthy men. A tycoon type will generally have a big ego, otherwise he wouldn't have the drive to make all of that moola. Therefore he would not allow his wife to be seen on the same block as that limping contraption you own, much less allow her to drive it. So why aren't you married?" he asked abruptly, while with his hand he gestured for her to be seated.

"Why aren't you?"

"Uh-uh, ball was mine to serve, making it your return. But, all right, as it appears you're determined to upset the rules, I'll tell you. I was married. At one time. Very formerly."

"So? And?" she persisted.

"So, and, that's it. Now, what about you?"

"That's not an even swap. Maybe I have dark hidden

tragedies in my past. You can't get away with making vague, nondisclosing statements and expect me to bare my soul.''

"No,'' he said, and took a sip of coffee. "But I can try, can't I?''

"Okay. Truth is, I'm not married because I eat crackers in bed and no one will have me.''

"Ah, now you've given away a secret. You aren't a virgin.''

"Not so,'' she countered, laughing. "Virgins can eat crackers in bed.''

"Any man would have to be crackers to turn you down for crummy sheets.'' He raised his champagne glass. She wasn't sure if it was to toast his pun, or in honor of her. Maybe both.

"And your wife? What happened to her?''

"Back to me again.'' He grimaced. "Well, we were young, actually. Too young for marriage. It wasn't anything heavy between us, no drinking bouts, wife beating, running around with the milkman. Very tame, prosaic. One day we woke up and realized we had nothing much to say to each other. The next day we shook hands outside of a lawyer's office.''

"How civilized,'' Jennifer said.

"The only way to be.''

"Only I don't believe you.''

He looked up, feigning shock. "Really. See, no battle scars.'' Michael displayed his arm for her inspection.

"Maybe not on the outside. But inside. Otherwise you would have remarried.'' Jennifer noted that the humor had faded from his eyes. She had gone too far.

He glanced at his watch. "Excuse me, there's something I've got to catch on the tube.''

Leaving her, he entered the living room to switch on the television.

For all intents and purposes, after that, she may as well have disappeared. His attention was trained on the broadcast.

The announcer from the *Today* show was just concluding the national weather forecast. Almost immediately, the next spot came on. The camera did a close-up on the New York hostess.

Michael was staring at the screen, his eyes dark, intent on the telecast. She brought him his unfinished coffee. He took it without comment and slipped into a leather sling-backed chair.

Darla Hart's face appeared on the screen. Jennifer flicked her eyes from Darla to Michael, trying to understand from his visual responses what the relationship could possibly be.

"She's beautiful, isn't she?"

It seemed he didn't hear her at first. "She has a quality," he said finally.

"But not your type," Jennifer said, fishing.

"My type?" He looked up at her. There was a wariness behind the dark eyes that had not been there before. "I'd have to know her to say if she was or wasn't." He snapped his attention back to the screen.

He had lied. Why had he lied?

Whatever questions she had were forgotten momentarily as Darla Hart answered her first question from the interviewer. All questions were reputedly derived from man-on-the-street solicitations by the station prior to the show. Darla fielded each question with the grace of Queen Elizabeth and the wisdom of an ancient sage. Jennifer had been in the people-watching business too long to be impressed by much, and this was a rare instance. The rest of the country would most likely be bowled over by the presentation.

Morosely, she thought of the effect *Today*'s triumph would have on her boss at *Everyday*. Enderall had been on the warpath at the station for the last month, exiting each board meeting more dyspeptic than when he went in. Last week he had resorted to firing one of their seven staff researchers, an employee who had been with the station for eight years. A pall had hung over the staff ever since, and Jennifer (as well as the others) sensed the purge had only just begun.

The interviewer had just finished delivering a string of profuse compliments to Miss Hart, and now she was asking whether Darla might answer a question she had—a personal, kind of impromptu question that had cropped up previously in her life.

Michael suddenly leaned forward in his chair, his jaw rigid with tension. A slight tick played at the corner of one temple.

As for Darla, she seemed perfectly relaxed. Smiling, she considered the question for a very long time, too long of a time, Jennifer determined. Michael had risen from the chair now, and was standing just a foot or so from the television.

"Say something, will you?" he muttered under his breath.

Jennifer realized he had entirely forgotten she was in the room. His whole being seemed trained upon the woman whose dress matched her emerald-green eyes, whose lips were smiling and were also, unfortunately, absolutely mute.

Even the interviewer began to fidget. She filled in with some small talk, then rephrased her question. Anyone involved with on-air interviews was familiar with noted personalities blanking out on camera. There were tried and true methods of bringing the drifting interviewee back to life, and that is precisely what Jennifer was witnessing now.

With success.

Darla Hart's lips finally began to move again. Only there was a certain glassiness, an unconnectedness to the wide green eyes that radiated danger to Jennifer, just as surely as warning lights had been switched on.

"Actually . . ." Darla was saying, "your question is very interesting. I've often had people write in—"

And that was that. Darla Hart stopped mid-sentence, appearing for all the world as comatose.

Michael Casari sank back into the chair just as the station cut to a commercial. Panic-time in the engineering booth. Jenny could almost hear the turmoil, the expletives bouncing off the walls. Since, after all, it was *Today* and a competitor, she couldn't keep the grin from spreading over her face. On the other hand, Darla Hart . . . her icon . . . had just managed to disgrace herself before millions of her public.

She looked down to Michael who was leaning forward, his head drooping between spread knees, both hands locked into a deadly-tight knuckle-clasp. Wearily, still paying her no attention, he rose and punched the television knob to off.

One thing, whatever his relationship was to Darla Hart, it had to be intense. Unless it had been his own career on the line, Jennifer couldn't imagine a more empathetic response to the disappointing interview.

"She kind of blew it," Jennifer said.

"Like a bloody volcano," Michael returned, the words snapped out as a rebuke. "Sorry," he said immediately, and raked one hand's fingers through his hair, looking to Jennifer vulnerable and miserable and in need of some serious comforting.

"Why don't I, uh, heat up some more coffee?"

"What?"

He hadn't even been listening to her.

"Coffee," she said again.

"Yeah, that's . . . look, excuse me. Got to make a call. Be back in a minute . . ." His words trailed behind him as he disappeared through a door leading to a hallway.

Left alone, she scanned for clues to what his relationship might be with Darla Hart. Darla was obviously much older than Michael, but the older woman, younger man combination was a popular trend these days. Perhaps they were lovers; an intense emotional relationship between an older and wiser woman and a younger and confused man. No, unlikely. Jennifer shrugged off that premise without a second thought. First of all, this Michael Casari did not seem to be in the least unsure of himself. If anything, he seemed too much in control. If he had an ego, it was well under wraps. It was a rare man who did not immediately launch into a familiar litany of personal triumphs, exhibiting whatever status he had as bait for the intended game.

But besides knowing he had money and manners and was somewhat, somehow connected with Miss Darla Hart, she knew relatively little about him. The disclosure about once having been married was not a typical spilling of one's marital guts. He could have just as easily told her that he had been forced to repeat algebra in tenth grade, for all the emotional angst he displayed.

She was ruminating over the lack of telling clues when the doorbell rang. Michael didn't show. When the bell kept ringing, she went to the door herself.

"Hey, how's it goin'?" An older-looking teenager stood opposite her, holding a large iron box, secured by a combination lock. Before she could reply, he hefted the box forward. "Give this to Mike, okay? It's the Darla stuff from Morey."

"Sure . . ." Jenny stood in the open doorway, the box in her arms. Deep in contemplation, she watched the messenger bound down the walkway running the length of the house to the street.

This was not fair, she thought, staring down at the box which in her imagination had taken on almost animistic properties, its dim voice insistently whispering sweet words of temptation. With each passing second she was feeling more and more like Pandora debating the wages of moral transgression against the passionate desire to discover what treasures the box possessed.

Whereas some of the others on the staff went by the "anything goes" standard, she had developed her own code of ethics. She would not take advantage of a personal relationship, and although she did not know this man well, he had been kind to her and her decision to accept his offer of a ride had been based upon personal factors rather than professional. Granted, it was a fine line that divided truth from deception, and in some instances the line wavered, but for now . . . she was obligated to play the relationship straight.

She marched back to the living room. As she delivered the box to a safe place on top of the coffee table, she wouldn't have been surprised to have heard celestial harps and a deep, unseen baritone voice commend her saintliness. All things considered, it was damned hard to be that good.

Michael slammed the door to his study. With the shutters drawn into a closed position it was dark in the room, almost as dark as his mood as he grabbed up the telephone receiver and punched out the number he knew by memory from having dialed it a million times during the past five years.

On the third ring a secretary answered.

"Let me speak to Morey," he demanded.

"Michael, that you?" came the unsure response.

"Yes."

"It doesn't sound like you."

"Just put Morey on." Distractedly, anxiously, he ran his fingers through his hair as he waited.

"Mike, how're you?" Morey Greenbaum's voice was cautious.

"You saw it?"

"Mike . . . she was just—"

"Don't make excuses for her, Morey. She's crucifying me."

"No one even knows it's you," Morey said, trying to sooth him, his voice a shade unsure.

"I know it's me, and that's enough."

"Look, Mike, give her a chance. She was frightened. It's been a long time—"

"She was loaded, Morey. Loaded," Michael repeated again.

"A couple of Valium, I think."

"A couple? Try a bottle. She blanked, dried up in front of millions and millions of people. She fell flat on her face, Morey." Michael couldn't remember being so angry in years. Somewhere in the back of his memory a banner flew by with the slogan *cumulative repressed hostility*. And so what? he countered with his conscious self. He was a human being, wasn't he? He could get angry just like anyone else, couldn't he? Damn right, he could. And what was more, he was angry.

Morey was hemming and hawing on the other end of the line. "Well, it was *her* face, Mike. There's no need to go on about the whole thing. Relax. I had a doctor friend of mine rush over to the studio and do a number about her having to recuperate from some weird bug. He took her with him and they pumped her stomach. Just in case. She wasn't looking too swell by the time he got to her. Besides, she appeared courageous. Regardless of what you and I think, the public adores Darla Hart. No matter what Darla Hart does, they'll read some redeeming element into it. She's a bloody saint as far as the public goes. Besides . . .'' Morey broke off for a second. Michael could hear papers rustling in the background. ''Here it is . . . got some statistics in just this a.m., Mikey. Looks like Darla's readership expanded by two point five percent, just from her appearance yesterday. That's dynamite . . . dyn . . . a . . . mite.''

''Have you ever heard of a concept called integrity, Morey?''

''Me? You're talking integrity to me? Listen here, Michael, don't go getting huffy and sanctimonious on me, guy. It was your idea to write this column anonymously. It was your idea to hire Lena Stephens. It was your idea to hire a neurotic, has-been actress to pose as Darla Hart. I could have gotten you plenty of normal actresses to sub for you. But, no, no. You had to play God. You wanted that used-up fruitcake—''

''Lena Stephens had a decent career at one time!'' Michael flared suddenly, his protective instincts for his former patient awakened. ''I guess she just wasn't ready for this yet.'' And of course that was the real reason he was so angry; he felt guilty for letting her down. Lena hadn't failed him. It was the other way around.

''Look,'' Morey said. ''What the hell is this? You're attacking or defending her? You're making me crazy too, Mikey.''

Michael slumped down into the padded executive's chair behind his desk. ''Okay . . . okay . . . forget it. I was out of line.''

''Look, you're just tired, is all. And you spend too much time alone. Ginny and I are giving a party this weekend—''

"Thanks, no. I'll talk to you later."

Michael closed his eyes and leaned back in his chair. Of course Morey had been right. It was all his own doing, this intolerable situation. But it had gone too far and there didn't seem to be any way now to back out of what he had begun. This Darla Hart charade, this fiasco of his, had simply grown too big for him.

And Morey was right about another thing. He *was* lonely. There had been a time when he thought he would just as soon live in a cave, free from all human beings and their various and assorted miseries. He had had all he wanted of hysterical outbursts, fevered confessions, all the waste of good emotion turned sour, that seemed to be the universal condition.

But that part of his life, too, had grown sour; had gotten away from him. He had gone to the best schools, taken the most rigorous course load, done a grueling apprenticeship, and in the end was satisfied that he was a capable psychologist.

Now that he thought back on it, his naiveté was incredible. To think that he could become a savior to all the hurting souls who walked with such childlike hope through the door to his office, was the greatest of conceits.

What he had told Jennifer had been true. His marriage had been short and had ended in a pink cloud of courtesy. The truth was, his wife had been glad to unload him, relieved to abandon him to his obsessive drive to play God to the confused souls who threw their lives at his mercy. He hadn't exactly been an attentive husband.

But no one could say he hadn't done his very best professionally. What he couldn't do was work miracles like a true savior. He would lay awake at night, thinking of his patients, of their problems, feeling their pain as his own. And so the failure ate away at him until he finally closed the door to his office for good. He took a long trip after that. He couldn't even remember half the places he went to during that period. He just drifted, let his hair grow, even cultivated a rather rakish beard and mustache for a time. And then, when it seemed he had become soul-mated to the Lost Dutchman, that he would go on circling the globe forever, he suddenly ended his journey to nowhere.

One day he sat down and began to write. He wrote to himself, about all the things that enraged him; he wrote about the futility he felt in trying to help people who wouldn't be helped. A strange thing happened then. He began to write solutions to the problems he couldn't solve during regular therapy sessions with patients.

A friend fished a couple of his prescriptions for happiness out of the wastebasket one afternoon. The same friend said he ought to do something with what he had read. Like he should take it down to the local paper—a small-town Eastern publication. So, because he needed the money by that time, he did.

And the rest was, as they say, history.

One thing led to another and Morey became his agent and soon enough Darla Hart became a media legend.

Providentially (or so it seemed then) he ran into one of his ex-patients in the agency's lobby. Lena Stevens was still neurotic as hell, but she'd come a long way since the time Michael had worked her out of suicidal depressions over her lagging career. The thing of it was, she actually had talent. She had done some pretty outstanding work in the past; only her craziness kept her from sustaining her professional life. There was only one explanation for what happened after that: once stung by the Messiah-bug, the fever would linger on forever. Lena said only he could help her. She pleaded with him to take her on as a patient again so that she could get herself together and act again. The chance to help a human being tottering on the edge of an emotional chasm was too much of a temptation to resist. And so Darla Hart was born in the person of a fading, neurotic actress, grateful and humble and actually ecstatic to play an ongoing role with Michael there to give her constant emotional support. It gave credence to her life, and it kept him from having to face the public. Whereas Darla never appeared before an audience in the flesh, her voice was heard on countless radio shows, giving prearranged answers to prearranged questions that had been carefully worked out by Michael. All Lena had to do was emote from the printed script. The commercial packaging of an anonymous Darla Hart was wildly successful, and for five years the deception worked.

There were several major advice columnists—Abby, Anne Landers, others—all of them good. What separated him from the others were three things: the first was his writing style. In fact, as a psychologist, he had published articles in major magazines, the content often lapsing into an editorial mode for which he received surprising recognition from the literary establishment. Two self-help books published early on in his career garnered favorable reviews from both academia and the general public.

The second attribute setting him apart from the other columnists was, of course, the wealth of concrete knowledge he possessed relating to the psyche. Sprinkled along with what came across as good commonsense, humorously prescribed folk wisdom were scientific or philosophical references relating to the problem at hand.

And oddly, the third reason for his astounding success with the public was that however subtle the difference actually was, he was able to bring across the male viewpoint. It was this unfamiliar slant in perspective that separated his column from all of the rest. He took in not just the typical predominantly female readership associated with such journalism, but also collected fans from the male sector.

Like any success, this too had its price. Not satisfied with merely the voice, the public began to clamor to see Darla. Morey pulled some statistics out of the air which said that the public would be offended to discover at this late date how they had been duped into believing Darla Hart was a woman. The public did not like to be tricked. "They'll turn on you," Morey predicted. "They'll rip you and your column to shreds."

So Michael hadn't objected to retaining his hidden identity. In fact, he had been relieved. His state of anonymity had grown on him. He worked for days with Lena, who was both terrified and eager to perform again. Bleak hours of reassurances, of pulling every trick he had out of his therapy bag, were spent in rehearsing Darla Hart's debut. It was the cleverest of compromises; he could save souls and yet not face souls. No more personal misery with which to contend.

Except his own.

He opened his eyes, remembering the young woman who was waiting for him in the living room. Jennifer. Jennifer Winters. She was very pretty. Shaking his head, he sighed, thinking that he was insane to have actually picked up a strange woman at barely the crack of dawn. In a way he felt shabby for having used the excuse of her car to have some company. It was not a class act on his part.

Yes, he thought, she was very pretty. Beautiful? Possibly. Desirable? Definitely. Would he try? Would he actually sink so low? From a male viewpoint, the idea was tantalizing. He felt himself stir, automatically picturing her body as it might appear unclothed. Michael . . . Michael . . . to what depths have you sunk? Defrauding the world, contemplating the ravishment of a woman who came to your home . . . your home, Michael . . . on the premise that you would offer her help.

It was you who was seeking help. Be honest, Casari.

There was something in the eyes of Jennifer Winters that held him. A soul within, some element that drew him out of himself for a fleeting instant. And that was what he needed. He needed to be drawn out of himself.

He threw open the door to the office. The light from the hall entered the room like rays signifying the miraculous in old biblical epics. Happy to snatch at any straw, he counted the mundane phenomenon as an auspicious portent.

"Sorry it took me so long," he said, sauntering into the sun-flooded living area.

"That's okay," Jennifer said. She had been standing by the glass wall, looking out. The sun was warm on her arms.

Michael had to force himself to keep from staring. It was as if each pale strand of her hair had trapped the light. It fell softly around her face, and as she moved, the golden mantle caressed her shoulders in a way he wanted to do with his fingers. It was a strange impulse he felt, as if he were actually jealous of the sun for touching her body. Even her skin glowed tawny and burnished.

She turned to him and the blue eyes caught his, specks of green-blue bursting out like rays of joy, filling him.

"You should catch the show from the deck," he said, making his way across the room to where she stood. He opened the sliding door and guided her through, his arm lightly encasing her waist. It was a gesture certainly within the grounds of propriety, except perhaps that his hand grazed the round swell of her hips. An unexpected and fierce mixture of lust and excitement flamed in him.

Outside on the weathered redwood deck a gentle breeze played through the hanging baskets of creeping Charlie, swayed the spider plants, tendrils sweeping long and graceful with green star bursts at the end, and ruffled the brilliant red and purple blooms of the fuchsias.

Jennifer stood absolutely still, the scene taking her in its spell. She closed her eyes, wanting to hold in the moment just the way it was, forever.

"Do you like the ocean?"

She turned as her eyes opened, accidentally moving into him just as she had done in the convenience store. Only this time there was no pulling away. His arms enfolded her gently and certainly, a sea anemone caressing its treasure.

"Jennifer . . ." he said, her name voiced as both a question and its own answer.

His fingers swept through her hair, pushed the strands away from her face.

"Michael, I don't think—"

"Then don't think," he said. "Thinking is hazardous." He bent himself into her, brushing her lips at first lightly, then with more force, and by that time she was not able to think very clearly.

The sun and the breeze, the sound of the surf, the distant cries of children playing below, all seemed to meld together and finally to disappear entirely as she opened her mouth to his.

His hand pushed against the small of her back. She could feel the reaction their closeness was having on him. The thought of that hardness in her made her shiver, encouraged her to meet his tongue with the same urgency.

"Jennifer . . ." he began, then had to stop. She could see him physically fighting for resolve to continue with his message. His breathing came ragged and short. One hand was still on her waist. The curl of his fingers burned into her, making it difficult for her to pay attention to what he was saying. "I honestly didn't mean for this to happen like this. It wasn't my intention."

"No, of course not," she said, sounding sane enough but feeling wildly off-kilter. She wanted to make love to him. Her body was aching, on fire for his.

"I'll take you back now."

Neither of them made a move. She didn't know what to do. Oh, she knew what she should do, the prudent advice she would give to anyone else: Scram out of there. A slam-bam encounter with a stranger had only one way to go. No place.

"Come on," he said, his voice edged with the same frustration she was experiencing. He moved ahead to open the door for them to enter the house.

She passed by him, both of them judiciously avoiding any contact with the other.

When they were inside again, Michael said, "I'll get my keys."

Jennifer waited, staring beyond the glass wall to where they had been on the deck. The feel of his body had magically dissolved the lonely ache of that morning and that of other recent days.

It took her a moment to realize he hadn't moved more than five feet away from her.

From his expression, he appeared to have been struggling with himself. "What if I didn't take you back?"

"Then I'd stay," she said.

"You'd want that?"

She nodded. "Yes, I think so. Yes," she said more definitely.

He was with her again. "Jennifer . . . Jennifer . . ." He

repeated her name between kisses that flew urgently over her neck and down to the folds of her blue turtleneck in which her body now seemed like that of a condemned prisoner longing for freedom. Her breasts felt heavy, swollen, straining to be lifted in his hands. She moved against him, lost in sensation, unaware of her suggestive, undulating rhythm until Michael responded by moaning softly.

His hands were traveling over her hips, down the swell of her buttocks, moving more rapidly, lost as he was now in his own fever of desire.

He pushed her back slightly and bent his face to her breasts where he rubbed his face across them, then buried his face in the crease between.

"It's okay," she said, "I want you to," and with her consent he began to peel the sweater up, off her body.

She stood before him in her bra and jeans, her nipples hardening as his eyes took in the fullness straining against the pale blue lace.

"You're so beautiful," he said, not able to take his eyes from her body as his hand slipped around to her back. His breath was hot on her neck, and the small gentle bites sent jets of ecstatic warmth into the lower regions of her stomach.

Dimly, as he unhooked her bra, she cautioned herself one last time that what she was doing was madness.

But then his hands were lifting both breasts into his palms, running thumb and forefinger over the peeked tips, making her close her eyes and moan even as she kissed his shoulder, the curve of his neck, tasted the sweetness of his ear. She was seized with an almost savage need to savor the flavor of his skin. She wanted to wrap her legs tightly around his waist, to take him into her.

"No."

At first she thought she had misunderstood, but when he repeated the word again, the single sound stabbed her like a knife.

"No, my beautiful, desirable Jennifer." He pulled her tightly against his chest, stroking her back as they both struggled to calm themselves.

She could feel his heart beating a wild tattoo, almost in counterpoint to her own heart's rhythm. And against her stomach, there was no doubt he was still fully rigid with desire.

After a time, during which he stroked her hair and periodically kissed her head, the outline of her temple, he finally said, "It would ruin everything for us. This is too soon, too fast. It isn't the way either of us wants it, is it? Outside of the—" And here he broke off, trembling. "We want each other, but we should build something between us first. Something real and true."

Looking up at him, into the dark glistening pools, she saw the remnants of his physical desire reflected clearly. Touching her fingers to his face, she said, "You're a romantic . . ."

He returned a half smile, one that was not happy. "Is that a complaint or a compliment?"

"Both. But mostly, the truth."

"You know I want to make love to you," he said, and closed his eyes tightly; a small war was being waged within his body at the reference to what could have been—what still could be—between them.

"I know."

"But you understand?"

"Ummm." She nodded. "I think I'd better get my-self together." Pulling away, she crossed both arms in front of her breasts. The demure gesture was out of keeping with what had just transpired. It brought home the unreality of their brief encounter, and of Michael's wisdom to stop.

He handed her her sweater and bra. "The guest bathroom's down the hall, if you'd like to make any repairs."

"Thanks," she said. "Not a bad idea."

The repair she had to make was less physical than psychic. Looking at herself in the bathroom mirror, she had to question what on earth had made her give into . . . well, the word was *lust*. Only a dolt would believe in love at first sight. Lust at first sight, that was plausible and believable. What it wasn't was forgivable. Her standards did not include casual sex with strangers.

She scrubbed her face with soap, removing all remants of makeup. The Lady Macbeth syndrome. Out, damn spot. Only the spot was in her heart.

She liked him, genuinely liked him. So what if she didn't know him well? She had instincts, didn't she? That's what made her good at her work: right-on assessments of people and situations.

The very thought of work was sobering. Romantic feelings dissolved in the presence of such tangibles as paychecks and car payments. There was to have been a mandatory staff meeting that morning which she had risked missing only because she was going to march in later as a conquering hero with her Darla Hart story.

Her hand trembled slightly as she took out the mascara wand from the small makeup pouch she carried in her purse. She realized a truth of life then: It was damned hard to make up a face when your stomach was turning over in circles and your head was spinning in reverse direction.

The man she had almost made love with was a man who could literally make or break her career.

But could she use him? Could she do that?

For the first time in her life, she really wasn't certain of her morals. That fine line between what was right and what was prudent had never appeared more tentative.

Chapter 3

"YOU LOOK WONDERFUL," MICHAEL SAID WHEN SHE walked back into the living room.

To Jennifer his expression said that and more. Even with the lecture she had so recently delivered to her mirrored image, she found her resolve crumbling in the glow of his presence.

"I've got to be going. Things to do, people to meet. You know, that sort of thing." The jaunty delivery rang false.

"You're angry," he said, the happiness fading from his eyes.

"No, no, I'm not angry."

"Then upset."

"Okay, upset. I don't even know you. What happened . . . that is, what almost happened . . . I'm not used to—"

"Neither am I."

Jennifer turned her back on him. He wasn't going to let this be easy.

"Honestly. I'm not in the habit of collecting beautiful women at the crack of dawn and taking them home to make love to. I'm not even in the habit of collecting women." He came up behind her. She could feel him wanting to touch her, but he didn't and she was both glad and regretful. "Don't let the surroundings fool you," he went on. "I actually lead a very circumspect life. Perhaps too circumspect." The last was said more as an aside to himself than to her.

She didn't reply because she couldn't. There was nothing really to say. It wasn't only that she didn't sleep with men upon meeting them; it was because he wasn't just any man, nor was she any woman. Michael Casari was her link to what could possibly be the biggest story of her career. The true basis of their relationship was as natural enemies, not natural lovers. But he didn't know that. If only things hadn't gone so far.

"Okay," he said when she made no reply. "We'll take off then. I'll just go change into another shirt."

A door closed softly down the hall. The sound could have been Fate taunting her. There, across the room from her, was the box where she had left it earlier. It was the same, but for one difference. The combination lock had been removed.

No. She couldn't.

Turning, looking for something physical to do, she removed a lipstick and compact from her purse. It made no difference. The box was framed in the mirror just as it was in her mind, a glittering jewel waiting for her touch.

She felt like an emotional wishbone, fingers pulling her in opposite directions. Every part of her was warring with every other part.

She dropped the makeup back into her purse and crossed

to the far side of the room, away from the box. But her eyes were magnetically drawn to it. She stared at it, worked the top up in her mind, pulled out a piece of paper that would give her a handle on a story that would knock America's socks off. Well, maybe nothing that great. What could a person expect from one little piece of paper? But it might be a beginning anyway, some clue to Darla which she could follow without involving Michael in her "research."

And that, she knew, was it; the excuse, the justification she had been searching for all along. Her plan had never been to expose Michael Casari. He was only to have been a thread leading her to the source. And he had.

The lid to the box groaned slightly as she lifted it. She cringed, almost hissed "shussh." Inside were perhaps twenty or thirty envelopes addressed to a Los Angeles post office box. All looked personal with names and return addresses included. She ran through them quickly. Every one of them was for Miss Darla Hart; all but one, that is. One envelope had Michael's name on it, scrawled in blue ball-point ink. There was no reason to open one of the Darla Hart letters, obviously from fans; it was the envelope addressed to Michael that intrigued Jennifer.

The envelope made out to Michael had already been opened. A portion of the contents was visible in the space of the triangular flap. She held it up, debating with herself. All she could see were three words, "answers to these." And with that, questions tumbled through her mind like chaparral on fire.

"Looking for something?"

Jennifer reeled around, the envelope still in her hands.

"I . . ." but she had nothing more to say. The expression on Michael Casari's face had removed all thought.

If he had come only a moment earlier or a moment later,

perhaps he would have spared himself the crushing disappointment. It was one of those totally unexpected images incomprehensible to the brain. For a moment he found himself reacting with classical response. He attempted to rearrange the observed to fit a more acceptable reality, that being, of course, one which would match his expectations. But no excuse his mind could formulate was strong enough to defeat the facts.

There, on the other side of the room, a woman whom he had almost made love with a few minutes before, whom he had been willing to trust with his emotions when he had long since shut himself off from such folly, was going through personal papers containing professional dynamite. In the wrong hands the letter to him from Morey would explode into headlines all over the world.

"You don't have to check the silver. I can explain," she said.

"Can you?"

"Yes."

"That's good." He was waiting.

Desperate, she was trying to formulate a plausible excuse to match her bravado. And then she had it, a flash of inspired genius: The best defense was an offense. "This came for you while you were on the phone. The boy who delivered the box said it was for Mikey. From Morey. The Darla stuff. That's pretty interesting since you told me you didn't know Darla Hart."

"Go on," he said.

To Jennifer, he seemed either amused or stricken. She wasn't certain which. The letter she held burned in her fingers.

"So I was curious. That's all. I mean I'm a fan of hers, you know. You don't need to look at me that way. It was a perfectly natural thing to do. Who are you to be so holy, anyway? You lied before. You told me you didn't know her.''

He was just staring at her from across the room, looking bereft and betrayed and she wanted to take back what she had done to cause that expression. Only she couldn't.

All she could do was to drop the letter back into the box and close the lid.

"I don't like having my privacy invaded. By strangers," he added, and she flinched.

Jennifer lowered her eyes to the floor. It was an excruciatingly embarrassing moment. It was also somehow painful in a way she could not understand. Sunshine filled the room. Patterns of light filtering through hanging plants on the outside deck danced gaily about on the carpet. The simple display of nature's spontaneous joy startled her.

When she looked up, Michael was on his way to the kitchen. "Look, I've got to take care of some other business now. I'll call a tow truck, have the expense billed to me."

"I'll pay you back. I will," she insisted when he said nothing in return.

"Forget it." He had his keys now. "Chalk this up to a mistake on both our parts." It came out too harsh. He had wanted to project disinterest. Anger was only inverted passion. He busied himself with looking up the number of his local garage, which had a tow service.

Jennifer snatched up her purse. "I'm not a thief," she said. "And I'm not a deadbeat, either, if that's what you're thinking." A slight film of moisture had formed at the corner of her eyes. *What I am,* she thought, *was one sorry human being who's lonely and scared for her job and who's wishing she had made love with you instead of being a miserable sneak.*

Michael dialed the number and gave the instructions for the billing and the location of the car. "They'll take the car back to the station and see that it's fixed."

She followed him out of the house and into the car. The ride back to the convenience store couldn't have taken more than six minutes; it seemed to last forever in the stony silence.

"Thanks," she said, and got out. Before closing the door, she leaned back into the Cadillac. Their eyes touched again, just as they had earlier that morning when everything had been so different. In spite of what had gone on she experienced that same joining as before. It was, Jennifer thought, as if they had only been playing out their roles, with both of them knowing the actors were feeling something quite separate from the lines they had delivered. Oddly, she went blank, forgetting whatever words she had intended to say in parting. Instead, she said again, "Thanks. And I'm sorry."

He nodded, turned his face ahead to concentrate on his fingers clutching the steering wheel. The door slammed shut. From the corner of his eye, without giving in to the impulse to take a full, last look, Michael caught Jennifer Winters walking away from him. The fine line of her chin was in profile. The blond mane picked up by the sea breeze, tossed, streaming freely. The nose, slender and straight and small. And of course those startlingly blue eyes in which he had lost himself briefly but could no longer see.

Freedom, he thought, and put his foot down on the gas pedal. Freedom. The word had a hollow ring to it. He said it with more force. Again and again. Freedom.

Jennifer watched the white Cadillac fade from view. When it was gone, she leaned against the MG and waited for the tow truck to arrive. The twists and turns of life, she thought, should come as no surprise to her. Her life, anyway, consisted of a series of endless meetings and partings. On and on. There was always that sudden intensity when she delved into a new project, the total consuming commitment of all her faculties and passion directed to the job at hand. An interview with a woman who was getting the shaft from a landlord. A luncheon with a multimillionaire accused of embezzling investment funds from the life savings of blue collar workers with no other resources. On and on. That was the life she had chosen and loved; to ferret out the truth, to live on adrenaline, to explore and achieve, to go on and on . . .

In the distance where the Cadillac had been a moment before, she now saw a tow truck headed in her direction. Partings and meetings . . . God, she missed him already.

He should have gone to see Morey. It was what he had intended to do as soon as he let Jennifer out. Instead, he had turned back home, or in essence, turned back into himself the way he wished he could have pushed back the clock to that morning. It would have been better to never have met her at all than to have had it end like this.

He stood looking out the plate glass wall of his living room. Usually he could take solace in the ocean. It was vast and eternal, and as he had said to Jennifer, it cut everything —from one's ego to one's problems—down to size. Impatiently, he willed it to work its magic on him.

His view of the Pacific was as expensive as it was spectacular. Neighbors of his had paid up to three million dollars for their twenty-four-hour-a-day peek at the ocean. Even he had splurged extravagantly when he had dipped into the bulk of his Darla Hart funds to purchase the hideaway, a compromise between holing up in a Himalayan cave and being accessible to his Beverly Hills agent, his accountant, and his attorney—each of whom kept tabs on the other two as their main function in Michael's life.

But at that moment the million-dollar view was invisible to him and the ocean had yet to salve the emotional wound. How ironic that he, whose daily pronouncements on the human condition made psychological sunshine for half the world, was lost in the darkest universal angst.

Topic for consideration: He had offered help . . . correction . . . he had picked up a pretty blond-haired woman outside a crummy roadside store. The other was just a rationalization to allow him to get to know her. The sexual gesture was totally out of character for him. Sure, lots of men did the same, always on the ready to score. It just wasn't his style.

He had been overcome by an attraction to the woman. And if only his interest had been purely physical, things would be less complicated. He had liked her enough to wait. And now there was nothing to wait for. What a fool. He who knew people in and out had been taken in. He had considered their interest in each other to be mutual. Nevertheless, they hadn't exactly built an enduring relationship, had they?

Why had the whole thing happened? Why had it been necessary for her to snoop into his box containing the letters from Darla Hart's readers? That attempt to infringe on his private life had infuriated him. She had no right. And he had every right to be angry.

But perhaps he had overreacted.

People weren't perfect, even if he had a hang-up about wanting them to be.

He opened the sliding door leading to the deck. An ocean

breeze caught him full on, a biting astringent that momentarily cut through his melancholy. For a while he watched the children playing on the sand below. It wasn't long before the brisk wind died. Sailboats that a moment before had been racing close in, parallel to the coastline, stalled, their canvas falling slack. It was a signal for the mood to return, and it hovered over him like a black cloud dampening his spirits.

Damn! His fist came down upon the wood railing. He missed her. Or the idea of her, anyway. How could he be sure? Hell, he didn't even know this Jennifer Winters. She was a beautiful woman who drove a rotten car and had some kind of lousy job that obviously didn't pay her peanuts. Suddenly a sadness filled him, a feeling of wanting to help her, of wanting to protect her. Thinking of her that way, he smiled. She was a tough little cat on the outside . . . that wild she-lion mane of hers . . . the air of independence, not wanting his help at first. The outside, the outside. And now he would never know the inside, never know what fires burned behind the sparkling eyes. Damn! And he hit the wood railing again.

Mentally, he stretched out on his own analyst's couch.

"What is the problem, Mr. Casari?

"I don't know!

"Yes, you do. You know. Why are you afraid to admit it?

"The lady was very pretty, okay? A good-looking female, and she was also nice. Seemed to be, except for that incident with the box. And so, yes, I was kind of getting to like her. It's been a long time since I've . . . since . . .

"Since . . . since?

"All right, dammit! Since I felt at all open to maybe having a relationship.

"Ahh . . .

"You probably think that's very funny, don't you? The ultimate romantic fool. Meeting an attractive woman who —but, look, that's not the only reason I was turned on to her. I mean, it was more. The soul. The eyes. I don't know. And now here I am feeling really lousy. I want her back in my life. Yes! I want to get to know her and I want her to know me. But she's gone. And, hell, I can't believe I'm actually thinking these things, feeling this way.

"Is there anything wrong with feeling warmth for another human being?

"Don't be cute. You know damn well there isn't anything wrong. Love makes the world go round. Haven't you heard? God. I'm really getting into this, aren't I? I mean, wow. Cool it, Casari. You've got the answers, man. It was yours truly who wrote the book on how to deal with romantic illusion. Beware starry-eyed innocents! Build a cloud castle in the sky, then watch it scatter in the next wind. That's exactly what I told the woman who wrote in last month. Met a trucker passing through on his way down the back-road wilderness of Indiana, fell hard for him in a truckstop, had two glorious days, the man split, end of story. 'Deal in reality,' I wrote back to her in my column. The message: Easy come, easy go.

"Amen. Very wise, indeed. Now I can understand why you are so successful.

"And lonely. Don't forget emotionally isolated, either.

"Now we're getting somewhere."

The voices in his head grew dimmer. Maybe because he didn't like what he was hearing.

And suddenly the sea came into focus. It was like glass, with the sun's rays bursting off its mirrored surface. The sailboats were becalmed, drifting easily in the slight, imperceptible swells. Everything was waiting. Including him.

Jennifer picked a dime out of the change Michael Casari had given her and dropped it into the telephone's slot.

The KZAM switchboard operator connected her to the *Everyday* offices. Enderall's secretary came on a second later.

"Edith? Jennifer Winters. Sorry I couldn't make it for the meeting this morning."

"Yes, Jennifer." Edith's voice sounded pinched. Like her face, Jennifer thought. "You're aware that the meeting was mandatory?"

"Well, yes. You see, my car—"

"Jennifer, I suggest you come in and speak with Mr. Enderall personally."

"My car—"

"Jennifer, I really think you should make every attempt to get in here. As soon as is humanly possible."

Jennifer was about to try to explain for the third time, but the phone had gone dead. Humanly possible, huh? The old bird ought to think about behaving like a human herself once in a while.

She glanced around the corner of the booth to her car in the garage. It was still up on the rack where it had been for an hour. Her spirits fell even further than they already were, something which she had thought was an impossibility.

She stared dully off into the horizon, trying to deaden her emotions.

At first she didn't think anything of it. There had to be a hundred thousand white Cadillacs cruising the streets of L.A. Then she thought she was hallucinating because the man in the white Biarritz Cadillac just pulling into the station was the spitting image of Michael Casari. In fact, it *was* Michael Casari.

She was across the drive, rooted in place next to the telephone booth. Michael had gotten out of the Biarritz and was walking toward the garage. His attention seemed to be on her car suspended on metal tracks, looking angelic, as if it were floating in space.

At that moment she was seized with two impulses: one, to sink into the pavement and avoid any further confrontation with the man; the other, to run across the pavement and tell him the whole truth, clear the air, and see if something could be salvaged of the relationship.

The garage mechanic gestured to the car, as if that were the topic of the conversation, then shook his head. Michael nodded, turned, and with his hands in his pockets, his head down, started back to the Cadillac.

He had only come to see about the bill, she supposed. Again there was another wave of disappointment.

But he looked up then, stared. At her.

At that moment she knew exactly what he was thinking. She could feel his thoughts as surely as if they were her own. He was sorry things had ended badly between them. And he wanted to begin again.

They started toward each other at the same time.

"Hi," Michael said when they had met halfway.

"Hi." Neither of them spoke for a moment. Nothing coherent would formulate in her mind. Finally she said, "The car—"

"I didn't come here about the car," Michael said, and quickly, with something approximating a sigh of resignation, he went on, "I came back for you."

"Look," Jennifer said, feeling walls of resistance tumbling about her, "I'm really sorry about all of that. You know . . ."

"Yeah. So am I." His dark eyes danced merrily. "I have a habit of being insufferably smug sometimes when it comes to what I consider lapses in someone else's morality."

"I beg your pardon," Jennifer said, bristling. "I didn't exactly drive a stake through your heart just by looking at the outside of an envelope."

He gave her a curious look, as if she had said something profound, but his mood remained light. "True, and I take back my word. It was a poor choice."

She was about ready to mention that her action had also been a poor choice, when he said, "Maybe *sneaky* or *underhanded* fits more aptly."

Jennifer arranged her eyes into narrow slits. "Now, wait just one minute here . . ." And then she saw that he was only joking with her.

"I guess maybe the word I was searching for was *curious*. Overtly curious."

They both smiled shyly, awkwardly. A truce had been declared.

"Well," Michael said, "I thought dinner might be nice."

"Dinner?"

"The two of us. Dinner."

Jennifer nodded. She felt herself falling into his eyes again. When you tumbled about in black, velvety pools of light, there was nothing a person could do but accept. "Yes, that could be nice."

They stood there like two teenagers shuffling their feet; she a woman who had dated some of the all-time ferocious barracuda of the movie and financial industries, and he a man who would give Robert De Niro a run for his money when it came to sex appeal.

"Then, it's a date?"

"Yes, sure, a date."

They had both been so serious, anyone observing from a distance would have thought they were discussing nuclear disarmament rather than a social engagement.

"Great, then . . ." Michael started to back away.

"Michael? When?" She was thoroughly enjoying his nervousness. It took her mind off her own.

He tossed his head back, shaking it self-deprecatingly.

"Tonight. How about seven tonight?"

"That's fine."

"So where do I pick you up?"

"I'll meet you," Jennifer answered reflexively. Never had she allowed anyone connected with her professionally to know where she lived. It was a precaution she took for the obvious reason of safety. The emotions of human beings were never predictable, and when under pressure, as many—no most—of the people she was "researching" were, explosions could occur.

"Okay, then . . . make it Jimmy's in Beverly Hills. It's a great place."

Michael had agreed but was looking at her queerly, as if trying to read into her again. Only this time the gates to her soul were drawn closed. It was an instinctive reaction for her to guard against her own privacy, even while she invaded others.

They said their good-byes, the general tone friendly. But as Jenny watched Michael Casari drive away she felt the cold feeling return again. The notion of unraveling the mystery of his relationship to Darla Hart had not been entirely abandoned. She wasn't particularly proud of herself, but there it was. The habit of surviving was difficult to break.

* * *

It was two o'clock and Edith was at her desk when Jennifer stopped by to make her command appearance before Enderall.

Edith looked up, weak gray eyes peering at her over brass-rimmed half-glasses. Enderall's secretary had been with him since the day he had taken his job at KZAM some fifteen years before. They were a team. To the staff it appeared that what Enderall thought, Edith spake. Although some were of the opinion that it was the other way around.

Which is why Jennifer felt particularly uneasy. The look Edith directed her way was not encouraging.

As she buzzed Enderall's office on her intercom, Edith said, "I hope you have a good explanation." And then, to Enderall's cranky "Yes, Edith?" she replied, "She's here."

"So," Enderall said when Jennifer had taken the proffered seat opposite his desk, "what a marvelous day you must have had for yourself."

If he only knew, she thought, but said, "I'm sorry about missing the meeting. My car—"

Enderall stood, scraping his chair against the linoleum floor. The sound made Jennifer wince and she broke off her explanation, although Enderall would have preempted her anyway with the next breath.

"I've let Angela Demerast go."

"Angela . . . ?" Last week it was Terrance Young. Now Angela. A sickly feeling turned her stomach and she tried not to let the fear take hold. When Terrance had gotten the axe, they could all read the writing on the wall. Periodically these purges would occur and she, along with the other staff members, would step up their already superhuman efforts to perform. Hence her four a.m. sojourn at the studio's gate.

"I'm sorry to hear that," she said. Angela had been with *Everyday*'s research staff for eight years. She was considered a fixture. Plus, Angela was good. Almost as a eulogy, Jennifer said as much. "Angela always delivered fine stories."

"Past tense," Enderall said. "We can no longer afford to live in the past."

For a moment Enderall appeared to drift, exactly as if having entered the past himself. The life and times of Casius P. Enderall were the stuff comprising company fables—part truth, part distortion, and with each successive retelling, always fluctuating. As well as Jennifer could determine, sifting fact from fiction, Enderall had been a young, feisty, hot-dog reporter who had gotten his start covering some nasty business over in Europe and several assassination attempts on the life of then President de Gaulle. He had interviewed and supposedly befriended Fidel Castro before things heated up around the Bay of Pigs incident and had copped inside scoops on kingpin Mafia members when the justice department couldn't get the inside track, and so on. KZAM was the number one station in Los Angeles then. They outbid every other major network to sign Enderall. The salary he commanded and got was unprecedented, written up in all major magazines, his actual worth the topic of great debate among his peers.

But just as the people whose lives he had profited from faded from prominence, died, or became inaccessible, KZAM's position similarly changed, and along with its decline came Enderall's. Jennifer guessed he was in his early fifties and taking the downturn on life's calendar poorly. Once trim, he now had a paunch that strained shirt buttons. Although not bald, his brown hair, flecked with equal strands of gray, had receded a third of the way up his dome. Aging was worse for people in their profession because everything they covered was notable. Somehow the fame of others rubbed off; it made you want to keep up with the movers and shakers of the world. A candidate who kept up a manic schedule would make you run faster. A guy who beat the bank in Las Vegas would inspire you to beat some other unbeatable system, to get that un-gettable interview, to unearth a fact which others claimed did not exist.

Somehow, being perpetually in the shadows cast by giants made one strive to be either ahead, as quick, or as big. Otherwise you could look down on the pavement and see how picayune a human you actually were. There was a theory in psychology proposing that men engaged in law enforcement were equipped with the same basic personality structure as that of the criminal element, the only difference being that the impulse for violence and craft was turned to the public's welfare. Jennifer's hypothesis about her own profession was that reporters, interviewers, and researchers lived vicariously off the glamour and heartache and danger that comprised other people's lives.

Most of the people she knew in her business were single. Socially they were mobile, forming quick and intense alliances. But beneath the laughing surface of smiles and professional confidences were remote personalities, un-willing—or unable—to connect on any permanent basis with other humans who could possibly bring them heart-ache along with any joy. Therefore, the compulsiveness, the constant flux, the quest to find the story—all of it was a disguised effort to feed the emptiness within.

She was looking at Enderall, but she was thinking of herself as well. It was safer to keep Michael Casari in a professional niche, in a nice safe manila folder, than have him carve a permanent place in her heart.

With a shock she realized Enderall was dabbing a handkerchief to his eyes.

"Sorry," he said, muffling a necessary sniff as best he could. "I, uh, I've been under a bit of pressure from upstairs and—"

Enderall stopped in the middle of his sentence, seemingly at a loss for words. His eyes, which had been merely moist before, were full to overflowing. Regardless of the new standards saying it was okay for men to cry, healthy for them to give vent to their emotions, it was still a rare occasion when Jennifer actually witnessed the phenomenon. Even under extreme conditions the male species kept up a stoic front, perhaps weeping only at times of the most extreme crises—a death of a child, the loss of a spouse. But here was Enderall looking as forlorn as any of those men.

Actually she wanted to clear out of there. It was embarrassing for both of them. And it wasn't as if she and Enderall were close pals. If anything, they had both been thorns in each other's sides. To break down in front of her like that, he had to be in desperate straits.

"I apologize," he said, and sat down again at his desk where he began to riffle through loose papers and folders.

She wasn't sure if he was actually searching for something specific or was just indulging in a diversion.

"Here it is." Enderall's eyes were trained on a paper filled with grids and graphs and numbers. "The ratings . . . they weren't good. They were"—he cleared his voice, which sounded fogged from excessive emotion—"very low."

"I see."

"No, I don't believe you do. We are in danger of being canceled."

"Canceled?"

"We've been given notice by upstairs," Enderall said,

studying either his cuticles or the statistics. Jennifer couldn't make up her mind which. Preceded by a deep shuddering sigh, his words came out as a plaintive sob. "I never thought, couldn't imagine, you see. Well, it's just that this is so . . ." His eyes clouded over again.

Humiliating. Jennifer didn't need to hear him say it. It was written in his eyes, in the downward slope of his shoulders. Suddenly their Trojan leader was diminished to a middle-aged man whose life essense was seeping relentlessly from him, as surely as if it were sand from an hourglass. It would do no good to offer sympathy; what he needed was to feel strong, in control.

"How long do we have to make a turnaround?"

"A month. Maybe on the outside I can buy six weeks."

"We can do it," Jennifer said, wondering at the same time how the hell that would be possible. A month.

"We've got to. You've got to. And the others," he said. "Otherwise it will be all of your behinds, too."

Jennifer felt better. He was sounding like the good ole Casius P. Enderall, the man they all feared and despised, but respected.

"We're going to need something big."

"Yes, of course. Big."

"No, no. I mean big, huge. A colossus of a story."

"Something like—"

"What *Today* does."

"I see." And, of course, she did. He was referring to the Darla Hart interview. The only thing she could think of to rival that was to get a personal interview from Chernenko one minute after defecting from the U.S.S.R. Somehow she doubted the man would be so accommodating as to change allegiances just to guarantee their show's ratings.

"Miss Winters." The two words caught in his throat and he stopped to clear his voice before beginning again. His attention was fixed on the pencil he was twirling between both hands. "Miss Winters," he said, "this is a very, very serious matter." With effort, he brought his eyes up. "Please try."

"Oh, Mr. Enderall . . ."

A tear was trickling down his cheek.

The offices of KZAM were not real offices, except for those belonging to Enderall and a few other station heads. The directors, however, holding court on the fifth and top floors of the building, had beige high-low carpet and real plaster walls that met the ceiling. As the ultimate in prestige, they had windows, windows that overlooked the smog-filled Hollywood Hills. The other floors were large cavernous affairs, into which six-foot-high, beige plastic-walled cubicles had been bolted to the beige linoleum floor. Each show had its territory, although to the unschooled eye all territories looked identical.

More than anything else, Jennifer thought it was the personalities that defined the geography at KZAM. She doubted that any other corner at the station had seen more savage battles waged than where the special staff researchers for *Everyday* hung their hats. The station employed ordinary researchers, too, but the special researchers were the Green Berets, the SWAT team of newscasting who went after the long-term assignments. By nature her fellow staffers were competitive and mean and cunning. She wouldn't trust any of them with her lunch money. Jennifer had often thought Machiavelli's blood would have turned cold at some of their schemes and counterschemes.

As she came down the narrow aisle flanked on either side by identical rabbit warrens, she noted a rare gathering of staffers in John Rudran's office.

All eyes turned to her as she stepped into view at the cubicle's opening. No cubicle had a door. It was a regulation-size office, square and about eight by eight. There was barely room for John Rudran's imitation-wood desk, a file cabinet, and the chair on which he sat. Even so, the others had managed to squeeze in.

Rita Levett, who was small and dark and wiry, and reminded Jennifer of a clever rodent, was sitting on the edge of John's desk.

John was seated in his own chair. In direct contrast to the swarthy Rita, he had perfect white teeth, blond surfer hair, a tan that never faded even during weeks of rain, and clothes that no one on his salary could possibly afford. To Jennifer he looked like the lost Beach Boy.

Then there was Rita Levett's sidekick, Arnold Fine. Arnold kept a needlepoint coat of arms hung on the wall of his office. It was French. His mother had made it herself to remind him of the family's roots before they became commoners about three hundred years ago. Slightly built and no taller than Rita, the would-be prince was standing by the file cabinet, his stance, as always, close to military attention.

The last remaining member of their division besides Jennifer was Estela Garcia.

Estela had been raised in East L.A. and had gone beyond the definition of tough. She had belonged to a Chicano street gang called the *Brujas*—which literally translated as "witches," but figuratively conjured images dark enough to render absolute black pale. In 1974 the Brujas had spray-painted their name in blood-red over half of Los Angeles. It was still there on some freeway overpasses, scrawled malignantly over the sides of buildings and fences. A sensible person would sooner remove Mount Rushmore from the American landscape than tamper with the insignia of the Brujas. Estela had originally attended U.C.L.A. on a rehab program and eventually graduated twentieth out of a class of eight hundred. She would often lapse into Spanish just to be annoying. In fact, she had spent an entire year at Oxford and had a great ear for dialect—street talk, tea talk, you name it. If she wanted, she could speak the Queen's English so flawlessly, a subject would want to curtsy.

So there they all were, staring at her.

"Hey, Winters," John said.

"High court's convening?" Jennifer asked, looking from face to face.

"Did you hear?" Rita's black ball-bearing eyes gleamed across the cubicle at her. "Heads are rolling again."

" 'Tis the season," said Arnold.

"I know, I know. I just saw Enderall."

"He almost blew a gasket this morning," John said. "He hauled us into the conference room and made us watch the Darla Hart interview."

At the mention of the columnist's name, Jenny's mind flew instantly to Michael Casari. Tantalizing shivers raced through her as if someone had trailed a feather over every erogenous zone in her body.

John was holding a photocopy of an interoffice memorandum in his hand. "We're number five in the ratings."

"Six," droned Estela, who had a photographic memory.

John checked. "Six."

Jennifer winced. "God. Six. Really, six?"

"*Cousin Billy Bob* was five last week," Rita volunteered.

Jennifer felt her stomach turn over. It was scary. Also humiliating. *Cousin Billy Bob* was a children's show with no redeeming educational or humanitarian value.

Estela had taken out a file and was working diligently on repairing a nail. "Also," Estela said, *"Guiding Wisdom* beat us out. And *Good Morning America* and *Today* and *The Green Woman."*

Jennifer shook her head. "Not *The Green Woman.* She's such a jerk." *The Green Woman* was a daily gardening extravaganza hosted by a manic English woman who did features on the eradication of nematodes from tomato patches.

They all stood there, silent, as if in prayer. And that reminded Jennifer that they had been beaten out by an electronic preacher who wouldn't know an angel if it flew up his nose.

"So? Does anyone have any bright ideas? Like on how to make a miracle happen by the end of next month?" Jennifer's question was met by a blank wall of faces.

"Sweetie," Rita said, "you've got to move your little prom queen tail faster. You missed the meeting this morning, and you missed our little get-together this afternoon. You're behind the times."

"Okay, okay, Rita," Jennifer said. Rita seemed to hate a great many things and people just on general principle. Her animosity extended to taller people, richer people, people who drove any kind of sports car—in fact, people in general. As for the things Rita hated, that was more discretionary. If Rita didn't own it, it wasn't any good. "My apologies. But maybe someone might fill me in on the nature of the big pow-wow?"

"Sure," said Rita. "The bottom line is, we're all out to save our own skin."

"Oh. But wouldn't it make more sense to work as a team?" Jennifer suggested.

"Enderall is not chopping teams," Arnold said, his voice

as well modulated as Rita's was strident. ''He is chopping individual heads. One must therefore hold dearly to one's own scalp.''

Jennifer had claimed all eyes. It was disconcerting, but not unexpected, that they all seemed to be looking at her head with uncommon interest.

Chapter 4

JENNIFER SPENT THE REMAINDER OF THE AFTERNOON IN her own cubicle. She knew she couldn't afford the hysteria that had gripped the rest of them, but knowing something and controlling it were entirely different endeavors.

Brilliant ideas will come, she told herself, and spent the next ten minutes staring at the blank piece of paper on her desk.

When no idea materialized, and just to have something down in black and white, she wrote: *What do people want to know about?*

That was easy, easy. Why, the latest political sex scandal, of course. A Hollywood marriage or divorce. Heroes and villains. Exposés on famous people. Immediately, as if the thought had been waiting like an actor in the wings anticipating his cue, the image of Darla Hart took shape, to be followed in quick succession by Michael Casari's handsome face superimposed over the columnist's.

He smiled at her just as he had in the convenience store. It was a brilliant white open smile, and to see it made her heart leap, sent thrills of erotic sensation traveling through her body. It was a smile holding rainbows and brightly colored balloons that danced in the wind.

The next thought struck like a whip, slashing through her visions which broke apart and flew off to some purgatory for discarded dreams. *She was falling in love.*

Although she had never been in love before, the emotion was every bit as recognizable as having an elephant sit down beside her. It simply wasn't possible to ignore the obvious, if for no other reason than there was nothing at all like that feeling in the entire world. The thought of Michael brought forth a rush of exhilaration. There was the false impression that they had always known each other.

No sooner had her spirit flown with this untamed emotion than a vague uneasiness settled over her. Not far down the hall, Rita's strident voice was heard issuing some order to the group secretary. That was reality. Rita and Arnold and Enderall were reality. Love had little to do with the world she had grown to know so painfully well during the past five years. Money was important, and power. In Los Angeles the image of having both was as valuable as the commodities themselves. Love, whenever it did appear, seemed an aberration. In the past, Jennifer had reported on all varieties of humans who had gone on emotional benders because of love, losing their jobs, their families, sometimes even their minds, and at the worst, their lives. But even as she cautioned herself, a seed of hope growing deep within her could not entirely be denied. Maybe that was it, she thought; love was an alien germ, some virus that could not be eradicated once a person was infected. The fanciful idea both excited and frightened her; her crazy notion might not be all that far from the truth.

She forced herself to concentrate on tangibles, like paying her rent and eating and maybe someday even buying a new top for her car. The alien germ, she figured, would take care of itself without her encouragement or even her discouragement. Instinct told her love was independent.

What do people want to know about? To tame her thoughts, she underlined the question several times in black ink.

Whimsically, she marked down *animals*. And beside this she wrote a number one, followed by *zoo story*, not because she actually thought the topic would do for Enderall's purposes, but because it was a gentle subject. To think of millions of people tuned in to their television sets learning about innocent creatures, sympathizing with their struggles, investigating their mysteries, made the world into an infinitely better place than the one that Jennifer knew actually existed.

There was a knock-knock on her six-foot-high plastic wall. Looking up, she found John Rudran framed in her doorway.

"Hey, babe."

"Hey, John."

He stood in a sexy hip-shot pose, smiling at her with his beige unstructured jacket slung over his shoulder. As John rarely bothered with anyone or anything that couldn't advance his interests, Jennifer wondered what he was after from her.

"Time to call it a day," he said amiably, his eyes drifting to the paper on her desk.

"Already?" Jennifer glanced at her watch. It was going on a quarter of five. The hour conjured immediate sense impressions of exhaust fumes and bumper to bumper cars. "Right you are. Time flies when you're having a ball."

"How's it going?" John's eyes darted quickly up from

the paper to meet her face. In spite of the ingratiating smile, there was an undercurrent of tightly coiled desperation to his manner.

"Okay for quitting time." She left her chair to get her purse from the bottom drawer of the file cabinet. Like water filling a void, John slid into the space where she had been.

"Any ideas yet?"

Jennifer noted the hungry blue eyes sweeping over the paper on her desk. She crossed back, casually claimed the paper, and folded it in two, with the next motion making it disappear inside her purse. "A few," she answered.

"No kidding? Already." He sounded impressed.

She knew he wasn't, that he would be inwardly laughing at the topic he had seen scratched on her page, that as soon as he left her cubicle, he would burst into hysterics, probably sharing his hilarity with Rita and Arnold if he could make it that far without collapsing from glee.

Perversely she let him think what he wanted. "Yeah, don't you think something on animals at the L.A. zoo would be interesting, John?"

"Oh, yeah. Animals are a gas. I agree totally."

"Well, actually, John, I don't. What I mean is, I really do like animals, but that's not what this witch hunt is all about, is it?"

John looked to Jennifer like a man who had laughed prematurely at the wrong punch line, only to find himself the brunt of the joke. Unsure now, he said, "No. Guess not." His face clouded.

"Enderall wants something really hot. Got anything?"

He shrugged and shifted position in the doorway. "An idea or two." Holding out his jacket, he examined it for lint and said, "So what've you got going, Jen?"

"Oh, something . . ." she said mysteriously.

"Yeah?" John forgot about the hunt for lint. "Something what?"

"Something good. Maybe even pretty terrific." She was smiling to herself as she locked her desk and file cabinet.

"Yeah?"

"Could be." With her purse under her arm, she edged past him.

Following her out, he said, "Like what, Jen?"

"Secret, John. Every man for himself. Remember?"

Leaving him with a jaunty thumbs-up sign, she made her way down the aisle toward the elevator. It wasn't until she was on ground level that she realized she had forgotten her Thermos in the bottom drawer of her file cabinet. She pressed the up button and made the trip back to her floor.

Before she had even reached her cubicle, she heard the hushed voices coming from her office. They were so engrossed in their project, they didn't even hear her enter.

She stood just inside the doorway. There was barely room for all of them. John was crouched down by her file cabinet with a paper clip, trying to jimmy open the lock. Arnold and Rita were standing by her desk, on which they had placed her wastebasket. Both of them held previously discarded paper in their hands.

"Well, well. What are you doing in here?" she asked conversationally. Her anger was so acute, so fertile, that it had to be controlled or she'd end up making a spectacle of herself.

The other three looked up, startled, aware of her for the first time.

"Jenny, hey . . ." John flushed. He tried, but couldn't manage one of his perfect magazine smiles.

"Okay, I'll ask my question again. What are you doing in my office?" Jenny looked from John to Rita to Arnold. Only John had the grace to hang his head.

"We're playing trash collector," Arnold said, and removed her metal wastebasket from the top of her desk. With all the aplomb of a prince who had inadvertently touched upon something foul, he redeposited the crumbled piece of paper he had been holding in his hand.

"Were you? Well? What did you find?" Jennifer sauntered forward to snatch from Rita what she recognized to be part of an old report she had discarded from her file earlier that afternoon when she was searching for inspiration for new ideas.

"Garbage, what else?" Rita said in her usual calm and insolent fashion.

John was inching his way around the perimeter of the cubicle, heading for the door.

"John, once discovered, a sneak no longer needs to skulk about. Unless, of course, skulking becomes second nature."

"You know, Winters," Rita said, smirking, "it's not like you're protecting a gold mine of creative inspiration here."

"Perhaps not. But when you came in here, you didn't know that, did you?"

"All we were was just curious," Arnold added. "It's part of our job to be curious."

"Oh, come on, Arnold, you're starting to sound defensive. Next you'll be making excuses."

"So all right," Rita said, "we were hunting for little green men."

"Oh, I do like that," Jennifer said. She was smiling brightly, but inwardly she was trembling. It was just one more assault on her ideals. Honor and integrity and good will were text book values taught by professors isolated in their ivory towers. "You know, Rita, you might see little green stars one day if I ever catch you going through my things again.''

"You're overreacting," Arnold said, placatingly. "This sort of thing goes with the territory, Winters.''

"Not my territory, Arnold."

"Lighten up," Rita said in parting.

The three left together, like a malodorous haze drifting down the aisleway, Jennifer thought. She spent a minute sitting at her desk, fighting fury and tears, then got the Thermos she had come back for and headed out again.

On the way back to her apartment she stopped at the Stop N' Go market to pick up bread and milk. The little store had been robbed so many times—four during the past month— that it had become known as the Stop N' Rob to people in the area.

Jennifer paid for her purchases at the counter, smiling back at Sung Ock, the store's small proprietor, who nodded and bowed several times as he returned her change. They rarely spoke, as Sung Ock was not so fluent in English as he was with his cash register. He had come from Korea only six years ago. Jennifer had worked up a special news feature on him, which was presented by one of the anchor people as a spotlight on Los Angeles's divergent ethnic mix.

Jennifer admired Sung Ock. He was a fighter. Only a bit past five feet tall, the forty-three-year-old Korean had a crinkled, wizened face that made him look about a hundred. But the tiny person had fought in a bloody war, lived to emigrate to the United States, worked two factory shifts in an electronics plant for five years so he could bring his wife and six children to the Land of the Free, and, miraculously, somehow saved enough money to buy into the franchise. Whatever his past, Sung Ock looked happy enough when he handed her the bag with her bread and milk.

Traveling along Centinella Boulevard was like taking a tour of Disneyland's "It's a Small World." The Buddhist temple, with its stark exterior guarded by elaborately bonsaid conifers, gave way to stores selling raw fish for sushi, signs plastered on windows advertising *Sapporo* beer, and farther down the street, out of the business section, modest but immaculately maintained homes where Japanese had quietly settled after World War II.

But then the landscape suddenly changed, as if an invisible barrier had been erected. Meat markets sold chorizo and the beer being hawked was Dos XX. Manuel *con* Lupe. *La Raza. Los Vatos Mandan.* Graffiti on the sides of buildings and on bus benches warned and informed.

Farther along, the street's personality evolved into a mishmash of Korean and Vietnamese, finally giving way to a vague Anglo flavor of architecturally uninspired apartment buildings with grandiose names.

Jennifer passed The Kingsway Arms and The Ritz, pulling the green MG against the curb to take the only available parking space beneath a spreading Brazilian pepper tree—a particular favorite of all the neighborhood birds. Which was why the space was available.

She reached for her groceries, then remembered the other brown bag she kept on the floor for such occasions. She dug her hand into it and pulled out a handful of bread crusts which she distributed on the hood. Her reasoning was, they were going to get her anyway, so she might as well build up good will. Maybe they would keep the really big birds away. Gulls were genuine bad news.

The La Fortunada apartment building, where she lived, attracted mostly unfortunate beings. In the two years Jennifer had made it her home, residents had silently come and gone, slipping out the back door just as the skip-tracer slipped in the front. Once past the showy facade, a person found himself in a hollow courtyard no wider than perhaps twenty feet, its center dotted with smog-blighted palms. Apartments were arranged on either side of the courtyard. There were two stories to La Fortunada's configuration. Each apartment had one door and one giant picture window, as if in some mad flight of fancy the contractor had envisioned residents peering out at rolling lawns and blazing sunsets, rather than at an opposing picture window. Being so close to the Pacific there was no air conditioning, which was a mistake. For some reason, the La Fortunada had a propensity for trapping dead air in its courtyard. Indeed, it was a virtual tomb for fresh air, or as Jennifer had sometimes thought on her more discouraging days, a crypt for tired dreams.

It was necessary for all the residents to leave their doors and windows open. This made crossing the courtyard to her apartment at the farthest end a debilitating experience. She would run the gauntlet, bombarded by the static noise from game shows, Mexican soap operas, wrestling matches, and canned laughter from situation comedies.

But the trip was worth the sound effects. Her apartment was unlike the others. It was on the second floor and in the corner, where the stairs took an unexpected jog to the left and went up a half floor. In essence, it was a quiet, safe little place and she had fixed it up with great attention to aesthetic detail.

She secured her four locks, put away her milk and bread, and took care of rinsing out her Thermos. It was five-thirty when she put a record on her stereo, started to peel her clothes off, and allowed herself to think of the man she believed she was falling, seriously, in love with.

Her bath was accompanied by a running interior dialogue between this rash new self of hers that had suddenly reared its head and the sensible self who was unwilling to give into

emotions promising no more solidity than the pink bubbles
billowing over her raised kneecaps. The sensations that
arose as she slicked soap over her breasts, down her
stomach, between her legs, did nothing to further the
recommendations put forth by her staid self. It was not her
hand she felt on her body, but Michael's, and the heat that
filled her at the thought of giving herself to him fully made
her eyes close automatically. Slipping further into the
water, she lost herself to its warmth, thinking all the while
of Michael and of how it could be.

At five minutes past seven, Michael was sitting in the bar
at Jimmy's in Beverly Hills. His eyes were trained on the
entrance. He had begun his vigil twenty minutes before
seven, and now every second seemed a millennium.

She won't come, his mind said. In a different voice, his
mind answered, *But of course she will.*

The conversation was typical. His mind had run rampant
ever since the mysterious, lovely creature had entered his
life that morning. God, he thought, had it only been that
morning? An eternity had passed since then. His world had
flip-flopped.

After he had gotten his anger under control, he had called
Lena. She was, as usual, both repentant and ready to cast
the blame of her failure to him. Michael gallantly assured
her that no major harm had been done by flubbing her lines
before half of America. He didn't know if that was true,
only that Morey was frantically leaking stories to the press
to the effect that Darla Hart had been under severe emotional strain due to her involvement with her readers' problems.
Michael restricted his information to Morey's efforts,
disregarding his own doubts about professional damage.

"Well, that's the truth," Lena had mumbled, a past

master at piteous melodrama, "about the severe emotional strain."

After that, he had tried to work, but couldn't. Up to that morning, work had been his life. Glorious work. For him, the salve for all psychic ills. With Pavlovian response, his attention had focused on the mailbox (as he and Morey had come to call it during the last few years). Dutifully, he had taken it into his office and removed the batch of letters already screened for him by a professional reading service.

He skimmed through a few letters, selected a couple of promising topics, namely problems he hadn't addressed himself to during the past few months. After the first couple of years of writing the Darla Hart column, he had reached the conclusion that there was only one real problem in the world, one which illusively presented itself in myriad disguises, making it that much more difficult to deal with. As he saw it, the basic underlying issue in all cases was simply *love*. For lack of love, wars were fought, suicides occurred, men drank, and women wept, ad infinitum. All the learned psychological jargon and sociological treatises boiled down to one concept: that of love; how to get it, and once possessed, how to keep it.

That morning, he had turned on his word processor with the best of intentions, ready to meet his day's quota of dispensed electronic wisdom. And there he had sat, staring at the blank screen.

He simply wasn't interested in working. It was so much nicer to drift in his imagination, thinking his rose-tinted thoughts. So he turned off the machine and took off down the beach.

He had peered up at the sky, amazingly blue, bluer than he had ever seen it before. He watched gulls circle more gracefully than they had ever circled. He saw women, some

forms tight and sleek, others soft and voluptuous, all of
them desirable. The face of Jennifer Winters flashed before
him, then her body, now clothed, now unclothed as he
imagined it would look. His anatomical nature shifted into
gear, and thinking less of white clouds and more of black
satin sheets upon which Jennifer Winters's unclothed body
lay stretched out and available to him, he continued both
happily and dreamily on his erotic stroll.

A dark outcropping of black rocks, pitted by the nibbling
of generations of sea creatures during high tide, presented a
perfect spot on which to continue his dedicated musing. He
climbed up, finding a suitable perch at the highest point of
the colony of stone. With the sun upon him, and a swift
ocean breeze pulling in from the southwest, he felt a thrill
of elation lift him high into a state he had not experienced
since he was . . . what? A kid, really. A kid flying a kite.
Climbing a tree to the very top. Saving the life of a
wounded bird and setting it free, able to see it fly away
again.

He stood on the top of the rock, and at thirty-five years of
age he felt that same way.

Really good.

At that instant he strongly suspected that he had fallen in
love.

The valet at Jimmy's was obviously not a naturalist.
From the curl of his lip, Jennifer could tell he had been less
than impressed by her car, its hood speckled by white bird
leavings. His snobbery did not extend to her body, however. As she walked to the restaurant's front entrance, she
held his interest far more than the white Rolls-Royce which
had nosed up behind her MG's rusting bumper.

The season was entering late June, which wasn't truly
summer yet for Southern California, and the mornings were

plagued by low clouds and moist Pacific winds, but Jenny already had a tan started. It looked even darker against the soft-pink jersey she had slipped on for her dinner with Michael. The dress clung, molding to her curves as she walked. Slightly flared at the bottom, the garment whipped sassily about her legs with each movement. But basically, it was a plain dress, decidedly ladylike, which was why she had bought it in the first place. Unfortunately, the combination of the dress's innocence and her physical attributes created an effect more vamp than schoolmarm. To save time, her hair had been left to dry naturally. When she brushed it straight, it formed a pale, blond fluff around her face. That morning, she had looked like a stray cat; tonight she wanted to be beautiful.

The driver of the Rolls beeped his horn, commanding attention from attendants whose minds were obviously not on their work.

Upon entering the restaurant frequented by the wealthy and famous, Jennifer immediately felt herself the object of interest to many wealthy and famous eyes. It was not only the men who detailed her figure with frank stares, but also the women, whose looks were thorough and professional. Appearance, along with money and power, were commodities to be exploited. She felt like a walking monetary exchange rate as she looked for Michael.

She saw him in profile. He was sitting at the bar, engaged in an interchange with the bartender. Barely a second passed before he flicked his head to the door and their eyes met. The familiar current traveled the distance between them. Lost in the dark depths of his eyes, she scarcely noticed that he had left the stool and was coming toward her.

"Hi," she said, feeling weak-kneed and excited. "I'm sorry. I'm a few minutes late."

"Twelve," he said quickly, not having to look at his watch.

"Traffic. A real mess on the freeway."

They were standing near the entrance, oblivious to the pedestrian traffic they were blocking.

"No problem," he said. "Just now arrived myself."

"Oh, good."

"No, I didn't." His eyes reflected humor. "I got here twenty minutes early. When I wasn't looking at the door, my mind was riding the second hand of my watch."

If it had been anyone else, Jennifer would have interpreted his honesty as false, no more than a means to entice her romantically, and in the same classification of singles' bar talk. She had done a story on the singles' scene for *Everyday*. Although each bar had a different name, the patter was more or less the same. "Hi, my name is blah blah. I never come to places like this. Bet you don't either. All the people seem so plastic, don't they? How can they expect to find a real relationship here? I'm only interested in a real relationship. How about you? You want to go someplace else?" Like to a quiet apartment where a rumpled unmade bed was as cold as the soul who made what he called love on its sheets. Even the faces began to look alike to Jennifer: overbright eyes dulling when she turned down their offers for casual sex; tight smiles hanging slack as they scanned through the smoke for a new contact.

But behind Michael's smile she had read nothing false. His admission of his interest in her was presented without any expectation on his part.

With uncommon impulsiveness, she said, "I was looking forward to seeing you, too." Only, halfway through her declaration the words caught in her throat, and the remainder of the sentence came out guarded.

Michael cocked his head slightly. She realized his ears could pick up false tones as easily as her own.

Michael gave his name to the reservationist. They were seated at once. Michael ordered for them. They had caviar—beluga—and blinis, served in an enormous cut crystal bowl with individual crystal pockets filled with chopped egg, minced onion, lemon wedges, and sour cream.

Afterward, they had salads, followed by roast duck in raspberry sauce and a few steamed vegetables as a side dish. A sparkling rose accompanied the main course, and before dessert was served, Michael sent for a bottle of champagne, expensive enough to raise the eyebrows of the wine steward.

Throughout the meal their conversation had been sparce and sedate. The attempt at decorum was forced, a deliberate form of overcompensation for the silly smiles that seemed to erupt over each of their faces whenever their eyes touched.

Finally, with his voice edged in gravity, he said, "So, you got your car repaired. And then what did you do the rest of the day?"

Jennifer's grip tightened on her spoon. She had been about to dip into a bowl of fresh blueberries and cream. This was her opportunity to come clean with him, to let the relationship stand on its own. Away with all conflicting emotions. Away with all duplicity.

"I want to know what you do, where you go," Michael was saying with sudden abandonment. "What kind of a place do you live in? What television shows do you watch? Are you a Safeway or a Ralph's advocate? Did you study French? Did you have braces on your teeth when you were fifteen? I did. Killed my sex life for two years. It wasn't much to begin with though, not much harm done. Do you like Europe? Have you *been* to Europe? Let me take you.''

He laughed at his own exuberance, seemingly delighted with everything and nothing as he looked around the room at their surroundings, then back to her.

She was still holding the spoon in her hand, her spine a rigid column.

The happiness in Michael's face dimmed. ''What's wrong?''

Her left hand had been resting beside her plate. Michael reached across the table and covered it lightly with his own, then repeated his question. ''Jennifer, tell me. What is it?''

A sigh escaped as she closed her eyes.

''Ah . . . you're married,'' he said.

Slowly, reluctantly, his hand removed itself from hers.

''No,'' Jennifer said, and she had to force herself to look at him. ''Worse.''

He was saying nothing, only waiting. She could sense him prepare for whatever she had to tell him.

''This morning I was following you.''

His brows furrowed slightly, trying to make sense of her statement.

''Yes,'' she went on. ''I'm a researcher like I told you. Only, I work for *Everyday*. I do special assignments for the show. Our ratings have been falling steadily. Panic's so thick at KZAM you could slice it with a knife.'' Now it was Michael who glanced away, who couldn't meet her face. It was a mistake, this honesty. She should have kept her mouth shut and let whatever was to happen take its course. But once begun, she had no choice but to continue. Reluctantly, she went on. ''Yesterday I watched the Darla Hart interview. I knew she'd be taping another segment today, and I knew where.''

''I see.''

"No," Jennifer said, the single word violent in its objection. "You don't see. Or at least, not far enough." She lowered her eyes to the table. As she spoke she could feel his pain. That cut her more than if he had denounced her with a biting remark; she knew the pain of disillusionment too well not to take his hurt as her own. She faced disappointment every day, with every story she turned in to Enderall. It was odd, but she had never become immune to the pain of watching her dreams butchered.

"You're right. I didn't see far enough past the pretty face." Sorrow surrounded them like a haze.

"When I went to your home, it was because of you."

"Certainly."

"It was."

"Would you have made love to me to get your story?"

"No, no. Please, let me explain."

Michael was very calm. Too calm. Jennifer imagined him folding in on himself like a brilliant flower retracting petals that had been luxuriating in the sun's warmth. Her words were the sudden chill, the darkness responsible for spoiling all the beauty.

"Jennifer, it's not necessary. Really, I can understand what happened. You're in a tough business. If you want to succeed, you've got to go with the rules of the game you're playing."

"I wasn't playing any game. It's called earning a living. Putting food in my mouth. That sort of thing."

"Yeah, sure, sure." Michael reached for his glass.

The champagne had stopped bubbling. Like everything else between them, it too had gone flat. Jennifer's mind fell back to the morning. There had been champagne then, too. Lively. Fresh. And Michael's mouth had been smiling, instead of being set into its current grim acceptance.

Jennifer dropped her hands into her lap, folding her

fingers into a cradle. The tension between them was expanding like a balloon about to explode. Her mind felt sluggish, caught in some nightmarish dream.

Michael's hand rose. He signaled for the check to be brought.

"So," he said, "you're in research. That much was true, anyway." His tone was laced with something approximating good-natured irony.

He also wouldn't look at her anymore. The black eyes which had shone during dinner, trailing languorously over her face, on occasion vacationing to the swell of her breasts, now restlessly toured the restaurant.

"Oh, look, you've got to believe this. I didn't come to your home this morning to seduce you into giving me information."

"Then why?" he asked. His words held a challenge more than a question.

"Do you really want to know the truth? Or am I just an insect under a glass?"

The waiter appeared with the bill tucked discreetly inside a leather folder. Michael opened it, then, as if remembering they had been having a discussion, closed it and looked back to her.

"Sorry," he said without sounding it. "I'm genuinely interested."

"All right," Jennifer said. On the chance that his frigid attitude was a mask for his disappointment, she decided to go for broke. And in fact, broke was what she felt— depleted of spirit, diminished of energy and will. "I took my job because I wanted to make changes in the world."

Michael looked down to his coffee cup, but not before Jennifer had seen a movement in the eyes. Whatever more he thought as she went on, she couldn't tell. His feelings

were made private by the veil of sable lashes, silken tips
curving slightly away from his tanned skin.

"I guess by nature I'm very stubborn. Tenacious. So
after I got my job at KZAM, I wouldn't give up my
illusions. You know, the illusions that get drummed into
you when you're a kid in school? The lectures from your
parents on how things *really* are, in spite of all evidence to
the contrary. About how this world is really a garden filled
with beautiful people who will respond to beautiful deeds.
How if you work hard and have nobility of purpose, you can
move mountains, reach the highest star." Jennifer
shrugged. "That sort of garbage." Looking up, she saw
that Michael's attention was fully focused on her. His eyes
glistened with what she took as the light of understanding.
A quiet warmth seemed to radiate outward from him to her.
She basked in it for a moment. Was it going to be all right?
She attempted to send him back that warm feeling, for a
moment wanting nothing more than to reach out and touch
her fingers to the side of his face, to trace the outline of the
lips she had tasted.

"Well," she went on, "the scenario played like this. I
would come in with some nice humanitarian story and it
would get a big yawn from the powers at *Everyday*. The
anchor people would rant and rave. They are like a bunch of
sharks hungry for bloody meat. So, I'd try to compromise.
I'd bring stories of interest about people who were doing
things, maybe not always good things. But they had their
reasons for whatever they did, and the way I presented those
stories, they were human beings not entirely good and not
entirely bad, but faced with life." Jennifer picked up her
spoon and saw a wavy reflection of herself in its smooth
bowled scoop. She wished she could see a nice flat image
with clean, definable lines. That's how she would have

liked all of life to have been. She went on. "Only, by the
time the story got aired, there was no semblance to what I
had originally intended to be shown. A small aside I may
have made about a man playing the horses, became the
grounds for an innuendo that the man was heavily into
gambling. If he had gone to the same high school with an
underworld figure, they'd blast that on the airwaves. It
wasn't that they would lie. They would merely present
disparate facts in such a way that no one would be able to
focus on the truth."

"But you stayed anyway."

Jennifer nodded. She had been judged prematurely.

"I complained, of course," she said in defense. Michael's look was blank. "And whenever I did, they'd hold a
carrot on a stick out to me. I would tell them what I wanted
to do and they would say, fine, that was admirable. Just
wait a while. As soon as the ratings got better, they told me
I'd be able to do my features. Exactly the way I wanted
them to be presented, too. Only our ratings didn't go up. By
this time it seemed that the whole media was into a war of
yellow journalism, each show bringing out bigger and more
deadly ammunition. It didn't matter where I went to work,
it was all going to be the same."

"So you gave them what they wanted."

"No. That was the problem. And I got called on the
carpet more than once for it. Was almost canned a couple of
times. I even looked around for other jobs. Nothing. A
wasteland. After Woodward and Bernstein's glorified reporting, every high school and college kid who could read
and write wanted to save the nation."

"Including you."

Jennifer felt herself coloring. "Yes. Including me. I
know that sounds egotistical, and not a little stupid."

Michael nodded, agreeing with her. Only it was more as if he were answering himself than her.

"So, I was elated when I saw Darla Hart on television. I figured, here was this icon, this perfect human being whom no one could make into a fool or a criminal. I'd be able to eat my cake and have it, too. The biggest and bestest story in the land—all mine. If I could get to her. Only I couldn't, not directly, that is. So—"

"You thought you'd use me."

"Yes."

"And you did."

"No. No, that's not true. I went to your home without any ulterior motive."

"You honestly expect me to believe that?" Disbelief stained his expression, which for a while had softened.

"It's the truth."

Michael fidgeted, picking up and putting down his glass, looking away, then back to her. "Jennifer, I would honestly like to believe you."

His heart was rushing to her through his eyes, and quickly, before the feeling was withdrawn into a place of safety, she said, "Michael, please, please try. I went with you this morning because I just felt totally whipped by the world. I needed to be with another human being."

"Jennifer, Jennifer . . . I was a stranger."

"No," she said, "you weren't. That is, there was something about you. There was a connection between us the moment we saw each other. I know that, Michael."

In the silence following her speech the words she had spoken in such a rush of fervor and conviction hung suspended in the air, an embarrassment.

He *was* a stranger; an attractive man who just so happened to be her link to a job that would set both her and her station high on the charts. Of course he wasn't going to believe her.

Michael slipped some cash between the covers of the leather folder. "We'd better call it a night." He stood, and immediately a waiter appeared to assist Jennifer from her chair.

"Everything was all right, sir?" the waiter asked.

"Everything was splendid."

The sarcasm was for her. "Sorry the company was off," she said.

Michael smiled wanly. "I'm sorry for a lot more."

The valet collected their parking tickets at the front entrance. They waited together like two strangers at a bus stop.

Her car was brought around first. It clunked to a stop. The valet held the door open for her. Michael came up and tipped the man a dollar. Jennifer stopped him as he started away. "I'd appreciate it if you'd send me the bill for the repairs. Mail it to KZAM, my attention. Only you'd better hurry. I don't know how much longer I'm going to be there."

She was in the car with the door closed, when he suddenly appeared by her side again. He leaned down and reached his hand around her head, fingers entwined in her long hair, to turn her face to him.

He kissed her hard on the mouth, then, glaring ferociously at her, said, "I'm not letting you go."

Chapter 5

A TIGHT KNOT UNFURLED AND CONTRACTED IN MICHAEL'S
gut as he drove down Pacific Coast Highway going toward
Malibu. He felt like the condemned driving to his own
execution. Now and then he would take a look in his
rearview mirror to make sure the MG still followed.

Jennifer, he thought. Then, *damn you*. He didn't mean it;
and yet he did. She had forced him into a corner. The
corner unfortunately had no escape route—the corner was
himself.

Driving behind the Cadillac, Jennifer did not know what
to think. So she did the opposite and tried making her mind
a blank. When that didn't work, she gave her thoughts over
to the lingering sensation of Michael's lips upon hers. The
kiss may have been a gesture of unbridled passion all right,
but anger had also been mixed in with Michael's fierce
display of sexuality.

Ahead of her, the red taillights of the Biarritz glowed like two eyes. Michael stepped on the brakes; the eyes grew brighter, angrier, flickering a subtle warning of what was to come. Still, she followed along obediently, all the while wondering why she didn't turn around and go home. She could only be letting herself in for more grief by going to Michael's house. It wasn't as if he had extended a warm invitation for some good wine and conversation. They were going to talk. "To have this thing out completely," he had said, after his prolonged kiss. When it had ended, she had been left with her hands on the steering wheel and the world swirling dizzily around her.

This meeting was a command performance all the way. She remembered the previous scene played on the same set that morning. Unfortunately, second acts always contained the crises. This might be one of those unfinished works with no third act to follow. No possible resolution. No satisfying denouement.

Actually, knowing what she did about life in general, there was no justification for what she was doing. Either she had become a masochist, or falling in love made a person do strange things against their better judgment.

The thing of it was, she felt compelled to go. She wanted to go. Even if it hurt. Left with the alternative of separating herself from Michael forever, this seemed the lesser of two unpleasant propositions. Alcoholism had never made sense to her. The need people had for drugs was incomprehensible. Given recent medical studies, she knew her bias was simplistic and unenlightened, probably even cruelly unsympathetic, but if something clearly wasn't good for you, why bother with it? Only now she had been educated, her horizons expanded. This present craving of hers provided a glimpse into the darker excesses of human emotions. If there was such a thing as a love junkie, she was it. She wanted, even for one more time, that sensation of his mouth on hers. She wanted to float freely outside of time and space in his eyes. And it was all so foolish and pointless.

They had reached Michael's house.

Jennifer pulled her MG into the garage, parking in the empty stall beside the Cadillac.

Michael left his car and headed straight up the steps leading to his kitchen. The light from the garage opener was still on. In his white dinner jacket and cream-colored slacks, Jennifer thought he had never looked more handsome. This time his black eyes gave no hint of his thoughts as he held the door, waiting for her to enter.

They were close enough to touch as she passed by. Neither of them spoke. The automatic opener's light went out as she stepped across his threshold. Her imagination was too vivid not to take that as an omen.

Jennifer wandered past him into the living room while he clanked around, looking for something in the kitchen drawers and cupboards. A moment later he joined her, bringing with him an opened bottle of Chablis and two glasses.

She watched him as he put the glasses on the coffee table, then removed them and took them to a sideboard. He was taking forever to do everything. She doubted he was deliberately trying to torture her with anticipation. From his expression, he appeared to be fighting inner dragons; and worse, losing the battle.

Abruptly, he turned. Her eyes had been on him, and for a long moment they stared at each other, two combatants scheduled for a round in the ring. Each sized up the other, both of them too professional to give away feelings that would give an edge to the other.

She waited for him to speak, not knowing if she would be

ripped to shreds or forgiven for her duplicity. The kiss could have been nothing more than a knee-jerk reflex to recapture the faded dream they had shared earlier.

Finally, and with obvious reluctance to open communication, he said, "Since this morning, you have more or less made a shambles of my life."

Having made the statement, he gave his attention back to the crystal glasses. Jennifer did the same. It was as if the glasses had spoken, not Michael. In all this time he had still only managed to pour one glass of wine, and that just halfway. Jennifer's heart went out to him. He appeared every bit, if not more, miserable than she.

"I'm sorry," Jennifer said, followed by a sincerely put, "I don't understand."

The Chablis bottle was again in his hand. Facing her, he used the bottle as a pointing stick, saying, "No, you couldn't, could you? Anyway, cheer up. You're about to witness the unveiling of the decade. No. I'm being immodest. My apologies—the old ego running rampant. Not the unveiling of the decade, but perhaps of the last five years."

His speech done, he spent a moment of silence pouring the other glass of wine. He presented it to her, saying, "To the real Darla Hart."

"You . . . ?"

"In the flesh, madame." There was little evidence of celebration in his attitude. But he gave a slight, mock courtly bow, then crossed to the glass wall and stared out to where the Pacific slumbered in a vast expanse of dark nothingness.

"I write the column," Michael said, his back to Jennifer seeming to act as a shield against second thoughts he might have about going on. "The woman you saw on television is an actress. Her name is Lena Stephens. She was a patient of mine. By actual profession, or more accurately, by training,

I'm a psychologist." He turned from the window, and looking at her, said, "Or at least, I was until I couldn't take dealing with my clients' problems anymore. No one in the world knows that except Lena and my agent, Morey Greenbaum. And now you."

Jennifer hadn't moved. She was still trying to assimilate the information. If she had decided to concoct the wildest story imaginable to blast over America's airwaves, she could never have come up with anything better than what Michael had just told her. And it was the truth.

She was a bounty hunter come face to face with the hunted who had just handed over his loaded gun with the safety undone. All she had to do was squeeze the trigger. The shot would be heard round the world.

Michael was watching her, waiting for her to respond.

"Why did you have to tell me that?" It came out angrily and she didn't much care. She was furious and she wanted him to know it.

She had told him about herself at the restaurant because she had wanted to set things straight. The truth was intended to end any lingering temptation to exploit Michael to get to Darla. But this, this! He had just offered up the biggest story of her entire career, gift-wrapped, no less.

"I thought we were into honesty tonight?"

He was playing with her. His eyes burned into her, full of canny insight.

"You don't trust me," she fumed. "And you're playing with me. I can see it on your face even now. You're just laughing at me."

"No . . . no." His open palm turned up in denial. "Believe me, I'm not doing that."

"You know what that information can mean for me."

She walked away from him. This time it was her turn to seek solace in the dark void lying behind the glass wall.

"I do."

Reeling around, she shot him a tortured look of despair, then found herself marching to the center of the room for no reason other than to be doing something physical. Stopping abruptly, she spoke to the air in front of her. "Why couldn't you have just let it be? I would have driven away tonight, out of your life. Out of each other's lives," she corrected. "I wouldn't have come skulking around your beach pad again. If I still wanted Darla Hart, I would have either found some other way of going after her, or dropped it. The whole thing would have been over."

"But I didn't want it to be," he said quietly.

Jennifer dared to look at him again. Michael's down-turned mouth twisted into a sad smile.

"Why have you done this to me?" Jennifer said, collapsing into one of the modern sling chairs.

"Because I wanted you to make a choice. You couldn't have made an honest one if you didn't know all the facts."

He said it so blandly, so matter-of-factly. For the first time, she saw him in his true professional role, that of a psychologist. So cool and in control, withholding his own feelings. Playing off the excesses of other people's emotions, off of their trials and tribulations, and all the while being safe from taking chances himself because he had his patients to make all the right or wrong moves.

"That's very good of you. I really appreciate that." Frustration bubbled in each word. He had manipulated her into being his prosecutor and judge, even his hangman, depending upon the outcome.

"I made a choice, too. To take a chance on you. On us," he amended.

Jennifer stared into the blank television screen, seeing it as the symbolic cause of her misery. Being fair about it, she had to recognize that his decision to come clean with her couldn't have been that easy. Giving her the power to destroy him could be looked upon as both a serious exercise in faith and a reckless gamble in human nature. Her hand had been called in a real-life poker game.

As if he had read the thought in her eyes, Michael said, "I was listening to your story in Jimmy's. And suddenly I realized something. We're alike, you and I. We both started out with these wild, high hopes of how good things were going to be. I was going to be the healer of messed-up heads, setting lives right. And you were going to tout good words to a nutzo world. Two optimists. Flagrantly out of step with the rest of the universe."

Jennifer looked up, the pain lifting slightly. She managed a faint smile of agreement.

"Oh, Jennifer, Jennifer . . ." Coming before her, he looked down, black eyes twinkling with warmth and humanity and a certain amount of sad humor. He squatted on his heels and took her hands into his. She made no move to pull away from him, the recent anger having receded. It was the same as before. His presence wove a magical spell over her. What had seemed urgent became mundane, not worthy of further consideration.

As for Michael, he was no longer looking at her. His head was bent, and turning her hands over again and again in his, he resembled a nervous fortune teller unable to find his customer's heart line.

"Let's try," he said. "I want to, if you're willing. I want to do the impossible, make this work between us. At least to try." He looked up. A light shone in his eyes where only sadness had been a moment ago. "What do you think? One last no-holds-barred crazy fight for the right."

"It's good you're a shrink," Jennifer said. She freed a hand to push back a strand of black hair from his forehead. "Because you're totally wacko."

"Look at us," he went on urgently. "At what we've become. We started out as a couple of renegade crusaders. Now I don't deal with other human beings. I talk a good talk, but they're only words on a printed page."

"They're great words," Jennifer said.

"I'm a great coward."

"Maybe. Still, you help people."

"So I'm told. But I do it dishonestly."

"Because you hide behind the Darla thing?"

"It's not what I do so much, as why I do it. I tell people to feel, to open up, but I've become an emotional clam. Except . . ." He looked down again as his speech faltered. "Except that something happened when I met you this morning." His gaze drifted off into mid-distance and held. "It was like I had a small trap door in my heart. When I saw you, it opened. You slipped inside of me." He shook his head, knowing how stupid it sounded.

But Jennifer understood. It was the same for her. She thought back on that morning, of how she had felt him enter her soul through her eyes. There had been that connection. It was a recognition of belonging to each other. Weird. But it was real. Or at least it seemed to be real.

Michael rose now and paced, the words pouring out rapidly. "What a joke! I set out to help everyone, and I'm the one who's become the emotional cripple. I cower behind newsprint. Sometimes I despise myself," he said vehemently. "But then I remember how it was, having to look in a patient's eyes and see my own failure reflected back." Michael became silent, considering something. With less fire, he said, "This isn't a man's home you're in. This is a goddamned fortress to fend off feelings."

Looking at her, he said, "And you, Jennifer? What about you? You're in danger, serious danger, of becoming the very thing you say you hate in your profession. Someone who'll profit at the expense of another human being, all for a good story."

Jennifer rose from the sling chair.

"Okay, okay. I don't want to talk about me," she said. "I can't. I can't figure anything out now and I don't want to be pushed."

"Yes, you do," Michael said. "Otherwise you wouldn't have come back here tonight. You were willing to give up using me before, when you thought I was just a lead to Darla. You want to put the brakes on."

"Look," she said, long buried fears colliding inside her, "I am not one of your patients." She started away toward the kitchen, her pink skirt making frantic whipping noises around her legs as she tried to make good her escape. She had full intention of going out the door and down the steps to her car, out the garage, and straight down Pacific Coast Highway. Good-bye, Michael Casari.

But her plans were interrupted when Michael caught her arm and swung her around to him. He held her close, and neither of them spoke for a moment.

"Thanks for the free analysis," she said, pulling herself away. "But I really don't want a shrink in my life." The tremor in her voice countermanded the authority of her words.

He still held her arm. Slowly he drew her back into him.

She forgot what she had just said. Whatever it was no longer seemed relevant to the situation. The lovely spell was upon her again. The warmth of his body radiated out to her. The scent of his skin and cologne mingled around her in a tantalizing cloud.

She was wanting him to kiss her. She was wanting him.

Instead, he spoke. "We've both had equal time now. The pot's called the kettle black, and the kettle's had its say. Where do we go from here?"

"Home. I want to go home," Jennifer said, trying to think through all the conflicting emotions and sensations bombarding her. "I don't want to know anymore," she said, managing to free herself completely this time. "I don't know what I'm going to do."

"Well, know this, then, this one thing." Michael caught her again, bringing her back, this time with more force than before. He took hold of her chin, raising it. "I think maybe I've fallen in love with you."

It was utterly quiet. Softly, in a voice that denied her words, she said, "Michael, that's not possible."

"Yes. Yeah, right. Too soon. Too improbable. I've never felt like this before." He laughed. "It isn't the flu. The flu I could deal with. Not this."

"I've got the same bug," Jennifer said morosely. "It hit like the plague the moment I saw you in the store."

Neither of them was smiling, both lost in consideration. It was a predicament. They were adversaries in love.

"You could ruin me," Michael said.

"Yes."

"Will you?"

"I don't know."

"That was honest," he said, smiling gently now, and negligently tracing his index finger along the side of her face. The eyes which had gone from bright-angry to contemplative suddenly clouded into a mist. "Let's not deal with the future tonight."

"Tonight isn't real, Michael. It's . . . it's attraction. It's moonlight."

"Not much moonlight." A thin sliver of a moon bore out his words.

"This is wishful thinking on both our parts. You know that. You're the head doctor. This is just magic."

"Okay. Granted. But we've made the magic ourselves.

And if we want, we can make it last into daylight as something real.''

"Michael, I hate to sound jaded, but real is having to pay my dentist. Real is a deadline. The rent's going to come due as surely as the sun's going to rise tomorrow."

"And for all we know there may not be a tomorrow. You want to project the future? Okay, let's. Tomorrow I may be a headline, appearing as a scabrous lout to millions of betrayed fans who liked me as a green-eyed blond female.''

"And I may be out of a job."

"True. So what will not living tonight fully have accomplished?"

"It'll make tomorrow a lot easier for both of us. No complications."

"No pain, no gain. An old shrink saying," he said. "Jennifer, I'm willing to risk hurting."

"Maybe it's too big a risk. You know what this story could mean to me."

"I know I want to make love to you," he said. "Now. Tonight. I want to hold you and touch you and love you."

His lips found hers, at first softly, almost reverently. But the pressure changed. She felt the tension in him grow as they opened their mouths to each other. Bringing her tighter into him, his rigidness grew against her groin. A searing heat flamed through her. It felt as if hot liquid coursed like a rushing river to her loins as she allowed herself to meld into the slow movements of his pelvis.

"Tell me now if it's not what you want. This time I'm not going to be able to stop," Michael said, the words almost a rasp in her ear.

His hands brushed over the pink material of her dress, moving rapidly, with increasing demand, sweeping the curve of her buttocks, pushing his palms lightly up and against her breasts.

In answer to his question, Jennifer captured one of his hands, held it firmly on her breast.

He shuddered. Her nipple had peaked, hard and erect. Closing her eyes tightly, she became lost in sensation as his finger slid over her nipple, back and forth. Gasping, Jennifer twined her hand around his neck, bringing her mouth harder against his.

His other hand slid lower down her back, exploring the round curves where her hips flared gently out from her waist. He moved her slightly from him, making space for the flat of his hand to lay hard against her stomach. The fabric of her dress bunched in folds, but even so, she could feel the tension in those hands, imagined the heat, and wanted to feel his fingers against her flesh. As if reading her mind, his fist caught up the dress's material, hiking it ever higher as they kissed.

With Michael's breath flaming against her neck, she leaned back, giving him the access he wanted to explore her breasts fully. With one free hand, he worked down her zipper.

The pink material fell from her shoulders with a soft whisper.

"Oh . . . Michael," she murmured. His fingers moved to the band of her bikini briefs.

The bodice of the dress slipped to her waist. Her breasts were taut, their fullness spilling slightly over the top edge of her pink lace half bra. She closed her eyes and gasped as his tongue licked her flesh.

With his other hand, he worked the briefs down. His hand was against the soft furry mound, then traveled lower. Their breathing quickened as she tipped her pelvis to accommodate his reach.

For a moment while he explored, they both trembled with

a mix of anticipation and excitement that was almost painful.

"All night," he whispered in her ear. "I want to touch you like this all night." Scooping her into his arms, he continued to kiss her, almost out of control, his fevered lips pressing against hers.

Jennifer looked into his eyes as he brought his face away. They were black, so black, glazed with a primal need to connect his body with hers. It was what they both wanted.

"I need you," she said, "want you."

Their kisses continued down the hall as he brought her into a darkened room. There was only the slightest light from a half moon beyond the room's glass wall.

Michael lay her gently down upon the king-size bed. He kissed her long and full, then reluctantly parted from her to cross the room to the wall of glass, where he slid open the door. The surf whispered up from the beach. Jennifer heard a breaker hit, its mighty weight pounding against the shore. The smell of the air was intoxicating, and the cool breeze against her skin was welcome. Feverish with desire, her body burned within and without.

Michael was coming forward in the silvery light. He had tossed aside his jacket, removed his tie, and now he worked at the buttons of his shirt.

Bare from the waist up, he lay down upon the bed beside her and brought her partially over him, kissing her hungrily. Her knee lay over his panted leg and he brought one hand down to run over her bare skin.

"Like silk," he said, kissing her ear with his tongue. "Very hot, hot silk."

Michael unsnapped her bra, removed it, and dropped it over the side of the bed. His palms covered both breasts, exploring their fullness. "Michael," Jennifer said, almost laughing except that her passion for him was so intense that it had become a dull, insatiable ache, "I don't know . . ."

"Don't know what?"

"Anything," she said. "Only this feeling. That's all there is."

"You don't need to know anything but this. Love me," he said. It was a wish, a command, a fact.

Their bodies seemed tuned to each other. She discovered she possessed something in her nature she had never known before. It was a reckless, sensual abandonment. There was passion, tempered with the lightness of play. The slightest touch, where his hand explored the crease of her bent knee, or where his mouth touched down on the inside of her elbow, elicited erotic shivers up and down her spine.

Michael's body was smooth and hard. Leaning over him, her hair trailing on his chest as she worked her way down his body, she kissed the smooth firmness of his skin, lay her face briefly against his flat stomach, heard him moan softly.

He arched into her slightly, encouraging her to continue her journey downward.

The touch of her lips made him shudder. "Jennifer . . ." He caught his breath. "Jen . . . this is . . ."

But he never finished what he had wanted to say. There was no reason. She understood. The closeness of their bodies was only a part of it. There was so much more. It was the intimacy, the freedom of being with each other completely.

When he began to lose his tight control, he made her stop, and brought her back up to kiss her. The gentleness had evaporated in the last moment, and she gave herself over to this new side of him.

It was faintly selfish, completely masculine. Swept away with a male lust, he took her breast, sucking, kneading the other with a firey palm.

"Oh, Michael . . . I want you."

"Not yet," he said, but she could feel that it would have to be soon.

His tongue traced the undercurve of her breast, slicking hotly over her ribcage, causing her to swallow deeply as his mouth descended to her navel. Fingers trailing over the silken smoothness of her high inner thigh, he slid the remainder of the way to kiss the place where his fingers had been.

Her head tossed to either side of the pillow, and she caught her breath again and again, her vision behind her eyelids fading into blackness, then sparking with light as his touch changed. Frenzied, she called out his name, asking him to stop, then in the same breath telling him, "No . . . don't stop, please . . ."

In one fluid motion, Michael hitched her pelvis high, with his hands beneath her. He lay poised over her for a brief moment, his mouth coming down hungrily on one nipple. Then his lips were upon hers, her tongue twining with his, and then with his easy thrust, they were together completely.

Upon that joining, a shock wave of ecstacy traveled through her. Michael moaned deeply, his kisses becoming more prolonged as his body undulated, spiraled, drove them both higher.

He waited for Jennifer to catch his rhythm. She did, her hips sliding in an automatic pattern that brought forth racking tremors as a response from Michael.

"My God," Michael gasped, "I never believed this existed . . ."

Jennifer kissed his neck, instinctively nipping at his smooth flesh, tasting the salt, wanting him all, totally, completely.

And then all thought ceased. There was the sensation of

holding him, of his body catching her in its magic, of his pulse leading her into uncharted territory. A fullness, a sudden cry—maybe from her, she didn't know—then an explosive release.

Michael was with her. His voice called out her name as he tightened, held, and finally lost himself just as the second wave of heat caught her. Her body trembled, arching into him. Her spasms held him to her, and she felt his fingers in her hair twining, grasping. His mouth was on hers, then on her neck, lower to her breasts. She came down slowly, degree by degree, the molten fire ebbing to a warm, safe reminder of what they had shared together.

She touched his back, beaded with perspiration, smelling sweet. "I love you," she said, tears starting to flow. They were from satisfaction. From release. From joy.

Michael held her tightly. "Don't forget that," he said, "tomorrow."

She awoke to the wail of a lone sea gull, followed immediately by the thunder of the surf pounding the shore. A momentary confusion filled her, then her thoughts assembled, and a joy sparked in her. Michael.

She turned her head, her arm reaching out for him at the same time. The place beside her was empty.

"Michael?" she called, and waited, listening for him. There was no sound coming from the shower. Then dimly, she heard sounds coming from another room and recognized the low buzzing to be Michael speaking on the telephone.

She slipped on her bikini briefs, thought about dressing, or at least using his robe, which was hanging on a hook on the back of the bathroom's door, but decided against it. Sensuous stirrings were already alive in her. She wanted to tease him, to make him want her.

So when she stood in the doorway of his office wearing

nothing more than the small patch of pink nylon, waiting for him to notice her, she expected more than the cursory glance he cast her way.

Already dressed in a white polo shirt and his regulation sexy, form-fitting jeans, he stood by the desk, the telephone in one hand. The screen of his word processor glowed with electronic print. Its steady hum merged with his voice as he spoke angrily into the phone's receiver.

"Morey, I understand the situation completely." He was silent for a moment while Morey had his say. Jennifer watched Michael's expression alter from one of righteous, positive conviction to a wavering uncertainty. "Then check the contracts. Get a lawyer to go over them." A beat, and then, "Sure, talk to you soon."

He put the phone down slowly, staring at it thoughtfully.

"Good morning," Jennifer said melodically, trying to rouse him from his reverie.

He looked up suddenly, his eyes taking a moment to refocus on the outer world. "Jennifer, ah!" His eyes ranged down her almost nude body, lingering on her bare breasts, before traveling farther to the small triangle of pink fabric. With a theatrically wicked smile, he started for her.

"You were off in space," she said, laughing, but he cut off further conversation by scooping her into his arms, bending her back, pirate style, and while kissing her passionately, roamed her body freely with his hands.

Both of them were short of breath when he finally brought her upright. "Let's have breakfast in bed," she said. "And skip the food."

Michael growled, biting her neck playfully. "Can't," he said, backing away, as if to prove his words.

"Morey?" she asked, referring to the telephone with her eyes.

"No, not Morey," Michael said, grimacing slightly.

"Morey's a separate matter entirely. Don't I only wish it were Morey. I've got to go see Lena Stephens this morning."

"Ah," Jennifer said, disappointed, but trying to be a good sport about it. "You mean I'm being jilted for another woman."

"Actually, it's the other way around," Michael said. "I'm going over there to talk to her about finding a new role to play."

"Oh, Michael . . ." Beneath his casual remark lay what constituted a major upheaval in his life. It spelled commitment, with capital letters.

"Yeah, 'oh, Michael,' " he mimicked, shaking his head and smiling crookedly. "Pray for me, little one." He patted her on the rump and ushered her down the hall and into the bedroom.

"Help yourself to towels, soap, water, food. Sorry I can't offer myself," he added, collecting his wallet from the dresser. Slipping it into his back pocket, he said, "Tonight. A seafood extravaganza. Lobster. Clams. Oysters. Any and all kinds of—"

"Calories." Jennifer laughed. "Where and when?"

"Come here. As soon as you can after your day of sleuthing is over."

Jennifer was sitting cross-legged on the bed, watching him. "You know," he said, "I'd just as soon have a peanut butter and jelly sandwich and you right here than any expensive meal."

"Yeah?" he grinned, coming to her. "Know what? I could do with just you. Skip the peanut butter."

They kissed again. Michael raised her up to her knees on the bed. He kissed her full, upturned breasts, went to the indentation of her stomach, but hesitated when he came to the elastic band of her bikini pants. His fingers toyed with the fabric.

"No," he said, with little conviction. "The entire morning will be shot if we start."

"I don't care," she said, grinning happily.

Backing away, he shook his head. "Uh-uh. You're the lady who told me all about the realities of life, last night. Rent? Dentist bills?"

Jennifer groaned. "Enough. Enough. Point taken."

He gave her a quick peck on her mouth, allowed one hand to linger on a bare breast, and with a sigh, reluctantly backed away.

Jennifer could only imagine what that brief joining had done to her appearance; Michael's eyes were slightly glazed, his complexion flushed.

"Michael!" she said, calling after him just as he went out the bedroom door. "Michael . . ." He had turned. "I love you," she said.

A slow smile broke over his face. "I was wondering if you were going to say it."

"I didn't really have to, did I?"

"No. I can tell."

Jennifer threw a pillow at him. Laughing, she said, "Get out of here, you conceited lout!"

He waved and slipped from her sight.

A faint aroma of aftershave or cologne remained in his absence. Jennifer savored it, closing her eyes to the daylight, remembering the moonlight. Falling backward on the bed, she stretched out, feeling free, feeling wonderful. Michael, Michael, Michael. Pulling his pillow to her, she hugged it against her skin. Tonight they would be together.

Chapter 6

HER MIND WAS A WHIRLING PINWHEEL AS SHE DROVE home to change into work clothes. With each spin, she imagined a new version of the future. Although the settings and the dialogue changed, certain universals held. Each blissful scenario contained Michael, just as every new frame flickering through her mind illuminated her as professionally victorious. In her most flagrantly hyped-up version of her success, Watergate paled in comparison to her Darla Hart story. But the best part was the real part. It was no fantasy that at this very moment, Michael was clearing the way for her rise to fame and glory. She was going to have it all.

She had almost passed the Stop N' Go when she remembered she needed nylons for that evening.

Sung Ock was not there. One of Sung's nephews, met previously while she was researching her story on L.A.'s ethnic mix, silently waited on her.

"Where is Sung Ock?" she asked slowly, over-enunciating each word to make certain she was understood.

"Not here." The cash register rang up the price and she paid. The nephew placed the nylons in the bag.

"Is Sung Ock ill? Sick?" she pantomimed, rubbing her stomach to make herself understood.

"Sung with policeman."

Jenny took the bag from the counter. "He's with policeman? Sung Ock is in trouble?"

"Sung show face of man with gun to policeman."

The nephew wasn't particularly friendly or chatty, but Jennifer finally understood. Sung Ock had been robbed again. Poor Sung Ock. He had worked so hard for his piece of the American dream.

"I'm sorry," Jenny said. "Tell him for me, okay? Jenny says she is very sorry about man with gun."

Sung's nephew gave no response. He pretended to be busy with paperwork. Jennifer left with her bag and the impression that Sung's nephew had probably earned the right not to trust anyone.

Enderall caught her just as she was coming out of the elevator. "Ah, hello," he said. "I was down at your cube looking for you."

Jennifer was shocked by the change in his appearance. Deep pockets of shadow rimmed Enderall's eyes. His round face no longer appeared robust. It sagged loosely with jowls. In fact, all of Enderall seemed to sag.

"Anything special?" Jennifer said, stopping near the drinking fountain. She felt invincible. Nothing Enderall or anyone else could say today could daunt her. She had only to summon Michael's image and the whole world became a gay carnival, flashing neon signs, fireworks on the Fourth of July.

"What's wrong with you," Enderall said.

"Wrong? Nothing."

"You look different, odd. You look happy. Why? Why are you happy?" he intoned glumly, obviously irritated by her good humor.

But before she could offer a reply, he said, "Our little talk the other day?"

Jennifer nodded.

"What've you got for me?" he pressed anxiously.

"I'm working on something."

"Something." Enderall rolled his eyes in exasperation. "What something?"

"I can't say yet."

"You can't say yet." He rolled his eyes again. "Miss Winters, trust me, there is no better time than this time to say what your plans are."

"I can't. Really." He looked so desperate. Relenting, she added, "But it's big."

From the corner of her eye, she saw Arnold Fine ease up to the drinking fountain next to her. Did she only imagine his ears pricking up, turning like radar scopes in her direction?

Not willing to share her conversation, innocuous as it was, with Arnold, Jennifer began to back down the aisleway.

Before her eyes, Enderall underwent a physical metamorphosis. The slack of his face hardened into a solid block of flesh. The old Enderall, tyrant of more optimistic times, faced her.

"Now, I'm not futzing around here anymore," Enderall said. His voice had also lost its faintly tremulous quality. Jennifer was aware of fear's miraculous restorative properties; here was proof positive. "I have a report to deliver upstairs, and I want something to put down beside your name. Unless you want that something to be 'Terminated,' I suggest you exercise your creative instincts.''

Jennifer transposed the last into: killer instincts. In Enderall's vernacular the two phrases were interchangeable.

"Will do," Jennifer said, saluting him.

"Something big?"

"Humongus, sir. Promise."

"Forget promises. Give me results." Enderall huffed away, marching in the direction of his office.

She was thinking of what to wear that night for dinner with Michael, when she passed John Rudran's cubicle. The thought forming on the edge of her mind dissolved, replaced by instinctive curiosity.

John also looked awful. Hunched over his desk, he was scribbling frantically on a yellow legal pad. Surrounding him on the floor, and strewn over the surface on which he worked, were wadded-up balls of discarded paper. His tan had faded to a sickly oatmeal color.

Sensing her presence, he looked up. Desperation radiated from his eyes.

"Have you heard?" The question was posed in an anxious stage whisper.

"No," she whispered back automatically.

She was thinking that John Rudran had never appeared so disheveled. His beautiful custom-tailored sports jacket was slung like an abandoned corpse over his small bookshelf. Dark orbs of perspiration ringed the underarms of his dress shirt, and looped around his neck, his unknotted tie drooped like a limp noodle.

With a nod he motioned for her to enter. "Enderall's begun to plant," he said.

"He's what?"

"Remember his speeches about how he was going to weed out the ranks?"

"Yeah. Just before the last hatchet job."

"Well, he's hired someone new. He's weeded and now he's planting. He's not kidding around this time."

"John, you're allowing yourself to become a wreck. Don't let it get to you."

Pushing himself up, he stood before her and with a sigh said, "What are you looking at here?" He had spread his arms out wide.

"You."

"Wrong. This is a weed. This body is the equivalent of a weed."

"All you have to do is to come up with a project for Enderall."

"I can't!" He kicked at one of the discarded papers, sending it flying over to a corner. "What do you think all this is? My mind is frozen. Thoughts don't come out of my brain, ice cubes come out. Clink. Clink. That's the sound of my brain working. Clink."

"I'm sorry, John. I don't know what to tell you."

"Do you have anything?"

"Yes."

"Is it good?"

"Yeah, it's good."

"Hell," he said, and kicked another paper.

She felt for John. Like her, she suspected he had at one time harbored idealistic notions of presenting world class stories, for which he would be lauded for his integrity.

Concern for John was driven away by encroaching thoughts of Michael. She was actually humming happily when she passed the cubicle belonging to Rita Levett.

The voices in the cubicle stopped abruptly. She felt gluey
eyes attach themselves to her as she passed the doorway.

"Oh, Jen?"

Jennifer swung around in response to Rita's melodious
voice.

"Hi," Rita said, stepping into the hall.

"Morning," Jennifer said, feeling good enough to be
pleasant, even to Rita. When Arnold appeared behind
Rita's shoulder, Jennifer understood immediately what had
prompted the friendliness. Arnold had of course overheard
the conversation at the drinking fountain. They figured she
had a good story and wanted to know what it was. As a
normal practice, neither of them was beneath stealing ideas
if it meant furthering their own interests. This being all-out
war, there was no telling what they might do.

"Jen," Rita began, "about the other day. You know we
really didn't mean anything by all that business. Still
friends?"

"Sure, Rita." When had they been friends? She started
away.

Arnold was next to summon her. "Jen?" he called.

"Yes, Arnold?"

"Sure are in a good mood."

"Sure am."

"Have a good idea for a project?" Rita asked.

"Sure do."

"Listen, Jen," Rita said, "I was thinking. Maybe we
ought to have a little talk."

"It's kind of important," Arnold added.

Jenny obliged. Once in Rita's cube, they closed ranks on
her like fans around their favorite movie star.

"Enderall's hired a new girl." Rita looked to Arnold to
confirm her news.

"So I understand," Jennifer said.

"She's unbelievable," said Arnold.

"Really? And why is that?"

"Credentials."

"Jenny," Rita said, "we're going to have to all stick together now. We're going to have to share."

"Really? I thought brotherhood among men was passé."

"It's the only way," Arnold concurred with Rita. "The thing is, this new woman is very, very sharp and she's going to wipe one of us off the boards very quickly if we don't all hang in there together. Now what I propose is that we all join forces on the best idea. That is to say, if we come up with something, we all work on it together. Make it a super story. We're an invincible unit. Comprende?"

"I do," Jenny said. "I do."

"So what's your idea, Jenny?"

"Well," Jennifer said, "I've got something fantastic." Exercising caution, she glanced toward the door.

"What's that, Jen?"

"Listen, guys, you know those houses in the San Fernando Valley? The ones being swallowed up by the ground?"

"The houses on the garbage fill?"

"Those very houses," Jenny said, nodding.

"What about the houses on the garbage?" Arnold asked.

"They're haunted."

"Haunted?"

"Yes. I met this man—an American Indian. He works in a pizza parlor. Well, he told me that the site where those houses are built used to be an old Indian burial ground. And that it isn't actually the garbage that's smelling. It's the revenge of old Indian souls. And that these souls are trying to swallow up the houses."

Rita and Arnold were quiet. They stared at her.

"Well? What do you think?" Jenny asked. "Isn't that a great idea?"

"Great," Arnold said.

"Great," Rita enjoined flatly.

"Super. Then we'll work together on my idea?"

"No. I don't think so, Jen." Rita was moving back to her desk.

"Oh? Well, then, what're your ideas?"

"Jen, just let's forget it. It wasn't such a good plan, working together." Rita was going through her desk drawer.

Arnold was acting as though she had already left the room.

"Well, in that case, I'll just work on my project alone. Every man for himself, and all that."

Since no one said anything, she left and continued down the hall humming her tune again. She didn't have to worry about spies anymore.

When she got to her office, there was a brown envelope on her desk. It was marked confidential. She tore it open and found a copy of what had to be the new employee's personnel application, along with a note from John Rudran: "Pray for us. All." John had underlined the "all."

Also shakily outlined in red ink were the most pertinent facts (as determined by John Rudran) related to the new employee's education and experience. It was all very impressive. Skimming through Madeline Renquist's application and resume was like taking a tour of one of those neighborhoods you'd never be able to afford yourself. Best schools. Extensive traveling. Multilinguistic. Hobbies were fencing, polo, yachting (not sailing, but yachting), rare-coin collecting. Why not? Jennifer shrugged. Madeline Renquist's father was on the board of the world's largest bank. Money was in the blood.

Still, even this new threat to her job security was no big deal. She had Michael and Darla Hart, all rolled into one.

Sinking back in her chair, she stared at her ecological posters. Save the Whales. Save the Great Lakes. Save the Baby Seals. Save the Planet. And the last, and most significant poster, of a droopy-eyed dog, with the slogan "Save Your Tail."

She smiled and began to work on the story that would do just that . . .

Michael wound his way up the narrow blacktop road. Incredibly, even narrower streets branched off from the one he now traveled. Checking the instructions Lena had given him over the phone, he slowed the Cadillac and took a sharp right which led up another hill on a road that zigged and zagged crazily.

The house, when he came to it, was at the end of a cul-de-sac. Michael got out of the car. For a moment he just stared at the place. It looked like something from a 1940s movie, an idyllic white frame cottage complete with a white picket fence. Rose bushes flanked the flagstone path leading to the front stoop, where small ivy clung daintily to posts supporting the heavy shake overhang.

He didn't have to knock. Lena was already at the door. She looked radiant, certainly not like a woman who had been in the hospital the previous morning having her insides pumped.

"Michael, I'm so pleased you could come," she said, stepping aside for him to enter.

She had on a long hostess gown in a small yellow and white and pink flowered print, suitable, Michael supposed, for entertaining during the day.

"We've got to talk, Lena."

"I know, I know . . . about last night." She bustled off,

calling to him over her shoulder. "Back in a flash, Michael. Coffee's just ready. And there's sherry, too."

Michael looked around, feeling uneasy. On the drive over, he had rehearsed the scene quite differently. It was to have been a somber, dignified meeting, handled with professional dispatch on his part. His opening would naturally have been Lena's immediately expressed remorse over her failure on the *Today* show the day before.

What he had not counted on was a sun-filled room, cut flowers everywhere, a coffee table laid with delicate china cups and plates, a platter of small tea cakes and thin triangular sandwiches, along with a dish containing what appeared to be homemade candies. All this hospitality was going to make things much harder. The idea did not escape him that Lena also knew this. She was uncanny sometimes, an emotional weather vane. If he went in for such things, he'd say she was psychic. However, in actuality, Lena was a sensitive, manipulative woman—qualities that would bring her a fortune in revenue if she capitalized on them in the acting profession.

"Here we are," Lena said, smiling brightly as she returned with a china coffeepot. "Oh, do sit down, Michael. And have some of the sherry. It's special, you know."

Michael did sit, taking a place on the sofa. He did not help himself to the sherry.

"Let me," Lena said, and poured him a glass.

Michael knew her act of cheerfulness was a deliberate defense. She was too sensitive not to pick up on his mood.

"Lena," he broke in, "this is all very lovely, but unnecessary. I came here to talk to you, not to be entertained. It's not social, Lena."

Her expression barely altered. Popping up from the sofa, she said, "How do you like it?" The full skirt of the hostess gown swirled gracefully as she moved about the room. "I did all the decorating myself. The needlepoint, too." She swooped up a pillow from a velvet armchair, displaying her accomplishment. "And look at this. Found it in a second-hand store down in Venice." It was a large ivory elephant. "It's very good luck," she went on. "And a real find. Cost pennies, Michael. It was covered in paint, you see. I stripped it myself and—"

"Lena . . . we've got to talk!"

She jumped then, seeming genuinely surprised.

Her face crumbled. For a second she fought to rebuild its previous cheerfulness, but failed. Looking down at the floor, she said, "Why do I try? You can read me. No matter what I do, you know what I'm really feeling. What I'm really doing."

"Lena," he said gently, and rose to join her where she stood. "You know I care about you, as a patient, and also as your friend."

Tears came into her eyes. Michael stiffled a sigh. He fought away the panic. He couldn't take tears. He had run from tears, had become a recluse because of other people's pain.

"I love this home, Michael. This home is my life. My whole life. I don't have any children. I don't have a husband. I have no career. This home is everything to me." She looked up at him then, sea-green eyes brimming. "The money from Darla gave me the down payment, you know. I make payments every month from my Darla check."

"You know, don't you?" Michael said softly, feeling like a cad; that had been her intention, of course.

"Yes. You came here to fire me. You don't want me to be Darla anymore because I let you down yesterday.

"It isn't just that."

"Of course it is!" she cried. "You were angry with me. Morey said you were angry."

"Well, okay. I was aggravated. No, to be honest about it, I was mad. We'd both put so much work into rehearsing for that appearance. You could have gotten through the show. But in the end you panicked. You took those pills because you didn't trust me. If you don't trust me, I can't help you, can I?"

"I was afraid. I didn't trust *me.*"

"It isn't just because of *Today,* Lena. I've got to be more honest with myself, too. I want to start dealing with the public again. It's hypocritical of me to preach honesty and then hide behind falsity."

Lena was looking at him. He could feel her antennae extend, probe him. "Kind of a sudden decision, wasn't it?"

Michael nodded. "A little."

"Why?" she asked. "What made you suddenly decide to be Mr. Truth?"

Michael hesitated answering. Instead, he walked back to the sofa and took up the glass of sherry he had previously refused. It was one thing to declare one's motives as being in the best interests of humanity—a righteous blow swung in the name of integrity; it was quite another matter to tell someone who was going to lose her job that he had met a beautiful woman who'd turned his head and heart and whole entire consciousness around.

"I want to make all my relationships straight," he said, hedging. For a guy who was turning over a new leaf, he was certainly not being straight with Lena now. He was being hypocritical. Specifically, particularly, he wanted to make one relationship straight. He downed the small glass of sherry in one long swallow. "I met a woman. I want honesty from her. She deserves the same from me."

"That's it?" Lena stood lonely and forlorn in the middle of the room.

Michael nodded. "Lena, I've a right to a personal life, just like anyone else." He sank down on the sofa.

"You have the hots for some woman, so you just throw me out of your life!"

"Cut it, Lena. You make it sound like you and I've been sleeping together."

"Well, you're very special to me."

"You're very special to me, too. But that has nothing to do with the issues involved."

"Michael!" she cried, rushing over to him and sitting down. She took both of his hands into hers, squeezing them like a dying person holding on to life. "Just give me one more chance."

"Lena . . ."

"No, I swear to you, Michael . . . just one more chance. You're right, you do deserve your own life and I have no right to interfere with your plans, if that's what you want."

"Lena, Lena . . . now we're into the act of nobility. Why don't you use your talent where it belongs? Do your stuff on the stage, behind a camera. You could. You're ready, Lena. Only you don't want to be ready, you don't want to let go."

"I know." Miraculously the tears dried in her eyes. In their place was a hard determination. "Michael, I am ready. And you've made me ready, too. I owe you everything. My very life," she said. "Remember?"

Michael remembered. She had tried to do away with herself three times in the beginning of her therapy. That was a long time ago, though.

"All I ask is this. I'm going to go out there and storm Hollywood. I'm going to get myself a fantastic job. On one of the soaps," she said. "I'd be great on a soap, don't you think? But people have got to remember me as a superb actress, Michael. I can't go knocking on doors as that stinko failure from *Today,* can I?''

Michael considered what she had said. Even if it was just another ploy to manipulate him, she did have a point. His conscience wouldn't allow him to cut her off from her chance of making it. In Hollywood, people needed any break they could get.

''All right,'' he said.

''Oh, Michael . . .'' She kissed him on his cheek. ''Oh, Michael, you're wonderful. I won't let you down.''

''Yeah,'' he said, rising. ''So, we've got a deal, Lena?''

''A deal. Scout's honor.''

''Why do I have the feeling you were never a Scout? I'll set something up with Morey for another show.''

''Make it *Today* again,'' Lena said. ''I don't want a black mark against me. They think I was sick when I blanked out before, so it'll be okay. They'll have me back.''

Michael walked to the door. ''This is important to me, Lena. We've got to handle this thing fast.''

''Oh, yes,'' she said. ''Absolutely.''

Chapter 7

THE SUN WAS A GREAT ORANGE BALL SINKING BEHIND THE water line of the Pacific. Streaks of deep purple and blue bled into the glowing flame-colored canvas. A large pleasure boat of some kind was passing slowly by, lights already on, twinkling as happily as Jennifer felt standing beside Michael on the deck.

"Quite a show, isn't it?" Michael said. He nuzzled his chin against her upsweep of loose curls. A few renegade tendrils floated down, playing against the back and sides of her neck.

"It makes a person believe," Jennifer said. It was a statement as defiant as it was wistful.

"In anything in particular?"

"In everything in particular. In things that are beautiful. In some intrinsic kindness in this universe. In people, just ordinary people like us." She paused, stiffening her grip on the deck's wood railing. "Do you think that's stupid? I mean, do you think there's any sense to believe in so much good actually existing?"

"What do you have to lose? Is it better to believe in the existence of evil?"

"No, no, of course not. But I don't like to be a fool, either."

"Why not? What's wrong with being a fool? Especially if we're both fools together!" he said exuberantly, bringing her into him.

Feelings of love swelled within her as she looked into his dark eyes. She touched her hand to his cheek, finding it wonderous and magical, that just by reaching out she could find such perfection at her fingertips. He kissed her nose, then her forehead, and as she closed her eyes, those, too. Her mouth opened to his and for a while all doubts about what was real dissolved in the kiss they shared.

When they came apart, the world seemed to have altered. The sun had diminished to only an arched sliver at the horizon. Even as Jennifer watched, it sank out of sight. With the sun's departure, an ocean wind had whipped up like an efficient time keeper whose duty it was to mark the division between day and night. Deprived of the sun's rays, the Pacific lost its sparkle, turning slate gray and churning white caps to the surface.

"Oh, too soon," Jennifer lamented, "it's over too soon."

"Not so. The show's not entirely over yet," Michael said mysteriously. He rubbed his hands briskly over her bare shoulders and arms, smoothing away goosebumps. She had worn one of her favorite outfits for her dinner with Michael. It was a sundress out of peach-colored cotton. The dress's thin spaghetti straps were almost invisible, blending in with

her tan, and the unstructured bodice followed the easy
curve of her hips down to the skirt which flared gracefully
to just below her knees.

"I want the sun back," Jennifer sighed. "I want the sky
filled with color again." It too had become muted, deepen-
ing to flat blues, a lifeless, fading indigo.

"But something special's coming," Michael said confi-
dently, taking her hand in his. He raised his other hand and,
pointing into the fast darkening night sky, said, "Out there,
somewhere . . . we can't quite see it yet . . . Venus."

Jennifer squeezed his hand, telling him she understood.
"Of course, it's always there, isn't it?"

"Always. We just can't see it. And that," he laughed,
"should answer your other question. About good things
being real. They're there. We just don't always have the
right perspective to see them."

It was too windy to stay outside, as Michael had planned
their evening. Together, they worked quickly to clear off the
table he had set for their dinner on the deck. Laughing, they
caught napkins mid-flight as they took off like eager white
birds.

"Storm's coming early," Michael said, carrying a stack
of dishes through the sliding door.

Jennifer followed after him with the silverware and the
extinguished candelabra. "Storm? Impossible. Storms
never happen during the summer in Southern California."

"Tell that to the evening news. They reported a hurri-
cane watch south of Baja. That's why we didn't see many
sails or powerboats tonight. Small craft warnings were
issued."

"Poor Venus. She won't have her night out."

"Don't worry; she'll still have time to make a brief
appearance. For us."

On Jennifer's next trip out to the deck, she found the wind had stepped up its force. Even without Michael's news flash, she could tell a storm was on the way. Besides the white caps, rising higher, and the swells hitting farther in on the shoreline, the air smelled different. There was a fullness, a heaviness to the atmosphere that had not been there before.

The wind whipped her skirt back and forth, catching the fabric between her legs, and making it difficult to walk back inside with the serving dishes. Michael was loading the dishwasher. That moment had a nice feeling to it—a sense of closeness. Outside, the elements raged, inside serenity reigned. She was feeling very good when Michael turned the television news on, listening for the latest on the weather. He went back into the kitchen, continuing to put things away.

She tried to help, but after Michael had bumped into her for the fourth time, he took her by the shoulders and ushered her into the living room. "Sit," he said. "Enjoy being a luxury item while you have the opportunity."

"Michael, can we talk?"

"What was that we've been doing all evening?"

"No," she smiled, "I mean talk about . . . I hate to say it . . . business?"

"Let me take care of this stuff first."

Jennifer watched him as he walked back to the kitchen. Something was wrong. He was being evasive. Up to the point of her suggestion, Michael had been so open, his eyes lively. He had responded to anything and everything she had to say, as if she spoke ancient truths or uncommon witticisms.

The newscast had reminded her of the papers folded in her purse. Dinner hadn't been the right time to talk to him about the Darla story. But she had worked on it all afternoon, and keeping it off her mind for this long had been an effort.

While he worked, now and then speaking to her from the kitchen, she got the typed seven-page manuscript from her purse and reread it in between comments.

The weather portion of the newscast came on. Michael rejoined her in the living room. What he had heard earlier was confirmed. A storm was coming. The first front had hit San Diego already, causing power outages.

"Michael, if you'd just take five minutes . . ."

He shut the television off and came over to her. Pulling her up from the chair, holding her close to him, he said, "Do you know how much I enjoy this? Having you here with me." Drawing her closer, he ran his fingers over her bare back.

"I was just thinking the same thing. That it feels good, very right."

"Nothing should spoil this, Jennifer," he said with a passion not in keeping with the situation.

He looked so serious. Instinctively, she reached up to smooth the wrinkles from his forehead, as if the action could banish whatever troubled him.

"Nothing could. Not ever."

"Remember that," he repeated solemnly. As if to imprint that vow on her mind, he lowered his mouth and kissed her softly. His hand moved up her back, and the initial gentleness became something more compelling as he buried his mouth into the hollow of her collarbone. Their breathing quickened simultaneously. Jennifer felt herself tossed in a whirlwind that drew her down into herself, finding unknown spaces. Tongues touched, then drew away, returned, speaking silent words to each other in a language only their bodies could understand completely.

"I had meant to have a leisurely, civilized evening of fine wine and mellow music, maybe some intellectual conversation on the meaning of life, too, before getting down to what I really wanted to do since the moment I saw you tonight in that dress." Demonstrating, he slipped one spaghetti strap from her shoulder. "What will you think of me now?"

"It's okay," Jennifer said, with as much gravity as she could muster. "I'll still respect you in the morning. Guess I'll have to live with your limitations. Some men are only cut out for certain things."

"Oh? Very well," he sighed, "you've got me pegged. Use me as you will."

Soft as velvet, she felt his hand slide over her, moving from the cavity of her neck, tracing its way lower to the rise of her breasts just above her bodice. His eyes burned bright and hot as he lowered the other strap from her shoulder. The soft purring sound of her zipper going down mingled with her rapid breathing.

With both hands, he guided the cotton away from her torso, letting it fall softly to her waist. She had worn no bra and her breasts sprang into view, high and full, her nipples already hardened.

Michael's eyes were fixed upon her body, then he looked to her face. He brought her to him again and kissed her deeply and reverently before touching her.

With one hand, he trailed his fingertips from her neck to her shoulder, while the other hand lifted one breast, cupping it, stroking her nipple. "Jenny," he said, almost as a gasp.

He found her other breast and she closed her eyes, dying a little from the agony of wanting more from him.

He kept his hands from her body now, deliberately torturing them both, and found her mouth with his tongue again, kissing her until she was being made mad with desire.

"Touch me," she whispered, guiding his hands back to her breasts. "Touch me . . ."

She shivered, yet at the same time a burning heat drove up from her loins and spread into her as he began to move his hands over her body with less studied consideration, with more male honesty for what he wanted from her for himself.

His tongue flicked over her skin, his fingers kneading and lifting the curving thrust of her breast until he took a nipple between his lips and sucked hungrily, losing himself in a pleasure which also became hers.

Gradually, he slipped the dress from her waist, lowering it to her stomach, his hand pausing, stroking there. The material drifted to the top of her lace bikinis, where he toyed with the elastic, teasing her. She arched her pelvis into him, encouraging him to explore further.

He took the dress the rest of the way down and she stepped from its folds on the floor. All the while caressing her, he guided her to the sofa. He leaned her back, settling her prone on it, and kissed the flat of her stomach as he worked the small triangle of lace down. The heat of his breath drove her to moan softly and call out his name. Her fingers twined in his hair, urging him to continue what he was doing.

She closed her eyes tightly, drifting with the feel of his mouth as he explored her body, one hand caressing the curve of her hips, then again sweeping like a wash of liquid fire to the mound where her legs parted.

At some point, he had unbuttoned his shirt. Now, one arm at a time, he slipped from it.

It was her turn to touch him now. She ran fingers over his smooth muscular chest, all the while kissing him, murmur-

ing his name. Again and again, as he kneeled beside her on
the sofa, she let her breasts fall into his hands, encouraged
him with small sounds to fondle her, offering her nipples to
his appetite, and then pulled away to make his desire burn
hotter, playfully denying him until he forced her back.

Bringing him down to lie beside her, she slipped her
body lower against his, and just as he had done with her,
pressed her lips against his skin, flicking and teasing, until
he gasped quietly, lost in some private world of his own.

Finally he shifted and lifted her off him, scooping her
into his arms as he stood. "You want to make me lose my
mind, don't you?"

"Yes. I do."

"Well, you won't. I'm a psychologist, remember? I
know how to handle these situations."

Walking with her, he kissed her neck, biting her ear, and
saying, "You're going to be made love to . . . completely
. . . like you have never been loved in your life."

"Hurry," she said, laughing. And then said, "Michael,
wait. I want a fire."

"That's exactly what I had in mind."

"No . . . be serious now. I mean in the fireplace."

He gave her a strange look. "It's summer."

"It's chilly. And the wind is blowing. And soon it's
going to be raining. Please," she wheedled. "I've never
made love in the firelight."

Michael shook his head, but she knew he was pleased
with her suggestion. He threw a couple of logs and some
kindling into the fireplace, obliging her just as she knew he
would.

They lay upon the white Flokati rug, the fur soft and
natural against their bare skins, the music from the stereo
easy jazz. Turning into the fire's glow, she saw sparks rising like molten bubbles, promising . . . perhaps dying

. . . perhaps, she thought, some of them reaching as far as Venus. Their star. Venus.

Michael drew her attention from the fire, kissing her deeply. A small patter began on the deck, so soft it was barely audible. It increased until both of them had to give it its due recognition.

"It never storms in Southern California in June," Michael said, slapping her butt lightly.

"That's not rain," Jennifer said. "That's the beating of our hearts." And she kissed him again.

Making love with other men had been heated affairs, born of desire and what she now recognized as only light infatuation. The physical drive had been powerful, but there was no poetry, there was no honesty. Motion without emotion.

This was different. This was making love.

Arching involuntarily, she kept her eyes closed as he moved his face against her stomach. He no longer spoke her name between his explorations. Beyond the verbal realm now, they moved in a universe of touch, of feelings that were at once physical and at the same time so much more than tactile.

Michael's tongue flicked hot against her, hotter, hotter, and with more purpose, finally probing into secret valleys now open to him. Raising her higher into him, he continued to taste, made new explorations which drove her to cry out softly, first to stop, then to continue, never to stop.

They moved against the white fur, weaving their bodies against each other like silken scarves, supple and soft, giving and receiving, aware of an "other" for a second, then in the next moment, fading into a place where there was only a sweet, driving anguish to satisfy the needs possessing them both.

He brought her hand down to feel him, keeping his

fingers upon hers, guiding her to please him. They wanted the same things. And so he let his fingers go slack, and in a minute the flicking of her tongue caused him to arch into her, giving himself completely. Seemingly unaware, he emitted a lost groan of hot, masculine pleasure.

He shuddered beneath her attentions, and struggling to maintain control, he brought her up from her knees, kissing her all the while as he lay her back against the carpet.

With her face held between his hands, he willed her to meet his eyes. He was over her, pressed against her body, her knees parted for him.

She touched him only slightly, her guidance unnecessary.

Hard steel and soft velvet. Mingling. Joined together in a single thrust.

And then, for a time which was beyond time, and in a space that had no place in the world, they met again and again.

Afterward, they fell asleep lying on their sides, their limbs twined together, lips barely touching.

But just before the veil of sleep fell, the fire sparked, talking to her. She answered back, ''Venus.''

In the morning they awoke together in Michael's bed. Beyond the glass wall the ocean lay flat and colorless, the sky above appearing just as drained and lifeless. The night had been violent. Once Jennifer had screamed, coming awake suddenly on the Flokati rug as explosions of thunder tore at the heavens and vibrated the foundations of the house. Michael had pulled her into him, making her feel both safe and foolish. It was ridiculous to be afraid of a storm at her age, but she was. From the corner of her eye she had caught great razor-edged slashes of light cutting across the sky's dark plains. Illuminated in the eerie glow were the swollen forms of thunderheads, ominous shapes like monstrous thugs crouched and waiting on thick haunches. The logs in the fireplace had died down to a few glowing embers. It had grown chilly. A crosscurrent of drafts seemed to meet in the living room. Jennifer had shivered, burrowing more snugly against Michael, who, feeling her tremble, lifted her into his arms and carried her to the bedroom. There she had remained for the rest of the storm, cradled safely in his arms. Sometime during the night her fear had given way to sleep.

When she awoke, Michael's eyes were already open, watching her. Neither of them spoke, choosing to communicate with a kiss, at first tender, then more seeking. She was still faintly drugged from her ravaged sleep. The fires of last night were slower to ignite, but grew under Michael's urgent caresses, until it was she who slipped atop him. She kissed his mouth, his neck, his chest, moving slowly to the rhythm he set. Last night, as they had lain before the fire, there had been fevered passion; now there was desire, just as intense, but with an added sweetness. The tension broke in both of them at the same time, and that closeness, that joining, was perhaps the best.

"Will that ever happen again?" Jennifer asked when their breathing had quieted. She lay beside him, partly nestled in the crook of his arm as he stroked her hair.

"Not within the next ten minutes, it won't."

There was hardly a beat before she felt his breathing change and knew he had fallen into a relaxed slumber.

She rose and found her clothes, then as quietly as possible took a shower and dressed. She was in the kitchen, putting a breakfast together for them when Michael walked through the hall door.

"Sorry," he said. His hair was still mussed, but he had thrown on a pair of jeans, leather moccasins without socks, and a soft, buttery-yellow polo shirt. "You've worn me out, woman. You not only look like a tigress, you make love like one."

"Is that a compliment or a complaint?"

"A fact."

He came up behind her and pushed her hair aside to nibble on her earlobe.

She laughed, doing a slight riggling shimmy from the chills he sent up her back, and slipped out of his reach. "How's your appetite for eggs and bacon?"

"My tastes run more to tigers," he said, following after her as she took the filled serving platter to the dining table. She had already put out a carafe of coffee, a dish of buttered toast, and glasses of orange juice.

"Sorry, not on this morning's menu."

"Then I'll have to settle, won't I?"

"Braggart!" She laughed, and sat down across from him. "Just be glad you got scrambled. My fried eggs are killers."

But Michael wasn't listening. His attention was on the pages she had placed beside his dish.

"What's all this?" he asked, leafing through the typed draft of her Darla Hart story.

It wasn't the reaction she had expected. The moment was supposed to have been a rite of passage for them, the two of them sitting together over coffee discussing her story about his life, which was to serve, in a sense, as a sort of moral glue binding both of their lives together from that time on.

A dullness crept over Jennifer. It was a familiar feeling acquired as a defense mechanism over the years, used to blunt disappointment in people and events not turning out the way she had hoped.

"You know what it is," Jennifer said.

"Yes," Michael said flatly. "I guess I do."

"And you don't like it. Give me a break. Most of my detractors read my stuff before they decide it's garbage."

The light humor failed for both of them. In fact, it had made things worse. There seemed a kind of desperation to the moment, as if a carefully constructed house of cards had begun to sway.

Michael was still staring down at the first sheet of paper. Neither of them wanted to be the one to topple the precariously balanced structure of their relationship. But it was coming; she knew it was. And so did he.

She recalled a different set of confident feelings. The day before she had sat at her typewriter, her fingers tapping energetically "The Real Darla Hart." So certain she had been of the future then. Well, it was here now, not bright as she had supposed, but bleak like the sky behind the glass.

That was one of the rules her teachers had drilled into her about her profession. It was foolish to expect. When you expected anything, you were invariably wrong, but worse, you were blind to what actually existed. And that could not only disappoint you, it could hurt you.

Slowly, Michael handed the pages back to her across the table. "This is premature," he said.

"Premature? Perhaps to you, but not to me. I have a deadline, Michael. We talked about it. I don't understand."

The papers were still there suspended between them. Jennifer wouldn't take them back, a hollow defiant gesture if ever there was one. She wanted to hold back time, to continue to bask in her illusions, even if that was all they were. She felt as if there had been music playing all morning, and suddenly it had come to an end. The silence between them mocked the intimacy they had shared during the night.

Finally, Michael put her papers down beside her plate. "Maybe I was wrong. Maybe I should have told you this earlier. But I didn't want to spoil last night for us." He met her eyes straight on. She could feel the effort that took for him. "Yesterday I talked to Lena about calling it quits. But she needs more time."

"She needs more time?"

"I know . . . you don't have a lot of time to spare."

"Michael," Jennifer said, leaning across the table, "I don't have *any* time."

"I can't throw Lena to the wolves," Michael said defensively. "Look, Jen . . . try to understand. You're talented and tough. A survivor. But Lena isn't. You and I both know what's going to happen. When that story breaks, it'll get more coverage than if Martians landed in Times Square. If we come out with that story now, she'll be remembered for that last fiasco on *Today*. She's an actress. She won't get one reading or audition once they equate her with bombing out like that. I can't do that to her."

"But you can do that to me? You can see me lose my job. I get penalized because I'm self-sufficient. Funny." Jennifer laughed wryly. "Funny what we're raised to think, you know? How we're told to develop all these admirable qualities. From the time we're kids. We should be honest. Right? So I don't go after the jugular in my line of work. Believe me, it's not easy when some of your stiffest competition is from co-workers who could moonlight in Transylvania as tour guides. But me? I look for some high principled story to warm the cockles of a cold American public who, I might add, would rather hear the exaggerated lowdown on a kinky sex trial or about a revenge murder in the drug world. Only I'm getting wiped off the boards for my high principles. And I learn independence, self-sufficiency. Well, I'm tired of swimming upstream against the current, while someone like Lena Stephens drifts along in boats paddled by other people."

"It's not that way."

"The hell it isn't," Jennifer said. "And even if it isn't, I don't give a damn. I've earned some self-pity. I feel like indulging, okay?" She leaned back in her chair, fully aware of how poorly she was behaving, maybe even ridiculously, but at the moment she didn't particularly care. The thing of it was, she was frightened. If anyone was being thrown to the wolves, it was she: A whole pack of them waited for her back at KZAM.

Michael sighed, shaking his head. "I have a professional responsibility to put Lena back on her feet, Jennifer. I've got my own moral obligations to uphold, just like you do. Lena understands she's got to get herself together fast. What's more, she really wants to." A light came back on in Michael's eyes. "She's come so far, Jen. . . . She's right on the brink now, right on the edge of breaking through. A few more steps, that's all it'll take for her, and she'll be free of the garbage that's made her an emotional cripple. You should have seen her when I left her. She's so hopeful now."

"That's terrific."

"Give me a little time. Clever lady, you can stall them."

"Michael, I don't see how."

"The story is yours, Jennifer. But it's got to break right. For all of us. For me. For Lena. And you."

"Sure," she said, without conviction. She rose from her chair. "It's late. I'd love to stay and chat about all the good times we're going to have. But you know how it is, the gladiators await me in the arena."

"That tough, huh?" Michael said, rising also, and coming around to her. He put his arms on her shoulders.

This time she didn't feel a thrill of magic. She felt sadness. There was such contrast between the sunset and firelight and the cool light now slanting in through the windows. In vain, she tried to imagine Venus, benevolently twinkling good will to lovers; there, but hidden. At the present moment she most certainly lacked the right perspective—that of a dreamer. The world, the real world, was too much with her.

"Yes, as a matter of fact. It is that tough," she answered. "I'm tired of the grind. I'm tired of being tough. I'm tired of being afraid of losing my job and tired of being alone."

"So is everyone. Believe me."

"Thanks," she said. "That makes everything okay."

"Look. You don't have a monopoly on jeopardy, Jennifer. Maybe it's crass to bring the little matter of my own situation up, but it so happens I've got something to lose in this exercise of wiping the slate clean, too. If the public turns against me, I'm going to be a virtual pariah in society for perpetrating this fraud. It's okay if you're a scoundrel out plying your trade with a black cape and a long evil mustache, because there's a certain expectation in dishonesty there. Some of those jokers actually become cult heroes. But I've been set up to be a kind of amateur saint. Dirty pool, you see. Saints do not trick people. They do not deceive. I can lose my ass on this deal." He looked around. "Including all of this." Then, brushing the side of her face lightly with his fingertips, he said, "But more than anything, I don't want to lose you. Give me time?"

"Time," she repeated wistfully.

"You're not being conned," he said. "If that's what you're thinking."

"Oh, I wasn't thinking that I was being conned. I was only wondering if you were being conned."

Michael shook his head. "Not by Lena. I understand her."

"Maybe you do. Ordinarily. But these are exceptional

times, aren't they? I mean, Lena wants to give a perfect performance before she makes her last, grand exit in the role of imposter. But maybe you don't really want her to take that final bow, because when she goes out, that means the real Michael Casari has to make his entrance into the world again.

"Want to stick around and see?"

"Only if this is going to have a happy ending."

"Jennifer," Michael said with a sigh, "again, my love . . . there are no guarantees in this crazy world."

"There are fools in love, though." She kissed him quickly and left for the wolves' den.

Chapter 8

ENDERALL HAD ASSEMBLED THE FIVE REGULAR MEMBERS of the KZAM SWAT team, plus Madeline Renquist, in the conference room. They sat on either side of the imitation burled walnut table, with Enderall standing at its head. Behind him was the station's oversized television screen, its blank white expanse protruding on either side of Enderall like great square wings. Even his hands were arranged together, fingers up, in a thoughtful, prayerful mien. Jennifer knew she had only to squint her eyes and her imagination would gamely transpose the fake burled walnut into a marble altar for sacrificial sheep. It was a discomfortingly apt analogy.

"I presume we're all acquainted by now?" Enderall began.

Everyone looked to Madeline Renquist, the sixth and newest member, and likely usurper of paychecks, as she was viewed by the others. No one said anything. Madeline smiled coolly.

Madeline, as everyone had already assessed, *was* cool. Frigid. She had been quickly appraised as an affected snoot who spoke with a finishing-school drawl, derived not from any particular geographic location, but from breathing in the vapors of great sums of money for most of her life.

But, as it appeared, the only person smitten by Madeline of the Maryland Renquists was Enderall. To Jennifer, it was a predictable affection, happening as it did that Madeline had an uncle on the board of KZAM.

"Good," Enderall said, taking silence as affirmation. He unclasped his fingers. "Then we can begin." But before doing so, he sucked in his lower lip, chewing tentatively on it for a bit, as he assembled his thoughts. Finally, in a dolorous voice, he made his address. "Well, we're finally up against it. Push has come to shove. Armageddon is upon us."

No one responded. Jennifer gave a surreptitious glance to the others. They could have been an assemblage of threatened ostriches, who without sand at their disposal, did the next best thing by lowering their eyes to the table. Only Madeline remained impassive in the face of terror. She was smiling her slight quarter-smile, pale gray eyes disinterested in the plight of her co-workers. Only in collective strife, Jennifer noted, was their little band a unified group.

"At four o'clock tomorrow I'm going upstairs. With a topic that'll knock their socks off," Enderall said gravely.

Jennifer understood far more than Enderall had volunteered. Poor Enderall. He was desperate, and probably for good reason. The guys upstairs had to be really leaning on him.

The others at the table raised their heads in surprise.

Enderall paused. He took time to look at each of them

directly. Jennifer was glad to see there was still a bit of the showman left in him. At least the boys upstairs hadn't squeezed all the razzle-dazzle out of him, along with everything else.

"Someone," Enderall continued in a sonorous voice, his confidence revived by his employees' obvious fear, "someone at this table is going to give me that story."

"You told us we could have a month," John Rudran objected.

"You've had three days to think," Enderall snapped back. "That's what you're paid for. To think. And to think fast. Supposedly it's this very quirk of your cerebrums that separates you from the lower primates and from the rank and file of your profession." As Enderall spoke a crown of moisture broke along his receding hairline. Every time he moved his head beneath the neon lights, his shiny dome glistened like a damp laurel wreath of an outgoing Roman emperor. "I'm not carrying any more dead weight on my back," Enderall complained. The wag of his finger encompassed all of them but Madeline Renquist. "You don't produce, you're out." To make sure they understood, he jabbed his thumb in the direction of the door.

Jennifer was fairly certain that the boys upstairs had presented Enderall with a variation of that same speech, more elegantly put perhaps, but the bottom line was the same.

"This is the way it's going to be." Enderall placed both hands on the table, leaning in on them conspiratorily. "Think of this as a game of musical chairs. Only you lose your job if you don't come up with something good enough to pass muster up there." His eyes went to the ceiling. Sighing, he looked back at them. "Look, you think I like this? I don't. The thing is, when they get itchy for action, they want to see things moving around—even if it's only a body moving out the front door with his pink slip. They equate activity with progress. They're a very nervous bunch up there.''

"So what exactly does that mean?" Arnold Fine asked. "In concrete terms. To us."

"It means the one of you who comes up with the most lackluster story, as perceived through my divine eyes, is going to get his ass fired. Is that clear?"

"Perfectly," Arnold said, casting his eyes down to his folded hands.

Damn right, Jennifer was thinking. She took in the pallor which had spread to each face like a fast-moving plague. What Enderall had in mind was as plain as the bombing of Hiroshima.

"That means one of you is out at the next meeting." A collective murmur passed round the table. "Which one of you? You want to know which one of you? That's up to you. So there it is," Enderall broke off abruptly.

"So," he went on, "since we're all of one mind on this now, you're free to go and pursue your projects. We'll reconvene here at the same time tomorrow afternoon. Either have your story ready or your desk cleaned out. And good luck."

Enderall left the room quickly. The others were silent for a moment, then began to speak excitedly amongst themselves. Only Madeline rose. Jennifer watched her saunter from the room, not a care in the world.

"We've got to talk." Rita said, moving to the head of the table and holding her hands in the air for silence.

No one paid any attention. Arnold was engaged in a heated debate with Estela over some notes he had once shared with her. Now, in return, he was demanding an introduction to a dignitary to whom Estela had privileged access. John was murmuring worriedly to Jennifer about how his mind was still frozen solid.

"Look, you guys, we've got to get together on this!" Rita persisted, pounding the table.

Jennifer rose from her chair. She left John talking to himself as she took her purse and started for the door.

"Where are you going, Winters?" Rita called indignantly.

"To work on my story."

"Didn't you just hear what I said?"

Finally everyone was quiet.

Jennifer looked around, reading desperation in each of their expressions. "It's too late to work together," Jennifer said. "None of you know how. You ought to stick to your original game plan, Rita. Otherwise, all you'll do is drag each other down. Even lower than you've already sunk," she added, not to be snide, but because it happened to be true.

"Terrific, Winters. Just what we need here. Another rousing speech filled with optimism. But go on," Rita jeered, "go on, Winters. Run out on us. I mean who the hell cares? You've been more of a goddamned pom-pom girl since you hired on here, than anything else. You think the world wants to hear about some lousy birds getting their beaks cut by some nut? Well, they don't. They want the dirt. Like it or not, honey, that's the way it is. And the way it is, you need us, Winters—not the other way around. We know the score. You're stuck in that cuckoo land of yours. So follow your yellow brick road. It'll take you right up to the counter for unemployment insurance claims." Rita's eyes were pin pricks of wrath.

Estela rose before Jennifer could respond. Estela looked frightening, black eyes sparkling malevolently back at Rita.

Jennifer imagined a younger Estela in East L.A., a switch-blade shooting out from the palm of her hand. But in a soft, pleasantly modulated voice, Estela said, ''My dear, some-one should cut your beak. It's too sharp, too ugly. Nature has obviously made a blunder in your case.''

Estela left the room. Jennifer followed after her. Behind them, almost immediately, a rumble and hiss of voices took up in the conference room.

''She was right,'' Estela said, as they walked together down the aisle.

''Yeah, I know,'' Jennifer said with a sigh. ''The world is not interested in a bird being unable to eat because some maniac is running around chopping off beaks. They want to hear about the film star Prince Andrew frolics with in Tahiti. People don't care about an old lady who goes out and collects weeds and plants them in little pots so that when the bull-dozers clear away the last patch of green earth in her city, there'll be a few scraggly survivors left of that insignificant species. People care about dirt all right, but not that kind.''

''Look, Miss Hard Case,'' Estela said. She stopped Jennifer with a hand on her arm. ''Where I came from, I can be cynical. I earned it. But you, no. You don't know what it's like to fight. Not just to fight for a better place to sleep at night, and to get a decent education, but for your life sometimes. Most of all,'' Estela said, a fire behind the black eyes, ''I had to fight to believe there was something good in this world worth a fight. And there is. People have just forgotten, that's all. They've forgotten about some of the good things. So they need people like you and me to remind them. You and I,'' Estela said, smiling, ''we're like those little weeds that lady collects. A dying breed. But weeds are very strong. They can spread all over the world.''

''Gotcha,'' Jennifer said, smiling back, and wondering

why they had never had this kind of talk before. "Thanks for the attitude adjustment."

"Too bad there won't be more opportunities in the future."

"Umm, I forgot about that. Only one of us'll be left, isn't that the way it goes?"

"You got it," Estela said, backing off with a grin. "And that someone's gonna be me."

Jennifer laughed and gave her the thumbs up sign. "For a gladiator, Garcia, you've got style." Jennifer was glad she didn't have Darla Hart.

For the rest of the afternoon there was nothing much for Jennifer to do. Like the others, who had eventually stopped their feuding long enough to do some work, she passed time in her cubicle. Through some refined sensitivity, she imagined she could feel her compatriots' frayed nerves as they scratched pens to paper, furiously made calls to contacts, gnawed on a nail or two. She, however, doodled. Like a teenager in love, she wrote Michael's name, connected it with an arrow to her own, and drew a further link to the image of a clock. She had nothing to worry about but time. And she had nothing to do but worry. This part was Michael's gig. And heaven help her if he didn't pull it off.

A couple of times, Madeline Renquist strolled languorously by, slowing to look in on Jennifer. Jennifer smiled calmly, and Madeline smiled coolly, with a certain annoyance even. Madeline probably would have liked it better, Jennifer figured, if Madeline had seen her tearing out her hair. Madeline was no threat to her, not as long as she had Darla Hart. But to the others, Madeline's studied cruise of the premises must have been like Death touring the aisles with a shopping cart.

Michael called her late in the afternoon. Just at the sound

of his voice, she grew warm, found it difficult to concentrate on his actual words, drifting instead with his cadence.

"Okay?" he said.

"Sorry. What was that?"

"Jennifer? Why do I get the feeling you're between
channels?"

"Yes, yes. I'm here! Totally tuned in, with you all the
way."

"Yeah, well. That's what I wanted to make sure about.
That you'd be totally with me tonight. I'll have a surprise
waiting for you."

Jennifer laughed. "Great. I love treats."

"Want to name one?"

"The best one. You," she quipped.

"Thanks. Try another one."

"Okay, how's about . . . Venus! Wrapped up in gold
paper and silver ribbons."

"Close," he said.

Jennifer showered and changed at the La Fortunada
before driving to Michael's. When she finally arrived,
having battled through the tail-end of rush hour traffic, it
was seven o'clock.

Michael answered the door. As usual he was wearing
faded and form-fitting jeans, and this time a light blue
garden-variety sweatshirt with short sleeves frayed at the
edges. He looked gorgeous. That, to Jennifer, was the
funny thing about people who could actually afford the best.
They would wear the really grungy stuff, bargain outlet
markdowns, and somehow look better in it than the would-
be snobs in their fancy designer rags. She had changed into
white jeans and a black and white striped top with a broad,
floppy sailor's collar. Her hair was swept straight off her
forehead and caught in a red ribbon at the nape of her neck.

"I love you," Jennifer said softly, melting into his arms.

"Me, too," Michael said, and the way he said the two words carried a suggestive intimacy. His hand slipped slightly lower on her back, and she pressed against him as he slid fingers over the curve of her buttocks. She was ready to be kissed, but then as if he suddenly remembered something, he pulled himself away with something akin to embarrassment. "Jennifer . . ." His eyes were dancing. "Your surprise . . ."

He stepped aside, giving her a view of the living room.

"Hello," said Lena Stevens. Fittingly, she stood near the television. She was wearing an emerald green jumpsuit made out of some shiny, flowy material. The actress's eyes glistened like green pools. Although she was smiling, Jennifer sensed apprehension.

That worried Jennifer. What she wanted to see—what she needed—from Lena was calm, collectedness, total togetherness.

"Hi," Jennifer said, finding it difficult to put aside her fears. It was also hard to remember that the striking silver-haired woman standing before her wasn't actually the one and only Darla Hart, but Michael's manufactured creation.

Michael started forward, taking Jennifer by the hand into the living room. He made the introductions formally. Jennifer felt awkward, as if she were the heavy who had disrupted Lena's life. In fact, she said as much finally, while Michael disappeared into the kitchen to get a pot of coffee.

"I hope this isn't too difficult for you. That it isn't premature?"

"It's really the best thing. Isn't it?" Lena said, looking past Jennifer to where Michael was standing in the kitchen. "I mean, for all of us."

"Michael's explained . . . ?"

"More or less. I mean I could tell by the way he looked at you how totally gone he was. In love, that is."

"But he's not just doing it for me," Jennifer said quickly out of guilt.

"We worked all afternoon," Lena said buoyantly.

"And she was great!" Michael added, bringing in a tray with three cups and a pot of coffee. He put everything down on the coffee table.

At his praise Lena beamed. "I did try, Michael. You know I want this as much as you do."

He gave her a fast hug. "And you're going to get it, too. This time you're going to make it."

"Yes! I am, aren't I? This time I'm not going to let you down. Woops! Goof. I mean, not going to let myself down." She winked at Jennifer. "You see, I'm supposed to think well of myself. I'm deserving of the best. The best of everything, he says." Lena cast a worshipful look to Michael.

"You got it," Michael said. "Coffee anyone?"

"I'm off," Lena said, picking up a notebook. "My script," she explained to Jennifer.

Michael walked her out to her car. When he returned, Jennifer was sitting cross-legged on the floor before the coffee table, smiling from ear-to-ear. "Wah-hoo! She's going to make it! We're going to make it! I'm going to make it!"

Leaping up, she ran into Michael's arms. They closed around her. Only there was little fervor behind his kiss and a second later he broke the embrace.

"Something's wrong," Jennifer said.

"No, not wrong. It's just not right. At least, not yet. Jen, I don't want to see you set yourself up high for a big letdown."

"Michael, what are you saying? I thought everything was 'great' just a minute ago?"

"Failure is a possibility. I just want you to recognize that."

"No," Jennifer said. "No, no. Lena looked fabulous. And she really wants this to work out. She even said so, Michael." She was fairly pleading her case to him.

"Yeah. But Lena says lots of things. Half of what she says is just to keep the heat off." Frustrated, he shook his head. "She's an actress, Jennifer. Performers are wonderful, warm, loving people. Super human beings. But most of them have this flaw—okay, all of us do to a certain extent—only they're a breed who's taken it to the extreme. They build up all kinds of clever defenses to protect that core inside where all the true emotions lie. They can stare you right in the eye, a smile as big as half a watermelon on their face, all the while crying inside.

"Okay, okay. Point taken. But Lena's specifically working on getting better."

"Exactly. And that's what makes this doubly tricky. She's getting right down to the soft core that she's been protecting all these years. This is real scaresville."

"So what you're saying to me is that I shouldn't raise my hopes too high, thinking that Lena's going to be ready in time to save my job. Is that it?"

"She may be. But then again—"

"She may not." Jennifer sat down on the sofa.

"You've got to keep the lid on this for a while longer."

"Michael, do you know what you're asking of me?"

"All life is a calculated gamble, Jen. I'm putting my whole career on the line, too. I'm willing to do that. For us."

"Oh . . . Oh, Michael . . ." Jennifer went rushing to him. "I know, I know," she said, snuggling against his chest. She kissed his neck. "It's just so hard, you know. The pressure at work is incredible. I know it's difficult for you, too, projecting what might happen in the future. But for me, well, it's like the future is already here."

"I can't do anything more than I already am," he said, stroking her back, kissing her temple lightly.

"Yes, you can." She looked up, finding him beautiful. Touching the side of his face, she said, "You can make love to me, make the whole world go away . . . your fans, my boss, Lena . . ." She kissed his neck, she kissed his mouth. "So there's only us remaining . . ."

Michael laughed at her earnestness. "It doesn't matter about the rest of the world. You're all I see anymore now." He freed her hair of the red ribbon. "I'm happy. Do you know that?" he said, his eyes searching hers. "For the first time maybe in my entire life, I know what it is to be happy. And it's so simple, so goddamned simple."

Tears came into Jennifer's eyes. "And a little scary, too."

"Don't you be afraid. It's all going to work out."

He kissed her, their physical response to each other building as his tongue twined in hers and she caressed the back of his neck. With his pelvis slanted into her, he made small spirals with his lean hips, bringing up the fire already racing through her body.

"God!" Michael said, squeezing her to him, trembling with desire. "I have never wanted a woman so much in my life as I've wanted you." He kissed her mouth. "Your lips." And then her nose, making her laugh. "Your beautiful nose. Your neck . . ." and he demonstrated. "And here . . ." His tongue flicked lower as his fingers undid each button of her blouse.

He slipped off her bra and, while kissing her, unsnapped her white jeans. "Take them off," he said.

She stood before him in only her white lace bikini briefs. Michael's eyes were scorching her breasts. His mouth found her nipples, and going lower to his knees, he slipped the nylon waistband off with his teeth, his hands roaming over her hips. She closed her eyes, swimming in the changing sensations he brought to her body, the warmth of his breath, the flick of his tongue, the pressure of his hand, his fingers knowing instinctively how to bring her higher and higher, to a point near total ecstasy and then at the crucial time, knowing when to let the pressure subside.

He carried her into the bedroom. When he came into the bed undressed, they touched for a very long time, with gentleness, with tenderness, before giving into the more urgent demands they both desired and took from each other.

His movements were fluid and demanding, knowledgeable. She caught her breath, feeling sometimes that she would pass out from the overwhelming sensations he stirred in her. "How do you do that?" she breathed.

"Like this," he said, moving in slow circles.

Jennifer moaned. "But how do you know how I feel?"

Michael deliberately moved deeper into her. "Because I love you. Can't you tell?"

"I can't tell anything but . . . oh, this is incredible," she moaned, throwing her head back and arching into him as he increased his rhythm.

Her hands gripped his back, and her legs moved against his. They were hard with muscle, like the arms that held her, but every male part of him was sensitive to her female wants.

She was not experienced, but he made her move with experience. Matching his rhythm, knowing instinctively, somehow, when to move forward, when to shift to the side, and soon it was Michael who seemed lost in a world of male pleasure. She felt his contractions, and the shuddering of his body, and somehow that was as exciting to her as the feeling that flooded through her shortly after.

Their bodies were slick with sweat, Michael's hair damp. Jennifer licked at his shoulder, tasting the salt, loving to taste him. "I love you," she said into his ear.

He said nothing. Instead, he kissed her. The intimacy of that deep kiss was shattering. She felt him inside of her, the way no physical act could ever bring closeness.

"I love you . . ." she said again. But words could not express what she was feeling.

Chapter 9

THE NEXT MEETING WITH ENDERALL HAD BEEN SET FOR two o'clock. It was usual for everyone to straggle in carelessly, five or ten minutes late. Jennifer took her place at the table, noting that all seats were occupied, also noting with amusement that it was ten minutes before two. Except for Madeline Renquist's, all expressions were grave. Madeline was leaning back in her chair, and with annoyingly calm precision, she drew a nail file back and forth over pale, unpolished nails. The others were studiously hunched over their notes. To Jennifer, they had the nervous, slightly wild-eyed look of politicians cramming for a public debate.

John Rudran rose suddenly. His chair gave a high screech against the linoleum. Without explanation he bolted from the room, but returned a second later to snatch up the yellow, legal-size pad at his place, then flew out the door for the second time. The hinges on the door to the men's lavatory down the hall could be heard squeaking open, then closing with a breathy wheeze. John's face was white when he returned. He took his place again, gluing his eyes to his pad.

Even Jennifer was less certain of her survival than she had been a day earlier. Ultimately, of course, she would triumph. But in the meantime she had to stall. That was going to be tricky.

Enderall appeared exactly at two o'clock. His presence in the doorway was like a thunder cloud, somber, heavy with foreboding. Jennifer recognized his suit as being one of his best. It was a navy gabardine, funereally dark, in keeping with the day's schedule of events. There was not only the matter of the staff's meeting; afterward, Enderall himself would be held accountable to the Boys Upstairs. In either case, he had probably decided it would not do to go larking about wearing the ice cream colors of summer.

"Ah, good. We're all here," he puffed, sounding out of breath as he entered. Enderall craned his neck around in the starched white collar. Its pristine brilliance shone in contrast to the mottled flush of his face. The familiar rim of moisture was already evident at his temple. In his hands he carried several folders which he placed before him on the table.

A quick glance and Jennifer recognized her name on one of the tabs. They were personnel folders.

"I just came from upstairs," he said. He lifted his neck higher again, twisting it. This time the movement seemed less a tick brought on by physical discomfort than one prompted by tension. Pausing briefly, he looked at everyone, as if allowing them air time to insert condolences on his behalf.

"Well, we may as well get at it," he said with a sweep of his hand. He retired to a chair set off to one side of the table.

To Jennifer, it seemed sadly ironic that John was the first to be offered up for sacrifice. But she had to give him credit; scared as she knew he was, externally he had certainly pulled himself together. Against the light-blue material of his suit, his tan had returned, pulsing health and well-being. He delivered his spiel with all the showmanship and confidence of a world-class surfer shooting a pipeline curl. The delivery, however, was more impressive than the subject matter.

When he had finished, Enderall gave no more than a grunt and a cursory nod. John did pale slightly then. He returned to his seat. Jennifer offered him a smile, but his attention was riveted to his clasped hands.

Rita Levett was next on the chopping block; or rather, the team of Levett and Fine.

On their own, Jennifer judged each of them dangerous, but together they were positively, gloriously lethal. They ran through their number like a pair of seasoned troupers from vaudeville: material committed to memory, timing down perfect. Rat-tat-tat. Patter-patter. Ta-da!

With some effort, Jennifer restrained herself from applauding when they had finished their number. She had to give them credit; they were pros at what they did. But then, she reminded herself, so had been Hitler and Attila the Hun.

Enderall, himself, seemed well pleased. He was grinning from ear to ear. "Yes, yes," he said, "that has definite possibilities."

Rita and Arnold were conspiring to expose the history of a woman who was running for a national office. Early in her life she had made several moral wrong turns. For one thing she had borne an illegitimate child and, because of her youth, had given the child up for adoption. Rita had used every means possible to track down the grown child and had plans for arranging a televised "showdown" of mother and child reunited, with no prior notice to either side. All the dirt had long been swept under the carpet of time and replaced by good deeds, but since Watergate, the American public had suffered an acute sensitivity to scandal. Jennifer didn't doubt the story would cripple the woman's political career.

Estela Garcia rose next. There was no trace of barrio accent as she spoke of her plan to televise an interview between the two warring sides of a South American country engaged in an inflammatory situation of global significance.

Clearly, Enderall was impressed. As was Jennifer. From the corner of her eyes, she saw Rita and Arnold exchange looks. John was staring straight ahead.

It was too soon for Madeline to be expected to contribute anything.

Jennifer stood. It was as if the floor beneath her had lost its solidity and she found herself ankle deep in swirling, shifting sand. Speaking with as much authority as possible, she addressed Enderall. "I have a story," she said. "A good story. Only I'm afraid at this point I'm not at liberty to disclose it."

"Really? Not at liberty?" The right side of Enderall's mouth quirked upward into something that did not in the remotest way resemble a smile. "Then perhaps, Miss Winters, I might suggest you may find yourself at liberty to search for a new job."

"It's only temporary," she broke in hastily. "I just can't tell you the details now."

"No details. My. How about just a smidgeon of a vague hint?"

"Mr. Enderall, that isn't what—"

"Oh, forgive us. We forgot. I forgot. You're obviously very special. Principled. Not like the other poor working

slobs who had to hustle to get stories in for today.''
Enderall's voice slid sarcastically over each word.

"Not special. No. But based upon past performance, I'd
think I'd be entitled to a certain period of grace, just as long
as I—"

Enderall flew out of his chair. His fist landed on the table
like a judge's gavel sentencing the condemned. "A period
of grace?" Enderall's voice boomed through the room.
"What do you think I am, the Pope? I'll tell you this, there
are a whole bunch of gods sitting up there—" he looked to
the ceiling "—who don't know grace from a snake. They
do know Dunn and Bradstreet, however." The silence
churned with his nervous fury even after the words were
gone.

It was Jennifer's turn again, and she spoke slowly and
coldly, her fear turned to indignation. "I've got a story that
will put this station on top of the ratings. The top. All I need
is time."

"And I don't have any time to give you," Enderall
returned just as slowly, as if he were speaking to a child. "I
don't have any time. I can't go upstairs bearing promises
under my arm. I need stories, Miss Winters. I need your
story."

Jennifer waited a long moment, or for what seemed to be
a long moment. For her it was some period of time
approximating eternity, during which her entire life's history was set before her in instantaneous review: the dreams of
glory during her school days as a journalism student; those
first heady months when she was actually working in her
magical profession, a profession which to her soul was the
latter-day equivalent of knighthood, the forces of light
triumphing over the forces of darkness; the struggle to keep
her own shining dreams from eroding in the face of the
ugliness and despair assailing others whose stories she told.

All of that had led to this moment of true reality. No matter how noble her intentions, she would be a knight without a standard to bear, tilting at windmills with a broken, ineffectual lance if she had no job. But Michael . . . Michael . . . he had trusted her to keep her silence.

"All right," she said. "You want a story? Then give them this." She spoke rapidly, defiantly, and with desperation, the swirling, imaginary sand rising higher to her calves, surrounding her thighs, inundating all that she was and had hoped to be. There would be no sign of her when she was done, only the tip of a rusty and bent lance.

"The pelicans," Jennifer said. "You know, the ones who've been found with their beaks mutilated? They're poor helpless creatures. They do no one any harm. And some maniac is clipping their beaks so they can't catch fish and they can't groom themselves. They don't have a chance of surviving, unless we do something about it. The police may catch the nut who's doing this, but we've got to do something, too. We've got to educate the public . . . reach the kids now, so when they grow up they'll have a sense of—"

"Miss Winters . . . please." Enderall sighed. "Spare us."

Arnold nudged Rita with his elbow. John looked hopeful again, his color returned. Estela, at least, had the decency to appear noncommittal. Madeline only seemed bored.

"I know," Jennifer said, feeling the anger building. "Blah, real blah, huh? Some poor dumb birds. Who gives a damn if they're going to be wiped out of existence?"

Enderall fidgeted, checked his watch. "I think we can wrap this up now. Miss Winters . . . Miss Winters, it gives me no pleasure to—"

"No. Wait."

Enderall raised his eyebrows. "Yes, Miss Winters? You have reconsidered?"

He was taunting her. That was the worst of it. She who had waxed so piously in her last breath was in the next ready to sell out like the rest of them. Anything to hang in there. Anything to be a guiding force in this mad, mad world which they made even crazier because they were no better, perhaps even worse, being the supposed defenders of truth and morality.

Around her, the faces became less certain. Madeline looked suddenly interested.

Mentally, Jennifer hoisted her bent lance, gripped it tightly and said, "Tell them . . ." She hesitated. "Tell them, Darla Hart."

No one said anything. They were all staring at her. Intently.

"Darla Hart, Miss Winters? What . . . about . . . Darla . . . Hart?"

"My story is on Darla Hart's personal life. I have total access, exclusive access to the most intimate details of Miss Hart's life story." There. She had done it. She had even compounded the felony by adding the trite little catch words so beloved in yellow journalism. Exclusive access. Intimate details.

If there had been silence before, now there was positively a void. After a bit, Enderall cleared his throat. "Are you serious?"

"Absolutely." She stood straight, looking ahead of her without seeing a thing. She could see herself as a traitor at a court-martial. Her allegiance to her conscience had been betrayed and somehow, she knew, she would have to pay.

"Well . . ." Enderall stroked his chin, staring off into the middle-distance, unfocused, visionary. Suddenly he looked back to her. "You're positive about this? This isn't some sort of hair-brained, last ditch effort to—"

"It's the truth," Jennifer said, adding for irony, "on my honor."

John loosened his silk tie. Both Rita and Arnold wore frozen expressions signifying panic and disbelief. Estela seemed impressed. Madeline's eyes held an unfamiliar gleam of respect.

"Well, then," Enderall said, "well, then . . ." He rubbed his hands together. "I think that's it. The story I wanted. Exactly what I had in mind." His eyes were very bright. To Jennifer, he appeared ten years younger, the old Enderall reborn to his prime.

"There's one thing, though," Jennifer said. "I'm going to bring this story in; but along with it I want your word that I can do my pelican feature." The good deed was as much a way to appease her throbbing conscience as it was a noble gesture.

"My, my, haven't we suddenly become cheeky? Bartering, no less."

There was no need for her to respond. The underlying threat was implied. KZAM wasn't the only station in town.

"Darla Hart . . ." said Enderall, appearing to chew over the name, and along with it the visions of success the name conjured. "All right. Pelicans."

Sedately, Jennifer took her seat. She knew she looked in control. So cool. Her moment of triumph, after all. But inwardly? A wreck. *Michael forgive me. I had to talk out of turn. You've got to see that. You've got to understand. And Michael, please, please, please . . . don't let me down.*

After that, it was a long day.

Shell-shocked, not feeling equipped to deal with the outside world until she had settled things within her inner world, she spent the afternoon in her cubicle. Her finger throbbed from dialing Michael's number. By four o'clock she would have lain even money on having listened to the pulsing, unanswered ring three hundred times. A full confession was in order. Only clemency from Michael could banish her headache, her heartache.

That same afternoon John was summarily given his week's notice. He didn't exercise the option. After the meeting, he emptied all personal things out of his desk and left KZAM without saying good-bye to anyone.

It was very quiet after he left. John's departure had made the abstract concrete. Enderall wasn't messing around.

Michael was on his second pass around the block, searching for a parking space close to his agent's office. He had already missed one spot, his mind drifting to Jennifer, her image then mingling with the future and all the consequences of the planned meeting with Morey. He was in love, yes. But he was not insane. Or perhaps he was. Never in his life had he felt so certain, so absolutely sure of his feelings. And yet, there was still that niggling worry that his emotions had skewed his capacity to make wise choices about concrete matters.

To the right was Morey's office. Unlike everything else about Morey, Morey's office building was low-key. When the money had started rolling in from the Darla Hart enterprise, he found he could afford better surroundings in which to sharpen his number two pencils. Whereas others reaping the Hart bonanza might have moved to streamlined Century City, Morey chose to invest in a squat, shabby office building on Sunset Strip. It was a two-story affair, its wood siding in dire need of a new coat of white paint, located in the shadow of an enormous billboard featuring a

leering invitation by seminude Las Vegas chorines to
sample various unspecified pleasures. Morey's rationale
was that sooner or later someone would want to buy the
dump and turn it into a parking lot; that, or oil would be
found in its location. Morey was hoping for the parking lot.
In the City of the Angels nothing was more valuable than a
place to stash one's vehicle.

Through bitter experience, Michael had come to agree
with that reasoning. After circling the block three more
times, he finally lucked out and slipped into a metered spot
across the street just as a car overflowing with bouncing
white poodles pulled away. The hapless driver of the Jaguar
behind him gave a rude gesture with his fist before zooming
on to continue his quest to possess a meter of his own.

After depositing a quarter for a half-hour's rent—the
meeting wouldn't take long, not unless Morey went crazy—
Michael jaywalked across the street and entered Morey's
real estate investment.

The bottom floor of the building was leased to three
tenants, one a rock concert producer, another who ran a
mail-order computerized horoscope business, and the third
lessee a mysterious oriental man, referred to by Morey as
his Shanghai connection. The man would arrive in his
Excalibur three times a week, always at the same precise
moment, and stayed no more than two hours maximum. All
he had in there, Morey related with wonder, was a desk, a
chair, a telephone, and an enormous potted cactus.
"Drugs," Morey had once confided to Michael. "So turn
him in," Michael had suggested. "I'm nuts? The guy pays
two months in advance. Cash."

Money, Michael thought as he reached the top of the
landing—money was always what it boiled down to. Maybe
even for him.

He passed through double doors (also in need of paint) and into the reception area. It was a large room and sunny. There were two sofas, long since frayed at the edges, four disreputable-looking armchairs, coffee and end tables strewn with dog-eared back issues of *Publishers' Weekly* mixed in with copies of *Variety* and *The Hollywood Reporter*.

Morey employed three underlings to represent television and screen writers, plus more pure literary types. The lobby was scattered with a few such clients now, chattily swapping industry horror stories while they waited to be seen.

They paused and nodded to him, following with their eyes as he crossed the room and tapped on the glass window, behind which the receptionist sat.

The electronic door lock buzzed, and Michael passed into Morey's inner sanctum.

Morey met him halfway down the hall. "Mikey, baby. You got parked okay out there? One of these days they're going to make that offer. They'll turn this dinosaur into a parking structure. A boon for humanity."

"A boon for you," Michael said, following Morey into his office.

"That, too." Morey gestured for Michael to sit opposite his desk. "You're lookin' good, kid . . . fabuloso." He hunted around for a thin cigar, stuck it in his mouth, and lit it while talking. "Must be the sea air. Wish I could afford to live in that kind of luxury . . . sea air . . . teenage girls, nothing on hardly, parading by my front door all day. Maybe I'd—"

"Cut the bull, Morey. Grinding me isn't going to make any difference to why I came here. You know that."

Morey made a flicking motion with his lips and the cigar traveled to the other side of his mouth. "My," he said, the cigar wiggling up and down, "aren't we in a cheery mood?" Morey shrugged. "So," he went on, "as you asked, I took a look at your contracts." He patted a manila folder on his desk.

Michael tensed. "And?"

"And it's like I said before. You have a clause stipulating your true identity not be revealed. In fact, as you will recall, it was you who fought tooth and nail for it. You didn't want anyone to scale your ivory tower."

Michael remembered it well. It had been the blackest of all times. He had been suffering from professional burnout from treating too many failed humans.

"What if I break the contracts? I tell people who I am. What's my position?"

Morey shifted his weight, the discourse uncomfortable to him. "They might just scream and holler. Maybe they wouldn't." He shrugged. "It depends, I suppose."

"On what?"

"If you lose readers for the publishers. You do that and they'll do more than yell. They'll sue your designer jeans off. Say bye-bye to Malibu, baby."

During the last speech, Morey's round face had taken on the hue of cooked oatmeal. Michael knew that Morey was thinking less about the loss of Michael's waterfront property than about his own Brentwood lot, on which subsisted a wife, two utterly stupid Afghan hounds, and a six-thousand-square-foot mock English Tudor architectural extravaganza.

Michael uncrossed his legs and started to rise. "Thanks, Morey."

"Hold it, hold it . . . whoa there, Mikey." Morey rose quickly, made a feeble gesture for Michael to remain where he was. There was mild panic in the agent's eyes. Morey ran a hand through what was left of his hair. Leaning over his desk, he said, "Look, Michael, what is this? This is not just an idle question and answer session here. Is it, Michael?" He looked like he wanted to be told a lie.

Michael couldn't oblige. "No. It's not."

"I didn't think so." Morey lapsed into silence. Picking at the edge of the manila folder, he said, "Look, you asked before about this. And I brought out all my numbers. All the data was from a top market research operation.

"The public is happy, Mike. They think Darla Hart is a female. They like the fact that Darla Hart is a female. Just like God is a man. That's the way it should be. Any other way is weird, you know?"

"Then it looks like they, and you, will have to bear some disillusionment."

Morey held up his hand, palm out, contrite. "Don't get hostile on me. I'm on your side. All I'm saying is facts are facts. You could do yourself great harm, you go shooting off your mouth. Hell! They'd think you were some kind of screaming Hollywood fanatic. Writing advice. What kind of a real man would do that for a living?" Morey stopped. "Oh, sorry, Michael. You know I didn't mean that. I know you're straight, right? People, though, you know how they think. They might have distorted vision."

"Yeah, well, thanks, Morey . . ." Michael rose again, started for the door.

"Thanks, Morey? Thanks, Morey?" The agent shot around his desk, blocking Michael's way. "That's it? You call me, ask me a question that makes ten more strands of hair fall out of my scalp, and that's all you can say? I mean, we're talking my life, Michael. I think I have a right to know what's going on inside your head."

"Know something? I'd like to know the same thing."

Michael crossed the room. Leaning forward, he rested both elbows on the high back of a chair.

"Oh, no. Oh, no . . ." Morey moaned and slapped his forehead. He traced his way back to his desk. Sinking into his chair, he said, "It's a broad. All this trouble because of a broad?"

"She's a lady, Morey."

"So, she's a lady. The world is filled with them. What's the big deal you've got to upset the apple cart because of this one. Take her to bed, enjoy yourself, fall in love—"

"I am in love," Michael said. "And this has nothing to do with sleeping with her."

"I see. This is serious." Morey shook his head, looking incredulous.

"Serious."

"So serious you've got to tear our world apart? I don't get it."

"No, you wouldn't. I hardly do, myself." Michael looked out the window. Five cardboard Las Vegas chorines leered provocatively back at him. Their faces blurred in his mind, each one becoming the same face, all of them his Jennifer's. Money. Pretty women. Fame. Fortune. His precious anonymity. They were all nothing to him compared with that single, beautiful face.

"I can't believe it," Morey was saying. "You. Mr. Ice Blood. Mr. No Personal Involvement. The man who came into my office five years ago and swore up and down all he wanted was to relate to a blank piece of paper that would be incapable of crying and swearing and calling him up at three in the morning. The man whose most intimate moments have been spent with his bank teller when he deposits his monthly royalty check. His vast monthly royalty check."

"Things don't always stay the same, Morey. My needs are different now than they were five years ago."

Morey's face turned crimson. "It so happens that my needs are still the same. Mortgage payments, eating well . . . keeping my wife off my back . . . not writing bouncers to my Mercedes mechanic, who besides being a wonderful mechanic is a vicious little gossip and at the drop of a wrench could and would ruin whatever reputation for solvency I've managed to build up amongst my Beverly Hills peers." He drew in a deep, agonized breath. "Get the picture? Look, Michael, this'll pass. Passion cools. You've got another two years on this contract. Wait two years, then give this dolly a whirl on the old honesty express."

"She's a lady, Morey."

"Lady, then. But don't be a jerk now. You be a jerk now, then phftt . . . it all goes."

"I get it, Morey. I get it."

"Good. Fine. You get it. Does this mean I can go to sleep in my nice big king-sized bed tonight and dream happy dreams, knowing the bed and I aren't going to be out in the street a month from now, just because my client has an adolescent lust?"

"You're free to dream whatever you want. I'm the one who doesn't have that option in my contract."

Michael started for the door.

"Michael, Michael, wait a minute."

Wearily, Michael turned around. Morey came forward slowly, looking small and suddenly older than Michael had pictured him before.

"Michael, this is cruel what you're doing. It's selfish. You have responsibilities to other people. Me. And what about Lena? Did you give Lena any thought—"

Morey had calculatedly struck a nerve. Knowing he was

being manipulated did not reduce the sting of Morey's accusation. Angrily, Michael said, "I am tired of responsibilities to other people. I have a right to my own life."

"I see," Morey said.

Michael wanted to walk out angry, but he couldn't. He knew Morey had done what he had intended; he'd hooked him into his old messiah ways again. The feelings he was experiencing were both comfortable and unpleasant. Comfortable because they were familiar; unpleasant because he had changed and old feelings rubbed against new ones.

"I'm working with Lena. She'll be ready for the *Today* telecast. There won't be any problem. Then, I want to make the announcement."

Morey blanched, but Michael continued.

"Lena will have a new career, one for which she can take full responsibility and get full credit. If all goes well, you'll still have me as a profitable client."

"And if it doesn't?"

"Then there'll be some changes in both of our lifestyles." Michael smiled. "Cheer up, Morey. Look at it in the biblical sense. Dust unto dust."

"I'm not religious," Morey returned. His whole being sagging, he returned to his desk. With his back to Michael, he said, "So maybe I should learn some prayers. Get the hell outa here."

Jennifer was almost ready to hang up the receiver when a melodic female voice on the other end said, "Yes?" For a second, Jennifer thought she had dialed incorrectly. "Hello? Hello?" the woman's voice repeated.

"Lena?"

A pause. "Who is this?"

"It's me, Jennifer."

"Oh, hi. Sorry," Lena said, laughing. "Can't be too

careful, you know. If I wasn't paranoid before, Michael's made me that way now. I feel like I'm guarding the secret passage into Fort Knox.''

Jennifer thought that might be an apt analogy, but all she said was, ''Could you put Michael on?''

''Not here yet. He hid the key for me. Told me to let myself in if he wasn't back to work with me yet. He went to his agent's.''

''Oh.'' Jennifer knew why. He was, of course, living up to his end of their bargain. If she had felt bad before, this piece of news only compounded her guilt.

''I'll give him the message you called,'' Lena said.

''Lena, how do you feel about . . . about what you're doing? I mean, do you feel confident?''

''Oh, sure, sure. Really confident. It's all coming along great. Michael's wonderful. The guy's like a saint, so patient with me. I'm gonna knock 'em dead next time. You can bet on it.''

''I think I already did.'' Jennifer could have bitten her tongue, but it was too late.

''What?''

''I'm just glad you're feeling so positive about—''

''No, you were serious, just now. You didn't tell anyone, did you?''

''Lena . . .''

''You did. You told someone.''

Jennifer could almost see Lena slumping into a chair. ''There were extenuating circumstances. I wanted to explain everything to Michael.''

''Well, hell,'' Lena said, her voice sounding at once defensive and frightened, ''explain it to me. I mean, like it just so happens it's my damned face out there in front of millions and millions—''

''No damage has been done,'' Jennifer broke in, sensing

Lena's hysteria mounting with every syllable. "It's all going to be okay."

The phone went dead on the other end.

Jennifer redialed. It rang, but no one answered. She put down the phone and grabbed her purse. "It's got to be all right," Jennifer muttered to herself as she tore down the aisle to the elevator.

Chapter 10

JENNIFER MADE THE TRIP TO MALIBU IN A MENTAL FOG, the MG practically driving itself as her mind spun various beginnings to the speech she was to deliver to Michael. And also to Lena, if she was there. When Jennifer finally did arrive, it was disappointing. The house looked dark, totally deserted. Jennifer took it as mildly odd that Lena's car was still parked in front. She knew it was Lena's because Michael had mentioned the newly purchased yellow Porsche, commenting on how it seemed incongruous to Lena's cautious personality.

After knocking several times, ringing the bell, and even going so far as to try the side entrances, Jennifer finally gave up and returned to her car.

It had been a warm day, but the evening was turning cool. Now the fog was rolling in from the sea, blowing across the highway, making it difficult to see very far down the coast road. She thought of waiting there for him, but just as quickly reconsidered. With no top to her car, she'd be soaked through from the dampness in no time.

So instead she drove down the highway until she came to one of the ubiquitous small roadside shacks that pass themselves off as restaurants along any tourist route. It boasted the usual fare on large red and white and blue signs slapped up against its wraparound glass windows: hamburgers and fries, a $3.49 steak special, and fish they claimed was fresh, but which Jennifer knew would be frozen. It, and other establishments like it, stayed in business mostly because the sea air made one ravenous and subsequently indiscriminate, or else the itinerant wayfarer was probably already confused by the sensory overload of Highway 1's exotic cars and bikini-clad women and tanned, muscular surfers with their giant, portable radios blasting out dreams of lust and love.

Jennifer thought of all this as she slid into a booth. She didn't belong to either group; she fit into no group, actually. She had always been a watcher, a bystander, a chronicler of other people's dramas. Well, tonight she certainly had her own.

How does it feel, Winters? the side of her who always stood apart as observer asked. She didn't answer herself immediately, instead giving the waitress her order for an iced tea and dinner salad.

It feels scary, she judged, looking out the window. She didn't know what was happening anymore. For once she was dependent upon others for her welfare, both physical and emotional.

On the other side of the glass the fog was thickening. Cars had turned on their lights and crept by cautiously and close together, like a slow-moving parade of lumbering elephants. The waitress returned with her tea and a small plate holding wilted salad with a garnish of dry, curling carrot peels. A single pale tomato wedge had been set off to the side. For artistic dash, Jennifer supposed.

She accepted the listless fare without comment. At any other time she would have sent it back; now the only thing that mattered to her was the black pay telephone on the other side of the room.

With one eye on the man using the phone, she sipped her iced tea. He wore a brown polyester suit, long out of style, slightly frayed at the cuffs and edges of the jacket. His short hairstyle had grown scraggly along the neck, and his shoes were worn at the heels, besides needing a polishing. Periodically he would respond to the person on the other end, occasionally writing down something on a small pad.

For a moment Jennifer became the professional again, losing herself in the stories of others. This one was a salesman, down on his luck. Borderline desperate. He probably had a wife whom he lied to, maybe a couple of kids to whom he still promised trips and toys that would never materialize. His wife already knew the truth. That's why he would sleep with a woman here and there, someone he met along the road, someone who would go along with whatever fantasy he spun out until the daylight came and he would be on his way. Or, Jennifer thought, he could be another one of America's unemployed, perhaps a transplant from the Midwest, a tired conquistador who had come to the fabled golden shores of Southern California looking for opportunity. He'd end up getting a job for one of the sham, quick-buck artists—as a salesman for some door-to-door sales gimmick, a phone solicitor for magazines or solar air, or a "realtor" for time sharing in Shangrila Villas, a fictitious desert condominium site which would never be built after the down payments were taken. Whatever, there would be the carrot-on-the-stick offer, there always was. He would grab for it, and they would use him, always smiling, always with the back slap, the firm hand-pumping that bound them together as brothers in commerce. Then, when it came time for him to collect his paycheck, the carrot would disappear along with the employer.

And suddenly, from her distant perspective, Jennifer recognized herself in the man. She was no better, no worse, no higher or lower; they were both equal participants in the complex game that people thought of as life. It was only that they were after different prizes. He wanted a long shiny car and a Mexican cruise. She wanted a story that would sizzle. Whether or not others would see their plans as sensible, even workable, was of no consequence. They, the dreamers, were bewitched by their desires. Perhaps that was why so many people failed at what they wanted. They were fair game to any words from any person who would support them in their illusion. An otherwise intelligent, monied woman would believe a young, handsome man without a penny in his jeans, when he said he was mad for her. A poor man of little significance would believe he could become a giant of commerce by sending in $29.50 for a book sharing a bogus philanthropist's secrets of success.

She sipped thoughtfully on her iced tea. Outside, yellow fog lights were a string of warm, friendly lanterns winking at her in the haze. She considered the fog, itself a treacherous gray veil. And she thought of a wilderness of snow, of being lost, and of the proverbial light that suddenly shone out in the dark. For her, Michael was that light.

If only, she reflected, there were not so many obstacles in the path she must take to reach him. And then, another thought, disquieting, slipped stealthily amid the others. Would someone else less involved than she, more objective than she, disbelieve Michael's sincere intent to help her? Was this all a stall? Common knowledge, elemental fact: a person's willingness to believe corresponded in direct proportion to how badly they wanted something. Knowing all she did about human nature, if things fell apart, she would have to accept responsibility for being her own victim. That was the odd thing, the truly mysterious thing about people; brains and experience counted as nothing when the heart had its say.

The man had concluded his conversation. Jennifer watched sympathetically as he slouched away from the telephone. Stopping briefly, he bought a pack of cigarettes from the cashier. He lit up one of the cigarettes, took a couple of short, nervous drags, and went out into the fog where he promptly disappeared from sight.

The phone was still warm from the man's tight grip as Jennifer dialed Michael's number again. She held her breath in the space of time before the call went through and the ring began, and continued to hold it prayerfully as it rang again and again. There was no answer.

So there was obviously nothing for her to do but wait.

Only, the prospect of spending even so much as another five minutes in sedentary stagnation seemed tortuous. Left with the alternative of becoming wilted like the lettuce— mostly left uneaten on her plate—or of literally and figuratively spinning her wheels, she paid the cashier and went out to locate her MG in the misty soup.

The fog was so dense she had to make three passes down the road before she was certain she was in the right drive. Lena's car was still where it had been before. Mostly to have something active to do, Jennifer repeated her earlier rounds of the darkened house, knocking, ringing, searching around the side entrances. Of course, no one answered. She was in the midst of planning new ways of killing time as she came back around to the driveway again, when she was caught in the beam of two headlights.

It was the white Biarritz.

Michael cut the motor as soon as he saw her standing there. The window went down as she came toward him.

"Michael," she rushed, relief flushing through her, "I can't believe you're actually here. I must have dialed your number a thousand times." Something made her stop. Even in the fog she could see his face in profile, faintly illuminated in the light from the dashboard, and knew something was wrong. He seemed to be only half listening.

"Michael?"

Absently, and after first expending a long breath, he said, "Yes, yes . . ." He was staring ahead, both arms partially collapsed over the steering wheel.

"Look, I can see there's something wrong. Why don't we go in, talk about it?" For the moment she had almost entirely forgotten her own troubles.

"No," Michael answered quietly. "I don't want to talk about it. I don't want to talk about anything."

"Oh." Jennifer stood there. "Is that a dismissal then?"

Finally he turned his face to her. His eyes were only two dark holes, now and then slightly glittery when the lights from a passing car caught him on angle. Those velvety brown eyes, so intense, so violent with feeling when they had made love and lively with fire when he laughed, were always his most expressive feature; they were the connecting link from his heart to her heart. They sent no signals now. And his voice was flat when he spoke. "I'm very tired. I don't mean to be rude, but all I think I can handle right now is my own company."

"I don't know about rude. But I'd say a little selfish." Her words sounded as cold as she was feeling, shivering in the mist.

"Goddammit!" Michael said, coming alive suddenly. The flat of his hand came down hard on the steering wheel.

"I have a right to be selfish. I'm selfish. So what?" he snapped, looking up at her, and almost at once said, "I'm sorry." He hung his head, shaking it back and forth. "I'm sorry, sorry, sorry," but now he was no longer speaking to her.

The Cadillac's headlights on the closed garage door created two luminous white spots, gray ghosts in the shifting fog. To Jennifer they could have been the fading images of her and Michael, their relationship seeming at the moment just as flimsy and transitory.

"I don't understand," Jennifer said, half desperately and half running out of patience.

"I am sorry for not being perfect. Sorry for being a sonofabitch right now and not wanting you to come in where it's warm and dry. But I don't want you to, Jennifer." He looked up at her. This time she was glad she couldn't read the expression in his eyes. Anyway, his words were icy enough to get the full message across. "I don't want to talk to you now."

"Well, you know, you're right about one thing, Michael. You're right about being a sonofabitch." Her voice shivered as much from anger as from physical clamminess. "It just so happens that I want to talk to you. I have to talk to you. And, quite frankly, I think I have a right to talk to you, regardless if you feel like going into your groundhog routine tonight, burrowing in until your bad mood passes—"

Suddenly, Michael sent the door flying open. Jennifer jumped back in surprise, and when he was out, he grabbed her, pulling her to him. Holding her by her shoulders at arms length, he said, "I have just returned from being with a woman who tried to kill herself today."

"Oh, Michael . . ." His words, muffled by sorrow and fatigue, touched her. "I'm so sorry. I didn't have any way of knowing." She touched his face with her fingers.

"Darling . . . I'm so sorry." It would have been the perfect time for him to fold her in his arms, to seek sustenance in their mutual love, only he didn't.

Instead, he removed her hand from the side of his face, and clasping her wrist hard in his fingers, said, "You're going to be a lot more sorry, I'm afraid. Come on," Michael said. "What the hell, let's go in. May as well get it over with."

They went into the living room, and Michael offered her a brandy. He took none for himself and stood facing her in front of the fireplace.

Only two lamps had been switched on, casting the room mostly in shadow. Streaks of tension creased the sharp, delineated planes of Michael's face, and dark pockets of blue weariness underlined his eyes. Yet, there was nothing weak nor beaten in him. There was a resolve, a forebearance as he began to talk.

"You're not going to be pleased . . ." he began.

For a brief moment she found her thoughts straying from his words, her mind momentarily dwelling on his physical presence.

Michael was handsome, even in his troubled state. One of Hollywood's most astute commercial ploys was the exploitation of men like the late James Dean or Tyrone Power, especially a man as darkly pensive as Montgomery Cliff, who reflected inner torment to the point of angst becoming an art form. Now of course there was De Niro and Pacino. A frown from them, backed up with the right orchestration, was worth a Mercedes in the garage to a studio chief. And Michael could have passed for one of their rank, just as compelling in that perverse, sort of smoldering way that turns psychic pain into profit and adulation. But she forgot the straight nose, the sharply delineated planes of his face, in the next words he spoke.

"I thought she was all right. But she wasn't," Michael said cryptically. "Lena cut her wrists this afternoon."

Jennifer's hand flew to her mouth. "No, oh, no." Her eyes strayed unseeingly to the glass wall. Lena's words of that afternoon replayed in her memory. At the start of their conversation, Lena had sounded so up, so positive, before concluding their dialogue so abruptly.

That meant that Lena's suicide was all Jenny's fault, caused by what she had regretted as an unfortunate, but basically harmless indiscretion. Anyone else would have gotten mad, perhaps, or pouted, maybe. They wouldn't have tried to kill themselves.

"But she's all right?" Jennifer asked. "Oh, Michael, tell me she's all right."

"She'll make it. She's in Cedars recuperating. But she could have died if I hadn't come back here when I did."

"For your appointment," Jennifer said listlessly.

"You knew?" Michael was looking at her strangely. "Jennifer," he said, taking a couple of steps forward, "did you speak with Lena this afternoon?"

"Yes." She felt like a butterfly with both wings pinned against the wall. There was no escape possible from the inevitable. She had come there to tell him the whole story, but not under these conditions.

"You spoke with her?" Michael pressed. "And how did she seem? Was she depressed? Did she seem uneasy in any way? I called her myself earlier in the afternoon, just to check that she'd gotten in all right. I'd left a key. She sounded great. Then. So something must have happened between the time that I called and—"

"*I* happened," Jennifer said.

Michael looked at her for a long moment, trying to read meaning into the two words. "Tell me," he said finally.

"Oh, Michael," Jennifer said dejectedly. "It's what I

came here to talk to you about. About . . . well, this isn't going to sound good after all that's happened . . .''

Michael came to where she was sitting. Looking down at her, he said, "Jesus, Jennifer, will you just get it out? A patient of mine almost killed herself and I don't know why."

"Okay, okay . . ." Jennifer rose. She strayed over to the window, wanting to dissolve into the black void beyond the glass. "Okay, Michael, I'll tell you." She turned slowly. "Today I went into a meeting with Enderall and the rest of the wolf pack. It was brutal. Believe me, the worst. You can accept that?"

Nodding, he said, "Go on."

"Please. Just try to understand?"

"Go on, Jennifer," he urged irritably. "Just say it."

"I was forced to tell Enderall I was doing a story on Darla Hart. It wasn't—"

"You what? You told them? After we had discussed—no, after we had agreed?"

"Michael," Jennifer pleaded, barely able to hold back tears, "I would have definitely lost my job if I hadn't have come up with something."

"That's bull, Jennifer. You could have stalled them." Michael turned and walked to the side bar, where this time he did have a drink. Scotch. A whole tumbler full. He drank it down quickly and was on his second when he faced her again. "You were so greedy for fame you couldn't wait."

"That's not true." Her fingers had gone cold and rigid. She could hardly bend them.

"So you told Lena, is that it?"

"It slipped out."

"Slipped out?"

"It did, Michael. It was stupid of me, I know. But I don't see how or why this could have happened to her. I mean we were talking and she seemed so up, so positive that everything was going to be all right. And then I said something. I can't remember what, exactly, just a little slip, and Lena picked up on it. She hung up before I could explain anything to her. When I tried to call back, she wouldn't answer. And I guess then . . . well, I came over right away. You must have found her in the meantime. No one was here," Jennifer finished, her voice reduced to a dull monotone.

"What if I hadn't found her?" he said, collapsing into one of his leather sling chairs. Seemingly at a loss, he ran both hands through his hair. "What if she would have killed herself? It would have been because of me."

"No, no!" Jennifer said, coming over to him. She dropped to her knees before him. Gingerly, almost afraid to touch him, she stroked the back of one of his hands fallen lifelessly to his lap. "It wasn't your fault. If it was anyone's fault, which it doesn't necessarily have to be, then it was mine."

"Lena was mine to protect."

"But you can't protect Lena, or anyone else, all of the time, Michael. It's impossible."

She thought he hadn't heard her, his eyes having become cloudy, their look faraway. "Yeah, I know."

"I love you," Jennifer said.

Michael sighed, as if having given up a long cherished resolve. Reaching out for her, he wrapped his fingers in her tossed blond mass, and pulled her to him. "How did this all happen?" he said. "You and me. And Lena. Why can't love be easy?"

Jennifer smiled crookedly, and without joy. "It's the old adage. Nothing good comes easily."

"Then this thing we've got going has got to be terrific."

"It is," she whispered. "At least for me."

"Maybe . . ." Michael looked past her shoulder, his eyes distant, "maybe we want too much."

"I only want you. Is that too much?" She took up his hand and brushed her lips lightly against the top.

"But you also want your story. And that might be too much."

Jennifer grew cold again, even with the recently downed brandy coating her insides. "Maybe we could compromise. We can announce the story on television, but not do it immediately." Her mind was working quickly, the seed of enthusiasm growing like a magic vine, shooting up to the sun a mile a minute. "Then when Lena's got her act together—"

"Jennifer!"

She stopped. He was glaring at her.

"You can't compromise with a human being's life. It ought to be obvious to you by now that Lena can't take the kind of pressure a public announcement would create. You want proof? Then look no farther than what happened today."

Jennifer exhaled. Hanging her head, she said, "Of course. You're right, I guess. I feel . . ." She looked up at him, the covering of moisture over her blue eyes blurring his face, "I feel mean. And hard. Just the same as the others at KZAM," she whispered. "I'm really no different, am I? Not if you really get down to it." Her voice caught, and she turned her face away, feeling ashamed.

Gently, Michael lifted her chin, made her look at him. "Hey! You're nothing like that. You're beautiful and sensitive and kind. And independent." He smiled. "And all of those reasons are just some of the reasons I love you."

"Even after what I did?"

"It was . . . unfortunate," he conceded. But the slight

pulsing at his temple, caught her eye, making a contradiction of his words. He was still angry, still concerned, not only about Lena's welfare, but most likely about her own suspect character. Well, he wasn't alone in that. She had her own doubts.

"It was almost tragic," Jennifer countered. "Let's call a spade a spade."

"Almost doesn't count."

Jennifer pulled herself free. "The thing is," she began, and rose from the chair, "I . . . uh . . ." She had to look away. Clearing her throat, she went on as best she could. "I don't know what does count anymore." Whirling back around, she said, "You know what, Michael? I know it's wrong, but I still want that story. Maybe I want it at any cost. I want to be a success. I've worked hard and honestly, and I deserve to reap the rewards for my efforts. You know something else? And this is the truth, and it may be vile and crummy and maybe you'll hate me for saying it, but the truth is, I care more about me than I care about Lena Stephens. And something else, Michael. I wish you did, too."

She didn't wait to hear what he thought. She knew what he thought. It was what her conscience was shouting to her, overlaying each word of her heartfelt confession with the accusation that she was no better than Rita or Arnold or Madeline. It had just been her conceit, her holier-than-thou, I'm-better-than-you arrogance talking all that slick talk about ethics and saving society from itself. She was society. And she was just as tainted, just as selfish, as the next guy.

She grabbed her purse on her way to the front door, and jerked it open as if fleeing from the devil. Her name on Michael's lips was cut in two as the door slammed after her.

She felt her way through the veil of tears and covering of thick fog, everything around her appearing obscured and indistinct.

The sharp crack of the door slamming reverberated in Michael's mind. He felt like he was two people, one of him watching the other. A part of him wanted to follow her, and the other part of him wanted to return to his peaceful status quo. Earlier that day he had known exactly what he had wanted. He had felt so certain, so sure of his love for her. But that certainty was pre-Morey. Pre-Lena's stunt. And pre-Jennifer's tirade.

At least she had been honest. She wanted her big scoop at any cost. And maybe he couldn't blame her. Hadn't he wanted his privacy at any cost?

The space around him vibrated with emptiness. An emptiness so familiar. An emptiness that had once been savored, cherished, desired, conjuring, as it did, safe impressions of a goose-down comforter on a cold, rainy night; or of a mineral bath, in which he could dissolve himself, troubles included. He had always sought sanctuary from real issues he felt incapable of solving.

But that was then, and this was now. And for some reason, in this particular emptiness, he was not merging into an emotionally safe harbor.

Let her go, he told himself. This is impractical. Illogical. Your fundamental standards are clearly at odds with each other.

Hell, he thought. What standards? His standards had changed twenty times in the past five years as his perspective broadened. What the hell did he know, anyway? What good was a closed mind? He had listened to his mind often enough in the past, and look where it had brought him? He was a lonely, isolated man in an unshared million dollar home surrounded by fog. Even without the heavy symbolism, he was lost.

He wanted someone. He wanted Jennifer. Yes, admit it, Casari, you want her, and not just emotionally, but physically. Tired as you were, a minute ago when she was close, you had wanted to make love to her. You had wanted to touch her bare breasts, you had wanted to feel her beneath you, her legs twined around you, squeezing you with that silken smoothness that makes your blood rush. You had wanted her body arched into yours as you made love to her. You're no saint, Casari. Face it, you're a man, just like any other, complete with runaway lusts and emotional longings. Damn.

He looked to the door and decided: to hell with the mind's advice. He'd give the heart equal air time.

The front door seemed to fly open at his touch.

"Jennifer!" he cried into the mist.

She was standing by her car, unable to get into it and unable to return to Michael, when the sound of her name cut through her miserable thoughts.

She turned, thinking that perhaps she had been mistaken, when, outlined in the light from a passing vehicle, she saw a figure emerge from a clearing in the fog.

When he saw her, Michael slowed and finally stopped a few feet away. They faced each other, neither of them speaking. A breeze swirled the mist between them.

"Where the hell do you think you're going?" he yelled, his voice low, not at all playful. "Running out on me . . ."

Jennifer shook her head. Her heart pounded. "Running out on me is more like it."

"You can't get away anymore. And neither can I."

"Michael, it won't work. I want it, too. But we're both on opposite sides of a fence."

"Then let's meet in the middle."

"I don't think we can."

"Try," Michael said, striding toward her. "Try," he said, and now in front of her, bent to kiss her softly.

At once the heat built in her. She returned his kiss hungrily, moving into him, and touching his hair. His tongue flicked deep and hungrily, a moan rising in his throat, even as she felt him rise hard against her leg.

She had wanted to make love to him all day, her thoughts conjuring pictures of his body, sleek and muscularly contoured, whenever she was not caught in her obsession with the Hart story.

"Come inside," he said, his voice a low throb, as he brushed his lips against her ear. His tongue darted out, licking at her lobe suggestively. "I want to make love to you . . . do things to you . . ."

"Michael, I want you, too . . . but the morning . . . it'll be the same problem."

He silenced her with a violent kiss. He worked both his hands through her hair, the kiss somehow taking on the promise of wild, abandoned sex. "Oh, God, Michael . . ." She moaned, her fingers slipping of their own accord to where she felt him straining full and taut against her leg.

He led her into the house, twice stopping to kiss her deeply, as they walked up the side to the front door.

In the bedroom she began to undress herself, but she was too slow and Michael took command. His fingers were hot as they moved over her breasts, one hand easing her shoulder from the red silk blouse she had worn. Helpless in her desire, she abandoned her attempt to remove her own clothing and became a toy to him, letting herself be guided into varying positions that allowed him access to her body.

With her breasts bare, he arched her torso back, and finding one hardened nipple with his mouth, began to suck, while the other hand cupped and fondled her other breast. His tongue slicked back and forth, periodically sucking, as now his fingers worked up her leg, through the deep slit on one side of the skirt's fabric.

Licks of flame rose in her groin, and she felt a ticklish swirling begin there, spreading upward, seeming to flow into her breasts. They felt heavier, fuller, and wriggling her chest slightly, she pushed her nipple farther into Michael's mouth.

"Wait," he said, partially breathless, holding himself tightly rigid for a moment. "Keep that up, I'm not going to last . . ."

"Neither am I," she said provocatively, and slanted her pelvis to accommodate the reach of his fingers beneath her skirt.

The nylon material of her briefs slid aside easily as his fingers moved past the elastic, and brushed along her inner thigh. She sounded a soft, pleasurable cry as his fingers entered, pressing a place which made darkness envelope her, then lights dance behind her closed lids.

When her legs were trembling and she thought she might expire from desire, Michael lifted her into his arms, carried her to the bed. He moved the white skirt lower, ever lower, his mouth trailing over each newly exposed area of bare skin as it came into view.

Jennifer heard the light drop of material as her skirt fell to the side of the bed. His mouth was hot against her stomach, his tongue at her navel, while his fingers slowly teased away the bikini pants she wore.

When they, too, were gone, he stood between her legs, and leaning over, he kissed her breasts, her mouth, her neck. In the pale light from the hallway, she could see the extension of his slacks, where the material strained outward.

Wanting him, needing him, she reached out and ran her fingers along his aroused length, feeling him pulse to her touch beneath the material. His eyes, which had been open, devouring her nude body spread before him, closed tightly. His mouth stretched tight, as he fought against losing control. Subtly, he shifted his weight, a prompt for her to reach lower.

"Come to me," she said, all the while touching him.

He undressed hurriedly, unashamed of his aroused state when he stood unclothed before her. He wanted her to feel him, and she did, feeling a sense of power, a freedom that was totally sensual, totally loving and unembarrassed as she continued to please him.

They were hot, on fire for each other, when he finally took her. He slipped into her easily. Jennifer caught back a cry of pleasure, the new sensation cutting off the sound, as Michael moved over her. He was powerful and assured. Relentless.

She wrapped her legs around his, rubbing her breasts back and forth against his chest, delighting in the strength of his hard body against her nipples.

Michael lifted her up, shifting her, until he could continue his movements and enjoy her breasts at the same time. The position made her cry out in ecstatic desire, and she clutched at his back, trying to make him an even greater part of herself.

"Jennifer . . . Jen—" Michael moaned, his voice low and guttural, a primal sound belonging with his steady thrusts.

She moved faster, along with him, unaware of anything but the heat she felt expanding outward and upward, filling her body, her entire being. Suddenly Michael shuddered, held himself in check, and with a drive and force he had never used before, brought her up to his level of desire.

"Michael . . ." She was panting, almost delirious. "Michael . . ." And then she was with him, totally. Her body arched and held, her legs forcing him deep within her, her love spilling into his as he tightened, held, and finally expended himself like a bursting flame.

Her mind disappeared. Her body disappeared. She dissolved totally, her spirit dancing and swirling in the heat of their joining.

"Oh, God, Jennifer . . ." he said when it was done, and he at last raised his head up slightly from her breast. Their bodies were both covered in moisture, but it was a sweet wetness that went with the feeling ebbing slowly from between her legs, draining away from the pit of her stomach. Her breasts tingled, and as he looked into her eyes, her nipples peaked slightly. "What you do to me . . ." He laughed lightly and shook his head as he rolled to the side of where she lay. "It's almost embarrassing."

"Embarrassing?" she asked, turning and sitting up to look at him. His eyes fell to her breasts.

"You are so beautiful," he said. He reached forward, cupping the fullness of one breast, his index finger brushing against her nipple. "Just the sight of you makes me want you."

"Again?" She laughed.

"Let's say . . . soon. The heart and mind are willing . . . the body's momentarily on strike."

"Do you know I thought of making love all day?"

"With me, I hope."

"What are we going to do?" she asked, suddenly pensive.

"Sleep. Let's go to sleep," he said, his eyelids slowly falling shut.

"Michael, no . . . wait. I can't sleep. Not until I know about Lena."

"Lena," he muttered. "Lena will be okay. She's at Cedars. A private room. Very hush, hush. No publicity to upset her. She'll probably be discharged Sunday. After breakfast."

"But, Michael . . . what about me? And my story. Nothing's been settled."

And she saw it wasn't going to be. At least not that night. Michael had drifted off. His breathing was easy and deep. She looked at him for a moment, thinking of how much she loved him, of how it would never, never be possible to replace him. Not just as a lover, but because he had become a part of her heart.

"I love you, Michael," she said. "Always. Always. Forever. No matter what happens. No matter what the future holds, know that I love you . . ."

He murmured, but it was only something in his sleep.

She had wanted more from him, but he was enclosed in an easy male sleep that evidenced his satisfaction. She had wanted him to somehow solve all her problems the way others had been able to come to him for solace.

"Michael? What am I going to do?"

The only answer was the silence, leaving it up to her.

Chapter 11

ALTHOUGH MICHAEL SLEPT SOUNDLY, SHE COULD NOT. She concentrated on the rhythmic wash of the surf against the sand. She tried to lose herself in the lulling in-and-out breaths Michael took beside her. It was no use, nothing helped to induce sleep. Her mind was weighted by her decision to either go ahead with the story, regardless of Michael's wishes and in spite of what it might mean to Lena Stephen's professional and emotional welfare, or else to abandon the project altogether, accepting the brutal consequences to her own career.

When dawn broke, she was still wide awake, her nerves jittery from physical and mental exhaustion. And she still hadn't reached a final decision.

She slipped out from beside Michael. He lay on his stomach, one arm stretched possessively across her chest. Some time ago, in his sleep, he had felt for her. She had curled into him, saying his name softly and waiting for a verbal response, before realizing his action had been somnambulistic. For a brief period his fingers had grazed her breast, stirring her desire, but still he was asleep, and soon after his arm relaxed over her in a leaden weight.

Now she looked down at him. He was so handsome. So desirable. But beyond the physical bliss they brought to each other, there was an excitement she felt when with him. His mind was sharp, his observations gentle, his humor light and always on the mark. She didn't know how much was instinctive, or how much was a byproduct of his trade as a psychologist, but he had the ability to see into a person and also to cope with the rough edges of a person's character. Still, no matter what he saw, Michael seemed to accept everything with compassion. She had never heard him condemn anyone. Not even Lena, who virtually held his life in her hands by way of her weakness.

That was what made everything all the worse. Because as she looked down at Michael, sleeping so gently, with an expression of such innocent purity, she was thinking horrid thoughts about Lena Stephens. Angry thoughts.

Shamed by her own uncharitableness, Jennifer retreated to the shower. She stood with her eyes closed, trying to make her mind a blank, as the needles of water pelted her body awake.

She toweled herself dry, wrapped her hair into a bun at the nape of her neck, fastened it in place with its own natural knot, and after dressing quietly in the bedroom, bent to kiss Michael.

"Bye," she said.

"Hmm . . ." He shifted in bed, but his eyes remained closed.

"I'd love to talk, too," she said, and smiled. "But I've

got to get out of here. Got something to take care of.'' She straightened. Watching him, she added, "Only I don't know how yet."

At the door she turned and allowed herself one last look. "I love you, Michael Casari," she whispered, hoping the words would be imprinted on his subconscious.

It was Saturday morning, and even at the hospital the weekend seemed to make an impression upon the staff. There appeared to be a psychological mind-set in operation, some cultural habit that had been ingrained in people's minds over the years, that demanded weekends be lived more lightly. If work was necessary at all, then it was to be treated casually.

Knowing this, Jennifer took advantage of the good-natured laxity of the lobby personnel who, bantering among themselves, failed to see her slip by.

The rest was easy for Jennifer, who had made a good living by being able to slide into places where she was not welcome.

Earlier, she had stopped at a pay phone and called the hospital to find out which room Lena Stephens occupied. They denied Lena's presence, of course. Michael—or Morey—would naturally have demanded confidentiality. And there was nothing particularly strange about the woman known publicly as Darla Hart registering as Lena Stephens. Anyone on a hospital staff was familiar with the practice of celebrities checking in under aliases in order to confound the press.

Jennifer figured her best bet was to approach a member of the hospital staff who was unrelated to Lena's immediate care. She stopped by the lab. A young orderly was there, restocking glass vials in a cabinet.

"Hi," she said, a bit uncertainly. "Seems I'm lost. Had

to bring an insurance form up to someone named Lena Stephens, only I misplaced her room number. Could you call the desk for me, and check?''

She was lucky. He did exactly what she had wanted him to do, identifying himself as ''Ronnie, in the lab'' before asking for Lena's number. He got it without any trouble.

''Thanks,'' she said, and bounded off.

The rest was riskier but turned out to be easy. She slipped past the nurses' station and into Lena's room without passing a soul.

Lena was seated upright in bed. There were two enormous bouquets of flowers, one on her nightstand, one on a dresser. The previous day's fog had burned away in the morning sunlight, which now streamed brightly across the white bed sheets.

Lena turned as the door swung open. At the sight of Jennifer, her mouth fell slightly slack. It was, Jennifer gauged, a peculiarly guilty reaction to what should have been construed as an innocent occasion.

''Hi,'' Jennifer said, shutting the door behind her.

''Hello,'' Lena returned. She continued to eye Jennifer with wariness.

''Hope you don't mind me visiting so early.''

''Why did you come?'' Lena asked defensively, bunching the sheets up around her, as if they afforded some needed protection. ''I'm not supposed to have visitors. Michael insisted I have complete privacy. And no pressure,'' she added. Clouds of fear wafted behind the green eyes, passed, and left in fear's place a vague placid veneer.

Jennifer noted the mascara, also the eyeliner and carefully applied blue-green eye shadow. Even Lena's silver hair was combed neatly, smoothed under in a sleek pageboy style. All in all, Lena did not resemble a woman whose life had recently hung in the balance. The only clue to what had gone before were the thin strips of white bandages on Lena's wrists. Otherwise there was no evidence to attest to the purported emotional crisis.

"I didn't come to hassle you," Jennifer said, suddenly feeling less responsible for Lena's predicament. Something just didn't jive with the image she had been given by Michael of a distraught, suicidal personality. If anything, Lena looked bright-eyed and bushy-tailed. "I came to see how you are. And I thought we might talk."

"About what?" Lena continued to observe Jennifer warily.

Jennifer crossed to the side of the bed. "Here, why don't I give those pillows a fluff?"

"They're fine," Lena said. She made a show of burrowing back into them.

"What about you?"

"Obviously," Lena said, sounding unduly affronted by the question, "I've been better."

"Oh, almost forgot." Jennifer opened her purse and pulled out a small wrapped box. "May your spirits rise." She handed Lena the Chanel perfume, purchased from a twenty-four-hour pharmacy on her way over to Cedars. "Wish I could be more lavish, but the powers that be at KZAM like to keep their employees lean and hungry."

"Thanks," Lena said, sounding less than grateful. She gave a disinterested tug on the pink ribbon.

"Your flowers are lovely," Jennifer commented while Lena toyed with the paper. She was taking forever to unwrap the gift.

At Jennifer's comment she perked up. Responding cheerily, she said, "They're from Michael. And Morey." Morey's name came as an afterthought. "The big bouquet's from Michael." Lena looked over to where it was on the dresser. "Michael knows how I love yellow roses."

"Michael likes you very much," Jennifer said. "You know, he's extremely concerned about you."

Lena's hands were trembling. She held Jennifer's gift, at last unwrapped. "Chanel Number Five. Thanks," she said, not looking up. To Jennifer, Lena's most notable expression was the lack of any.

"He feels responsible, you know."

Lena said nothing, as if, Jennifer thought, she was a suspect who knew that whatever she said could be held against her. Lena's only response was to look up, green eyes narrowed and contemplative. Jennifer knew she would be pushing things if she continued. But the same gut instinct that had led her on other successful fact-finding missions now told her she was onto something.

"That's what you want, isn't it? For Michael to feel responsible?" Jennifer continued.

Lena put the perfume on the nightstand. "It wasn't Michael's fault."

"You mean, your suicide attempt?"

Lena nodded. "It was your fault," Lena said, but she didn't look at Jennifer.

"My fault? Because of what I said on the telephone?"

"That. And other stuff." Lena smoothed the covers with her hands. She looked to the side, out the window. A blade of sunlight lay slashed across her covers.

In contrast, Lena's jaw in profile was set hard and trembled slightly from what Jennifer took as an overabundance of withheld emotion.

"You have no intention of ever becoming independent, do you?" Jennifer accused sharply.

Lena snapped her head around. "No!" she returned, just as hotly. "No, I don't. Why should I? It isn't what Michael really wants, anyway. He was quite happy with the way things were. Before you stepped into the picture," she said. "You've pressured him, turned his entire life upside down and inside out."

"That's what I thought," Jennifer said. She didn't feel triumphant, she felt saddened at having ferreted out the truth. She sank into a chair near the bed.

"And so?" Lena said, impatient for Jennifer to respond.

Jennifer appraised her. Lena seemed at a loss, waiting unsteadily. A blow had been struck against the opponent, but Jennifer had not counterattacked as expected.

"And so," Jennifer said after a while, looking at Lena full-on, "I think what you've done is pretty low and despicable."

"All right," Lena said, "I'll admit what I did last night was phony."

"That's one way of putting it," Jennifer broke in. "You knew Michael was coming back in time for your dramatic rescue. And even if he hadn't shown up, you'd have called for help."

Lena seemed suddenly energized, as if she had been holding in a wealth of thoughts for a long time, which she now wanted to share with someone else, even the enemy. She moved the sheets aside, and sat with her bare legs dangling over the bed's side.

Jennifer wasn't particularly surprised by the change in attitude. She'd run across criminals who had pulled off master crimes, gotten away scot-free, only to blurt out their accomplishment and subsequently land in jail, all because they wanted recognition for their cleverness.

"You think this is all pretty selfish on my part, don't you?"

Jennifer studied Lena closely. This last was Lena's reckless plea for understanding or sympathy. But all Jenni-

fer could think of was Michael as he had been the previous
night, miserable and distraught over his failure to make a
whole person out of his patient.

"Quite frankly, yes. I do think you're selfish and
unfeeling."

"Well, you're wrong," Lena said, suddenly defiant
again, since she obviously wasn't going to be molly-
coddled. "Michael needs me, just as much as I need him."

"Oh, no. You are wrong there," Jennifer countered. She
stood. "Michael wants to be free to live his life independently. He wants to be free of people who sap him of his
own happiness. Which," she said, staring hard into Lena's
now ice-green eyes, "you are deliberately doing."

"What do you know about Michael?" Lena scoffed.
"You suddenly came waltzing into his life, so now you
think you know everything?" Lena's voice cracked from
anger. Out of control, she had to begin over again. Pointing
a shaky index finger at Jennifer, she said, "I've known
Michael intimately for years. I happen to care about him
very much. I know his moods, and I know he can't take a
lot of people pressing in on him with problems he can't deal
with. He needs that column and he needs that anonymity.
Otherwise he's going to be miserable."

"Otherwise you'll be miserable," Jennifer said. "You
know what you are? You're a blood-sucker. You're draining
the life out of a man who genuinely cares about you, who'd
sacrifice his own happiness to stand by a phony, selfish
woman he's decent enough to believe in."

"Right!" Lena shrieked, with both fists coming down
hard on the mattress. "You've got it! Michael cares about
me. Me! And that's the way it is going to stay."

"Well, you're partially right," Jennifer returned with
surprising calm. "He does care about you. As a friend. As a

mixed-up human being. But you're dead wrong about things staying the way they've been, Lena. Things are different now.''

"I know Michael's in love with you," Lena said, her voice steady, the moisture glazing her eyes solidified into an expression of ice crystals. "But, like I said, I know him. And if it comes to a choice between loving you and abandoning me, he'll never leave me. He couldn't. That's the way he is. He's kind. And he's honorable. A totally good man.''

"I know," Jennifer said quietly. "That's why I love him. And that's why I'm going to fight for him.''

Lena smiled coldly. "You'll lose," she said.

Jennifer grabbed up her purse from the chair. She was headed for the door, when it swung open.

Michael stood before her, looking as surprised as she felt.

"Jennifer?"

"Michael . . . hello . . .''

His eyes passed reflexively past her, to where Lena was. Jennifer followed his gaze, saw that in that brief intervening period, Lena had rearranged her covers and the fierce expression on her face had dwindled to confused helplessness.

"Oh, Michael," Lena called weakly. "I'm so glad you've come.''

"I told you I would.''

"You never let me down," Lena said, holding out a hand to him, the white bandage circling her wrist saying more than any thousand words Jennifer could compose.

"Oh, spare me . . .'' Jennifer groaned.

"Jen," Michael said, not unkindly, but with a certain professional coolness, "you really shouldn't have come down here. You meant well, I know. But it's a delicate situation."

"Michael," she said, speaking in a confidential voice and feeling Lena's ears straining to hear every word, "I really have to talk to you." But Michael was only half listening. In fact, it was obvious that the greatest part of his attention was focused on Lena.

Large, silent tears were cascading down Lena's cheeks. Michael was right, Jennifer thought ruefully. Lena Stephens was a consummate actress. She was also a sick, conniving bitch.

"Give me a moment," he said, touching Jennifer on the shoulder as he started for the bed where Lena lay, looking more and more wretched with each passing second. Halfway to the bed, Michael turned back to her, saying "Jen, why don't you wait for me in the coffee shop. I won't take long."

"Sure," she said, because that was all she could say. As far as Michael was concerned he was visiting a sincere, emotionally crippled woman. But when she looked to Lena, all she saw, through the manufactured tears, was a woman who could barely restrain her smug victory.

She paused at the door, deciding to give Lena a parting shot, just to keep things interesting. "You're a wonderful actress, Lena. But there are some awards you just won't win."

Lena said nothing in return. She sniffed and wiped a tear from her cheek. The sun on her white bandaged wrist gleamed brightly. Jennifer closed the door quietly behind her.

When Michael entered the coffee shop, Jennifer was sipping idly on her coffee. He scowled as he pulled out the chair opposite her.

"Don't tell me," Jennifer drawled, "Lena has had an emotional relapse. And I am the blame."

"This isn't funny. Lena is sick, Jennifer."

"I'll drink to that. On both counts."

"So? Mind if you tell me why it was so necessary for you to come down here this morning?"

"No, I don't mind telling you. Only I don't actually know the answer to that one. You might say, I suppose, that I had mixed motives. Do you want any coffee?"

"No. I want answers."

"Michael," Jennifer said, leaning forward, serious, "I came here because I wanted to talk to Lena. I came prepared to offer my apologies, my heartfelt condolences. Honest," she said, and raised her right hand, palm out. "But I also came because I found it difficult to believe that the woman I talked to on the telephone yesterday afternoon was a potential suicide victim."

"Isn't that a little out of your line? I wouldn't say you're exactly qualified to give a clinical diagnosis of a person's emotional stability."

"So I don't have a Ph.D. But I've eyes and ears and common sense. And that's just for starters."

"Damn it, Jennifer!" He had raised his voice, and immediately lowered it when the heads of several other patrons turned in mild alarm toward their table. "I am a psychologist. Lena is my patient. I ought to know what I'm talking about."

"And I'm a woman. And a journalist. Put the two together and you have a sensitive ferreter of hidden facts. Besides which," she added, "have you ever heard of feminine instinct?"

Although whispering, they were as much as shouting at each other judging by the intensity of their interchange.

"I'll tell you what I've heard. I've heard of people who indulge in rationalizations to justify what they want, when they know it isn't right."

"Come on, Michael. Lena isn't any more sick than I am. She's just a frightened, lonely woman who's willing to do anything she can to hold on to her security blanket. Which just happens to be you."

"Congrats. It didn't take conferring with Woodward and Bernstein to figure that out, I hope. This is news? I'm her psychologist?"

"She thinks of you as her pal, her friend, Michael. And she's afraid of losing you. She'll never get well because she doesn't want to lose her personal relationship."

Michael was silent. Jennifer knew he was considering what she had just said, weighing it seriously. "And you don't call that being sick?"

But Jennifer noticed there was less assurance in his defense.

"No. No, I don't. I call that being mean and small and manipulative."

"I'm the only one she's had to count on for the past several years. It's typical and understandable for her to have developed a dependency pattern—"

Jennifer snatched her purse from the edge of the table. She had been perfectly willing to let him save face, but this was no good. She could see where his reasoning was headed. Talk about rationalization . . . talk about clinging . . .

She pushed back her chair and stood. Looking down at him, she said, "You just aren't listening. You want to talk about a dependency pattern? Then why don't you talk about your own? You're not stupid, Michael. But you aren't being honest. If you were, you'd admit you're afraid to let go of your goddamned messiah complex."

Michael reacted violently to her accusation. He pushed aside his chair so quickly and with such force that it almost toppled.

She knew she was right, and so did he.

He caught the chair in time. Gripping its back with white-knuckled tension, he said, "I love you, Jennifer. But I am not going to let another human being go down the drain because of my personal needs."

"And, Michael, I love you, too. Dammit."

"Then," he said, between clenched teeth, "if we love each other so much, what the hell is this all about?"

"It is about you letting something else, someone else, be more important than us."

"Now wait a minute," Michael said, "this whole thing is because you want that story."

"No. It's because I want you! Lena's not going down any drain, Michael. You are, though." She took a couple of steps backward. "Next time you speak to Lena, tell her for me, she's not just a great actress. Tell her she's a pretty fair psychologist, too. Because it sure looks like she had you pegged."

There was nothing for either of them to say. Besides, she left quickly before more bitter truths could be exchanged.

As she walked to her MG, she amended her opinion. There really wasn't anything in all of life that was true or false. There were only different perspectives colored by the shadings of different minds. Or, as the divorce courts put it: irreconcilable differences.

In spite of the sunlight it was not a good morning at all. Her heart was already broken. And now the MG would not start.

The rest of Saturday was spent having the MG patched up. Again.

"This baby's got more scar tissue on it than a war vet," said the mechanic who handed her a bill for 175 dollars. "Might think about putting this heap out to pasture," he advised while she scribbled her name across the credit card charge slip.

Tired, Jennifer looked up. "How could I do that?" she said. "To you this is a heap. To me this is the Rocky of automobiles. It's symbolic."

"It's a wreck, if you ask me."

"We're staying alive together."

He smirked. "Don't be so sure, lady."

As she drove out she gunned the MG loudly. If it had nothing else, it still had a lot of pride left.

Sunday dawned gray. A low cloud covering hung over the Los Angeles basin until almost two o'clock. The weather matched Jennifer's mood. Without enthusiasm she cleaned her apartment, restocked her refrigerator with food for the week, did some laundry, and generally tried to keep her mind off of Michael. Depending on how she looked at it, the rift in their relationship appeared either insurmountable or a mere interruption in what she knew was the love affair of the century. Her mind swung both ways, with vigorous, impartial defense given to each side.

Every time she passed her phone, she had to resist the temptation to call him. All Michael had was her work number; she had never given her home number to him. It was an oversight, of course. From the time they had met, she had either been at work or else at his house.

However, she thought, slumping into a corner of the couch with a glass of diet soda, there was always the chance that the omission had been more by design than she had previously realized. Her work had been her life, and her life had been characterized by its guardedness in personal relationships. Very few people had access to her home number.

That night she did not sleep. She thought. On Monday morning she had reached a decision.

She dressed impeccably for work that morning. It was going to be the beginning of a whole new life for her. For the occasion her best suit was called into service. It had been worn only once before, at her best friend's wedding to a Texas oil millionaire. At the time, Jennifer thought that to look less than knock-'em-out-grand would be a tacky slur on Susan, who was already battling the snobism of her new husband's ex-wife's friends. They had referred to Susan as a gold-digging, California hippy with the breeding of a wild mustang, and word got out that they expected her riff-raff friends to be the same.

Although Jennifer had rather liked the poetic image of a wild mustang, she had given in first to Susan's plea to "do her proud" and then to the saleswoman who kindly arranged for her to make payments ending (as far as Jennifer was concerned) sometime during the next millennium, for the twelve-hundred-dollar Adolfo original. There was also tax, of course. And a blouse, shoes, gloves, a hat, a purse, nylons so sheer they ran when she looked at them, and even new underwear. "Just in case," Susan had pleaded in her case for the expensive underwear.

So Jennifer had gone to Dallas, and when the proverbial Eyes of Texas were upon her, she had popped their sockets looking like the thoroughbred filly who had just taken the Triple Crown.

She expected to do the same that Monday morning, but for various and different reasons, as she piled it all on again. Each piece of her financial folly fitted together like an intricate jigsaw puzzle whose completed picture contained the soft perfection of a French master impressionist.

There she stood, hard-eyed and rigid, facing the mirror with her red purse clutched in her hand like a cudgel.

Her hair was up, with a draping of sun-lightened bangs stopping just above electrically vibrant cobalt-blue eyes, their charged effect softened by dusky blue eye shadow and outlined in a dark pencil. Through the pale layer of moisturizer prepared with a tawny tint for summer, her tan was allowed to glow naturally, her skin appearing radiantly alive.

The crimson glisten of her lips was the same shade as her purse and the color of the piping along the three-buttoned jacket of her white Adolfo suit. The outfit's front-paneled skirt hung soft and luxuriantly, barely grazing her knee in keeping with the season's current short fashion length.

Even in Texas, among the pampered and privileged in their diamonds and minks, she had stood out as regal and luxurious. In confidence, later, Susan had crowed out the excessive compliments Jennifer had garnered, how she had usurped the limelight from the snob Sissy Buckner and the Texas oil princess Priscilla Ralston, Susan taking Jennifer's triumph as her own through proxy.

Well, Jennifer thought, leaving her reflection and tossing her car keys in the air as she headed for the door. In another hour, she'd be knocking 'em dead in the aisles of KZAM.

"Tell Mr. Enderall there's going to be a meeting in the conference room in fifteen minutes," Jennifer told Enderall's secretary.

"Who's calling it?" she asked, reflexively taking up her pen and beginning to make a notation on the official slip used to announce meeting times and rooms and the subject of same.

"Me. I'm calling it." The response Jennifer had expected did not materialize. The staff never called meetings. It was a mutinous act.

"The subject?" Enderall's secretary asked, looking up without her usual glint of malice.

"The Darla Hart Story."

Edith's usually dry and tightly pursed lips broke into a fluid smile as she nodded. "Yes, of course. Mr. Enderall's so very pleased," she said, and added as if they had been chums for a lifetime, "and me, especially. It's marvelous, marvelous."

"Okay, then," Jennifer said, not knowing why she was feeling so uneasy.

"You look fabulous," Edith called out to her as she started down the aisle.

Jennifer disappeared into the conference room, arranging the chairs around the table herself, needing something to do to stem the excitement.

Rita was the first to arrive.

"My, my," Rita said. "Don't we look smashing?"

"Thank you," Jennifer replied.

"Miss Queen for the Day." Rita looked her up and down while she selected a seat that pleased her and sat in it.

Beneath the light snideness, Jennifer also recognized the signs of a grudging deference.

The others came in soon after. Their attitudes were as removed from normalcy as Rita's. In fact, they seemed to speak in code, bantering among themselves over Jennifer's new fame.

Arnold even suggested she'd throw prime-time viewers for a loop, looking the way she did.

"You have a wild imagination, Arnold," she replied. "You ought to stick to the facts, man."

"Hey," said Madeline, "you've earned it, so fly."

Jennifer was about to respond about clipped wings, but Enderall appeared. He beamed, seeking her out with his eyes immediately upon entering.

"My, you're lovely. Lovely suit. Like the hair. Everything."

Jennifer was afraid he might lapse into song.

Promptly, as if she had commanded it, Enderall grabbed a side seat against the wall, and sinking into it with a contented sigh, said, "Floor's yours, Miss Winters."

"Thank you." The uneasiness was growing in her. She felt like Alice, having fallen through the rabbit hole. No one was behaving with rational predictability.

All eyes were on her, respectfully, intently, waiting with patience for her to begin. She did. Standing at the head of the conference table, she said, "When I took this job, it was with the understanding that I—and all of you—would be employed to uphold the highest principles of our journalistic profession. Instead, there has been a steady degeneration of ideals, a total lapse in moral accountability to the enterprises embraced as esteemable by this station." She was using highfalutin language, but what she was saying was that they were all a bunch of low-lifes. Certainly that had to be coming across clearly. They might be scum-mongers, but they weren't stupid, not any of them. So why, Jennifer wondered, were they all remaining impassive. Why, especially, was Enderall smiling and bobbing his head gently up and down with her every insult?

Almost jittery now, she continued, her spiel committed to memory. "The purpose I had in calling you all here today was not to insult you, but to urge you all, as I have done, to reconsider the paths you have taken. I can't believe that any of you did not have the same shining hopes of influencing society for the better that I held when I entered this profession. We are all privileged, and we have a duty to ourselves, and to the public, to celebrate the gifts and the opportunity we've been afforded to use those gifts."

There was silence.

Jennifer's lips had become dry. The next few words flew ahead in her mind, just the way they had looked on the typed draft of her speech. Once out, that would be that.

Her heart was pounding so loudly, she imagined she had been electronically miked. "Mr. Enderall?" Gravely, she turned to him. It was disconcerting. She broke off momentarily. He was smiling that same bemused smile, a smile of the simpleminded, locked into an eternal, artificial bliss. "Mr. Enderall, I have come to withdraw my services to this station. My reasons are, of course, those I have just set forth."

She had expected a reaction, and so far none had been forthcoming. All that changed. Heads turned from her, whipping to where Enderall sat. His mouth hung loose, and he was white at first, then, like an ascending elevator, a red flush rose from his neck, seeping through his jowls and into his cheeks, exploding in a burst of moisture at the crown of his shiny dome.

Suddenly energized, Enderall shot from the chair.

Jennifer backed away as he came toward her, responding to the threat of over two hundred pounds of raw male fury aimed at her through his flaming eyes.

"You can't!" he shouted. His fist came down like thunder on the table.

"But I am," she said. "That is, I have."

"I'll kill you," Enderall said.

Jennifer thought he looked like he might, too. "I've said what I had to say." She reached for her purse. Enderall held on to one end.

"No," he said. "No, let's talk. Let's go into my office and talk."

"It's no good," she said, her eyes darting to the others, to whom it seemed their interchange was playing as a life or death volley for all of them. "I've made my decision."

"More money," Enderall offered desperately.

Jennifer shook her head. "I can't."

"What do you mean, you can't? Do you know what you're saying?"

"I'm saying that I'm going to leave here with at least some of my self-esteem intact." She yanked her purse free from his grip and quickly maneuvered around him.

She was walking through the door when Enderall's voice trumpeted behind her.

"And just what the hell do we tell the millions of viewers who heard the announcement on the KZAM news flash this morning?"

She was certain her heart stopped. She did not have the strength to turn. "What?" she said.

"You didn't know?" Enderall sounded hopeful. "Oh, you didn't know. She didn't know," he repeated to the others with relief.

Jennifer turned. "You told millions of people about the story on Darla Hart?"

"Yes," Enderall said. "Your story, Miss Winters. And we even mentioned your name. We're talking a special here!"

"You mentioned my name?" Jennifer felt dizzy. She had never fainted. She wondered if this draining feeling, this loss of all strength from her limbs was a prelude to a blackout? But a resurgence of anger saved her. "How could you have done that, Mr. Enderall? You shouldn't have. No one ever makes an announcement like that to the public, not until they have the story done and checked out and approved. It's just crazy. How could you have done such a thing?"

"Because I was desperate!" he said, his voice covering hers. "Because I wanted to save my ass—and all of these asses, too!" he shouted, referring to the others who had blanched eggshell white. "Winters, you walk out of here, you'll ruin our lives!"

She considered what he had just said.

"Why not?" she finally responded softly. "You've just ruined mine."

She turned, and somehow made it to the elevator. She pressed the down button. The doors opened. She got in. The doors closed, and the car gave a starting jolt. She may as well have been descending into hell.

Chapter 12

BY THE TIME SHE GOT TO HER CAR, SHE HAD FORMULATED A plan. She wouldn't call Michael. She would go to him. She would tell him the truth, that she had quit her job because she loved him, and that sorry as she was about the premature announcement, it had been made without her knowledge or her consent. That was the truth, wasn't it? But as she slipped into the MG, she reminded herself of another journalistic truism: the truth was rarely believable, always suspect; it was just too weird.

She flicked the ignition over. Nothing. Again, she tried to get the car to start. And again nothing.

"Look you," she said, tears beginning to form as she glared at the dashboard. "I have just experienced the worst morning of my life. At this moment I have almost no life. You and my apartment are all I have left. So now what? You're turning against me, too?"

She leaned back in the MG, closed her eyes. Tears pushed out from between thick lashes. Nearby, a bus braked at the curb. It took off, leaving a blast of noxious hydrocarbons in its wake. Jennifer choked back the fumes and wiped the tears off her cheek. She couldn't just sit there feeling sorry for herself all day.

"Please . . . make sounds like you're alive," she begged, leaning forward and trying the ignition again. The motor hummed to her command. The turn of good fortune was almost startling. She gave it a moment to die, and when it didn't she patted its tachometer. "Thanks, old friend."

The air and the sun and the MG's responsiveness helped to buoy her spirits, and by the time she was nearing home, she had convinced herself the end had not yet arrived. Whether or not her optimism was warranted was beside the point. She had to believe.

Her mother had been a great one for aphorisms. She had one to accompany every occasion, from scraped knees to spoiled cakes. What would she say now? Would her mother say that all seasons had their transitions? Yes, Jennifer decided, liking the sound of it. She would. A truth: Before spring, winter must end. The cold hard times had been passed through—with difficulty, but she had survived, just as the trees survive the frost. So it was poetic, maybe a trifle unrealistic. Still, it was something to go on in the present desperate moment.

Michael would believe her. Of course he would. He loved her. She loved him. So they'd talk it all out. And then, she thought happily, they would celebrate the beginning of their new season. It would be a glorious one, filled with flowers and blue skies and singing birds. They would launch this new beginning, this honest beginning, she revised, with champagne. Michael loved champagne, she loved Michael. Oh, yes, she thought, feeling a rush of happiness, she loved Michael.

She might not have a job anymore, but a splurge at the Stop N' Go for their finest vintage at under three dollars plus tax was a worthwhile extravagance. And, anyway, it was the thought that counted, not the label.

It was only eleven when she came up to the Stop N' Go. At noon, its small parking lot would be filled with the vehicles of construction workers stopping for premade sandwiches and beer. But now the lot was fairly vacant. Only Sung Ock's Toyota and a bad-looking El Camino, low and mean with rusting sides and deep gashes attesting to a disreputable history, were pulled into parking slots. The El Camino was backed into its place, its body slanted across two spaces, its nose aimed for the exit. She parked off to the side, avoiding the El Camino with the delighted hauteur of any poor person who runs across someone even less fortunate than they.

The MG shuttered and quaked to a stop. She had just closed its door, her hand still on the handle, when suddenly the world, which had just begun to brighten for her again, turned ugly.

A cracking noise tore through the air. The noise had come from inside the market.

Another burst of terrifying sound, identifiable now as the retort of gun fire. A man's agonized cry rented the sounds of everyday life.

From the Stop N' Go, a man backed out, moving quickly, gun drawn in one hand, the other hand stuffing money into his pocket.

Jenny ducked behind the MG. Her heart was in her throat, but she rose slightly, risking a peek.

The gunman was racing for the El Camino. He wrenched

open its door, was dipping to get in, when Sung Ock came
into view. The small Korean's stance was crazy, slanted.
There was a red stain spreading beneath his shoulder as he
raised the hand holding the revolver and fired at the El
Camino.

The first shot was not direct. It echoed *cah-chew* as it
richocheted off the car. The gunman crouched low behind
the El Camino. He bobbed up suddenly, gun gripped in
both hands. He took a moment to sight Sung Ock, who was
now staggering out from the door, a mixture of rage and
pain contorting his face. An explosion broke the tense
silence.

Jennifer couldn't believe it was all happening. Only it
was, and it was terrible.

Sung Ock clutched his belly. Silent, he began to go
down, then somehow pulled himself up and lurched forward.

The driver of the El Camino scrambled lithely into the
car. He looked over his shoulder at Sung Ock, who was
coming, weaving, but still coming at the gunman. The El
Camino's engine turned over.

Sung Ock raised his weapon. He squinted from the
exertion as he calculated his aim.

The El Camino rocketed forward, wheels spinning,
smoking rubber.

Sung Ock fired. The El Camino's window dissolved into
a network of crystals, then broke apart, glass blowing out,
shards catching sunlight, dancing gaily through the air.

In the breath it took for Sung Ock to fall to the pavement,
the car fishtailed into the street. The takeoff was too fast; the
car's engine stalled.

Jennifer started for Sung Ock. At the same time his
nephew ran screaming from the store's entrance. Behind her

Jennifer heard the El Camino's engine struggle to regain life. She looked at Sung Ock, now cradled in his nephew's arms, then back to the stalled El Camino.

Her keys were still in her hand. She made for the MG, jammed them into the ignition. "Go! Go!" she yelled to the car.

The motor roared to life, lusty and strong, a lion among engines. Throwing the MG into reverse, she screamed out of the parking lot. The El Camino had taken off. They zigzagged through traffic, the MG a stubborn magnet on the other car's tail. Traveling fast, faster, her mind replayed in slow motion the scene with Sung Ock, going down, pain on his face, red stain spreading. . . . She was going to get that man. Flooring the MG, she banished all other thoughts but one from her mind: She would get him. Somewhere, the high whine of sirens flew by in the wind.

They were moving like the wind themselves now, the MG going like a dangerous, reckless entity with its own goal, slipping around slower cars, braking rarely, its horn sounding passionate warnings to beware. And miracle of miracles, they were gaining. Up ahead, something was holding up the El Camino; Jennifer identified the problem as a tight parade of stodgy vehicles.

Still, she and the MG were coming up. They were going, going, hurtling ahead . . . but so was the El Camino, freed now from the bottleneck.

The light was red in front of him.

But the El Camino wasn't slowing down.

Jennifer swallowed hard. In her mind Sung Ock kept falling, falling, falling . . .

Insanity. The El Camino shot through the light, straight into the intersection.

More insanity. The MG streaked after it.

Holy! Jennifer gripped the MG's wheel. She fought the

impulse to close her eyes. A piercing wail was coming closer. But not close enough, or fast enough. The bastard, she thought, the bastard was going to get away. Unless . . . yes!

And in the middle of the intersection a new problem arose for the El Camino. A muddle of bewildered, frightened, and unaware motorists were locked in a deadly dilemma. The El Camino reversed, started forward again, the line of escape finally clear.

Almost.

Almost, because a tattered MG was moving up behind it like greased lightning. It slipped through the tangled maze of General Motors and Ford products, and slammed against the El Camino's left side, skidded in front of it, and locked fenders.

An awful scrunching sound ripped through the air.

And then, as thoughts of this is how it all ends, when you don't plan it, when you're thinking you're going to live forever, so crazy, but I'm still young, this can't be happening . . . only it is . . . flew through her mind, she helplessly watched the door of the El Camino fly open and the man jump out, gun raised at her.

A three-dimensional, technicolor image of Michael's face flashed through her mind. He wasn't ever going to know how much she loved him. She would die and Michael would never—

The air rang with a shrieking music.

The gunman was whirling around, confused.

Screech. Screech. Screech. Everywhere, on all sides, *screech.*

It was the good guys! Superman! A whole gang of them, dressed in darkest blue and flying out of their cars and making things all right. . . .

Which was the end of it. Jennifer checked out of the

scene, sliding down on the seat of the MG as she lost consciousness, the last sound she truly remembered, its engine. Gurgling softly. Proudly.

Like magic, the news camera teams appeared. They arrived even before the paramedics and barely allowed her time to be examined medically before they began their barrage of questions.

One of the paramedics suggested she be on the alert for whiplash. His uncle was an attorney. He handed her his uncle's card, and with a smile told her that "for the record" she seemed fit enough "for a crazy person" who would try to capture an armed robber.

The MG faired less well. Its right fender had been scrunched and ripped off. Other pieces of it lay like felled soldiers in the middle of the street. Looming off to one side were two tow trucks waiting for the police to finish detailing the scene.

The gunman was handcuffed and seated in the back of a squad car. Jenny saw him staring—glaring—at her. He looked as if he couldn't believe it had all happened; he looked like he would like to kill her.

She went over to the MG and touched its door gently. "Thanks," she said, "you were fabulous."

Mini-cams, emblazoned with the major network logos and KZAM, were hoisted atop the shoulders of film technicians. They were all aimed at her, as were the hand mikes being thrust in her face from all directions.

Reporters were screaming at each other, arguing, shoving. In the heat of the battle she felt momentarily forgotten. Then a voice rang out, "Jennifer . . . Jennifer Winters! It's me! Craig . . . KZAM. Hey, watch it, vultures, that's our girl!"

* * *

Michael closed the door to Morey's office quietly. The gesture was in soft counterpoint to the hysteria that had just characterized the scene with his agent.

One down, he thought, and one to go.

As he took the stairs to street level, he wondered at his feelings. Rather than remorseful, doubtful, guilt-ridden, he felt a light-spiritedness, a surge of exhilaration at having finally made the commitment.

But as he opened the Cadillac's door, he sighed. That was only one down. One left to go. And this one was going to be a killer.

Lena answered the door dressed in a robe. He had driven her home from the hospital yesterday afternoon. Then she had seemed in remarkably good spirits, insisting he come in for a sandwich and some coffee. Nevertheless, on the way over from Morey's, he had prepared himself emotionally for being greeted by a pitiful sight. But even at that, Lena looked awful and he had to force himself to go through the door. Lena's hair was uncombed. She wore no makeup, and there were deep blue rings beneath her eyes. Maybe it was from a bad conscience, but he noticed the white bandages taped to her wrists more than he listened to what she was saying. As she rushed away she was saying something about the television.

"Lena," Michael said, trying to keep up with her as she disappeared into her study, "I'd like us to—"

"Wait, wait," Lena said, cutting him off, and standing fixed before the television set. "Jennifer . . ." she said, barely audible.

"What?" And then he saw, too. Jennifer was being interviewed on camera. He couldn't believe it was happening. At first his mind did strange spirals, trying to land somewhere where the terrain was familiar, then, when he couldn't make sense of what he was watching, he gave up, and like Lena, stood gawking.

"What made you do it?" the reporter said breathlessly, thrusting a mike into Jennifer's face. She looked like she wanted to get away, but the reporter was insistent. "What made you risk your life for another human being? Against all odds. Without any weapon, pitting yourself against an armed man, a potential killer."

"Why?" Jennifer looked at once angry and disbelieving that she would be asked something so stupid. "Because it was wrong and he was going to get away with it if someone didn't stop him."

"But you could have been killed, too," the reporter argued.

And now Jennifer was angry. Michael could almost feel the sparks fly from her eyes. "And what's the use of being alive in a world where no one cares? It was the right thing to do. That's all." She moved away, out of the camera's angle and the interview continued with other on-the-spot coverage.

"Where's the telephone?" Michael barked at Lena, who was standing, as if in deep shock, staring at the television. Tears were streaming down her face. Michael didn't care. All he cared about was Jennifer. "Where's the telephone!"

Lena looked at him. "You can't get her yet. This was live."

"Jesus . . ." Michael said, and sank into the couch, feeling as if every ounce of strength had been sapped from him. "She could have been killed."

"She's okay," Lena said, and turning slowly, said, "And so am I."

Michael was aware of Lena talking to him, but all he

could do was think about Jennifer. She looked so beautiful. The brave little scrapper . . . going after that bastard. . . . "Oh, God . . ." he groaned, thinking of how it could have turned out.

"I resign," Lena said. "Michael! I said I'm through."

"What?" He looked up, seeing Lena standing before him. Her eyes were clear now, although tears still glistened on her cheeks.

"I'm resigning. Now. Here. I'm not Darla Hart anymore. I'm me. Lena Stephens. For better, or maybe for worse," she said, shrugging. "But I'm going to be me. I release you from being my therapist. And I release you—" her voice choked slightly—"From being my friend."

Michael rose slowly. "You mean it, don't you? This isn't another one—"

"Of my acts?" Lena shook her head. "No."

Michael let out a long sigh. "I don't get it."

"I want to be like her," Lena said. "Like Jennifer. You love her. But you also like her. And me? I'm just a drain. A pathetic charity case. There's nothing wrong with me, Michael. That suicide thing was just a stunt. Jennifer knew it. She saw through it as clear as can be. She's honest. I'm a phony."

"Thank you," Michael said. "That took some guts, right there."

"Oh, bull. It didn't take guts at all. You'd have gotten sick of me sooner or later anyway. My guess is sooner." Lena narrowed her green eyes at him. "Want some advice, shrink? You're getting it anyway. You gotta learn to let go, too. Just live your life. Don't live mine or anyone else's. You're a good guy, Casari, but when all's said and done, you're just a guy. You don't look much like a saint to me anymore. So," she said, turning away, her voice filled with emotion, "why don't you just get the hell out of my sight and find Jennifer. Tell her she's got a story to do on Darla Hart."

Michael started to go to her.

"No, Michael . . . no more helping hand. No more Mr. Nice Guy."

"Listen, believe me, I'm no saint." He realized he was saying it almost with pride. "I came over here to give you the sack."

"Sonofabitch," Lena said. She was smiling. So was he.

Michael stared helplessly at the phone in his office. Knowing she was somewhere on the planet, in transit and out of his momentary reach, was purely intolerable. Never, even at his most caring, most saintly moment, had he felt that way about a patient, never! The pain he experienced thinking that Jennifer might be frightened, even, God forbid, physically hurt, tore at his insides. Something primal and male was exploding in him. She was his woman, and she needed him, and all the help he could be was to dial a telephone number.

He dialed the KZAM switchboard again. The operator rang through to Jennifer's office. No one answered. The operator came back on. "Who's in charge down there? Wait a minute, an Enderall, someone Enderall's her boss. Put him on," Michael said, not caring if he sounded like a dictator.

"Mr. Enderall's office," a secretary's voice answered.

"I'd like to speak with him."

"I'm sorry, but—"

"This is the IRS calling."

"Yes, of course . . ."

Enderall answered a beat later. "Yes?"

"My name's Michael Casari. I'm not from the IRS. I'm

a personal friend of Jennifer Winters and I want to know her home number. It's urgent.''

"Mr. Casari—or whoever you are really—what do you think? That we at KZAM just fell off the turnip cart? Miss Winters is our exclusive property. If you want a story, get it yourself.''

Enderall put the phone down, missing Michael's expletive.

An hour later Michael had battled the traffic, battled Enderall's secretary, and stood before the man, himself.

"Look, I'd like to make myself perfectly clear,'' Enderall said, leaning over his desk. "You don't get her home telephone number. She's our exclusive property. Ours. And I don't care if you told me you were her guardian angel, you're still not getting it.'' Enderall leaned back smugly.

"You want me to shake it out of you?'' Michael said, hating violence, but at that moment feeling perfectly capable of batting Enderall's body up against the wall until he spilled out Jennifer's telephone number. He took a step forward.

Enderall's finger shot forward, pressed the intercom. "Get security up here. Now!''

"Save them the trip,'' Michael said. "I'm leaving.''

"Violence never gets you anyplace, Mr. Casari!'' Enderall called when Michael was half out the door.

"Want to bet it could get me a phone number?''

Enderall's finger flew to the buzzer again. Michael grinned malevolently and left the door open behind him as he left.

In her nightgown, curled up in the corner of the sofa, Jennifer watched the television screen with a kind of morbid fascination. She was observing her own character assassination.

The five o'clock news had carried pretty much the same story as the ten o'clock news. She was a local heroine; for all she knew, maybe even national.

All the networks carried something on the incident, padding the little they knew with half-truths and extensive film footage of the capture scene.

But now, in spite of her lack of cooperation, it was KZAM's shining moment. They didn't just stop with the news, but had put together a mini-feature on her being their tough-girl reporter. From their account she was a cross between Woodward and Bernstein, Marilyn Monroe, and a hungry barracuda.

"Incidentally, Carrie," the KZAM anchorman was saying to the KZAM anchorwoman, "this same crack reporter is responsible for some absolutely top-notch investigative reporting about to be aired on our *Everyday* show."

"Yes, so I've heard. KZAM's bringing its viewers the true, no-holds barred inside story of Darla Hart's personal life."

They both smiled at each other, then at the camera. Jennifer felt too sick to shut them off, as she would have like to have done.

"So stay tuned to your number one news station, folks. KZAM commin' at cha!"

A commercial cut off their smiles, the way Jennifer's hope had been severed.

Almost immediately, the telephone rang. She grabbed for it, her nerves raw and jangling. "Yes?"

"Jennifer? It's Casius. How are you?" he asked, each word honeyed. Jennifer pictured a Venus's-flytrap plant, sticky and lethal.

"How dare you!" she exploded. "I saw it, I saw that show. What they said—all lies, absolute lies! You know very well I quit this morning. I quit! And you made it seem like I was still on your payroll!''

"Jennifer, come back. Come back to us," Enderall went on as if he hadn't heard anything she had just said. "Everything can be worked out."

"Nothing can be worked out. Everything is over. Everything I ever wanted and worked for and believed in is gone."

"That's not true. The phones have been ringing off the hook for you here. You'll have a brilliant career. Just seize your opportunities."

"Who called?" she asked suddenly.

"Who? A thousand people."

"No, no. Personal calls . . ."

"We don't know who to trust. You know how people lie. They'll say anything to get what they want."

"No kidding?"

"Some bozo just left here, said he knew you. A violent type, dark, angry, Italian—"

"Who?"

"I don't know . . . oh . . . Casari. A regular fury. But not to worry, the station's behind you all the way, protecting your interests. I called security. He won't be around anymore."

"No," Jennifer said, feeling her stomach turn over, "probably not." Why should he? she wondered. He hates me.

"We're going to let you break the Darla thing yourself. You'll be another Barbara Walters."

"You can just go to hell with your Darla story," Jennifer said. "And do us both a favor. Don't call me again."

After that, only one thought repeated itself. It stayed with her all through the long, sleepless night. Like a printed banner whipping in teasing spirals, its slogan shined in the darkness of her mind. It was over, it said. It was over, her mind agreed.

The rest of the week passed in a haze. There were articles on her in all the newspapers, and she even found a photo caption in *People*, which angered her since she resented their right to exploit her as a newsmaker, as part of the public domain. By Monday whatever righteous indignation she had managed to savor had dwindled to the stale taste of reality.

The mighty crusader for The Right was out of a job. She had to face it: Jeanne d'Arc without an army to lead was just another unemployed lady.

The woman behind the counter for unemployment insurance claims gave her forms to fill regarding her employment history. Under reason for leaving last job, Jennifer wrote: Scruples.

"Scruples?" The department interviewer stared at Jennifer as if she had green wings. "Scruples? There are people out there who would kill for a job. And you quit for . . . scruples?"

Jennifer would get a notice in the mail telling her if and when she could start collecting unemployment compensation.

She filled out applications in three professional placement agencies. Her chances of landing another "glamour job," as they termed it, were approximately the same as being drafted as an astronaut on the next space shuttle. After a week of fruitless interviews, her only firm offer was a dinner engagement with the head of a motion picture studio's publicity department. Life was depressing.

The only good news was that Sung Ock was going to make it. He was out of intensive care and was going over the daily Stop N' Go receipts from his hospital bed. Jenny brought him a small African violet plant from the grocery store—all she could afford. When he wanted to give her "exclusive story on Korean Mafia . . ." she thanked him, but declined. "No good story?" he asked, seeming offended. "I don't have a job anymore," she told him. The following day she stopped by the Stop N' Go for cottage cheese and was given a large bag of groceries. Free. It was also the first time Sung Ock's surly nephew smiled at her.

Life was a little less depressing. But not much.

The newspaper was a necessary evil in her life. Every day she scoured the advertisements for possible employment opportunities. And every day she avoided the section containing Darla Hart's advice column.

But that did not stop her from thinking about Michael. At night she would lie awake remembering. His face. His voice. The laughter in his eyes. And she would brush her hand lightly over her breasts, remembering the touch of his hand. Countless midnight wars were waged between her body and her mind. But in the sunlight, reason ruled again, and she would abandon all notions of driving to Malibu to try to explain. Besides, there wasn't any room in his life for her; not with all those other lost souls clinging to him—the attachment mutual.

Had she decided to give into her romantic midnight delusions, she couldn't have anyway. To the insurance company the MG had been worth a good laugh and a check for $300. In three weeks she had used up the proceeds from the MG on a leased car and miscellaneous groceries.

Life was depressing again.

An unmarked envelope appeared in her mail. In it was a check for five hundred dollars and a note: "Dear Jennifer— From the Brujas' Emergency Fund for Indigent Gringas." It was signed "Estela." There was a postscript, actually two of them. The first said that Jennifer should keep the money, it was a matter of honor. It wasn't often a Chicano street gang got the opportunity to offer aid to a kid from a good neighborhood. The other news item was that Estela's story had been selected over Rita's and Arnold's.

"What the hell is this, Michael?"

"What's what?" Michael held the telephone beneath his chin as he stared at the glowing electronic letters on his word processor's screen.

"This rambling monologue."

"It's not a rambling monologue, Morey. It's Darla Hart's advice to her readers."

"It's crackers, is what it is! This is a . . . well, hell . . . this is a love letter! The ravings of a man in love."

"They still think I'm a woman," Michael corrected.

Morey groaned. "And when's the big announcement going to hit the airwaves?"

"You'll be the first to know, Morey. I promise you."

"Look, Mikey, other men fall in love. They fall out of love. They hurt. So they lift weights, jog along the beach, they find a woman or two or ten. They don't find it necessary to make public spectacles of themselves. Look, my friend, falling in love is a temporary mental disorder. Do not put us all in financial jeopardy, Michael."

"There are some things more important than money."

"Name something."

"You can read about it tomorrow."

"Oh, hell, Michael."

Jennifer was in the waiting room of yet another personnel office when the girl with straight red hair sitting next to her leaned over to a girl with frizzy short blond hair and said breathlessly, "Did you read Darla Hart today?"

The other girl nodded, her eyes growing wide. "Yeesss . . . wasn't it beautiful?"

"It gave me goosebumps."

"I cried."

"She must be in love."

"I had to take a cold shower after reading it."

"Do you think they'll get married?"

"If the guy can read, they will."

The receptionist called the frizzy blond in for an interview. The redhead smiled at Jennifer. "Did you read it?" she asked.

Jennifer leafed furiously through her magazine. "No."

"I thought everyone read Darla Hart. Darla Hart is wonderful. Darla Hart's—"

"Out of my life," Jennifer said, standing suddenly. She threw the magazine down on the coffee table and fled the room.

She went straight home, undressed, and even though it was only two o'clock in the afternoon, she crawled into bed where she remained for a full two hours during which time she intermittently cried and told herself to forget Michael forever, and then, burning for him physically, emotionally, she would reverse herself and give into the fantasy that everything about their relationship was salvageable. But it wasn't. It wasn't, because Michael felt responsible for the entire world, and that world he had invented to live in simply had no room in it for her.

At five o'clock she dragged herself out of bed, and against her better judgment, drove her leased car to the Stop N' Go, where she purchased the evening edition of the *L.A. Times*.

With Sung Ock's nephew eyeing her, she threw aside the entire paper except for the section holding Darla Hart's column.

And there it was.

She could hear him saying the words to her, could actually hear Michael's voice come out of the print. She saw his face superimposed over the column, his eyes bringing her into him, the invisible string tugging at her heart.

He wanted to marry her.

She started to cry. First one tear splashed on the paper, then another and another, followed by a torrential downpour.

"You hungry?" Sung Ock's nephew asked desperately.

"No," Jennifer said, shaking her head.

"You want something? Nice plum?" He scurried to the produce section and returned with a plum for her.

Jenny shook her head, the tears still coming.

"Apple?" he asked hopefully. "Nice apples today."

She began to cry harder.

"What you like?" he asked, his voice high and frantic.

"I want a job," she sobbed. "I want my MG back . . . I want Michael . . ."

"Ohhh . . . ahhh," Sung Ock's nephew nodded, finally understanding. "No got today."

The phone was ringing when she returned home. It was Enderall.

"I was hasty," he said, and plunged vigorously into his spiel. One word followed so close upon the next that there was no way short of hanging up that she could interrupt. "Everything you said was true, was right. Absolutely. You're a courageous young woman, an exemplar to our profession. I beg of you, I plead with you, Miss Winters, if you have even the slightest regard for our years of association—"

"I told you not to call me again," she said. The tempting vision of a paycheck danced before her. She was a fool.

"Name anything you want. It's yours. Just please, come down here."

"You're wasting your time. I have nothing to offer you," she said.

"Let me be the judge of that. Look, let me take you to dinner tonight. Where would you like to go? Ma Maison? It's wonderful there. Expensive. They have an unlisted number so only the right people get in. Come, Miss Winters, come . . ."

"Look, just tell me why this sudden urge to please me?"

"I have a proposal for you. And everything's on your terms."

"Oh, really? What if I wanted a pelican feature?"

"I adore birds."

"Make reservations at Ma Maison," she said blandly. "I'll meet you at the office in an hour, traffic permitting."

She put the phone down, cutting off Enderall's deep sigh of relief.

"Miss Winters!" Enderall fairly leaped up from behind his desk. "How good of you to come."

He was coming around the side of his desk, his hand extended, when Jennifer saw there was another person in the room.

"Hello, Jennifer," Michael said, standing. He came forward quickly, pushing the door closed with his hand.

They were very close. He looked down at her with those amazing, intense brown eyes, and she, in turn, felt her mind melting into a puddle of warm, yearning sensation.

"Jennifer," he said, his voice like a caress, very soft, intimate, his words not for Enderall's ears, "give me this chance." He moved closer. Shutting her eyes did nothing to dissolve the impact of his physical presence. They were inches apart, but just as on their first encounter on that first morning in the convenience store, which she had come to think of as her first time to be really, truly alive, she could sense the heat of his body, imagine the feel of his hard, masculine frame lying over her, feel his breath graze her neck, float over her breasts. . . . She sighed and, suddenly afraid her thoughts on her face were transcribable, took a seat in a chair facing Enderall's desk.

"What's going on here?" she asked, looking from one man to the other.

Enderall quickly took his place behind his desk.

Michael remained off to the side, his eyes never leaving her. She felt his eyes on her leg as she crossed it. The flap of her skirt's kick pleat parted halfway up her thigh. His desire for her was almost tangible. It was hard for her to concentrate on what Enderall was saying.

"Mr. Casari was good enough to explain the entire situation to me," Enderall began with a gravity belying the light of glad hysteria behind his eyes.

"Not the entire situation," Michael said, cutting in. Speaking to Jennifer, he said, "But I'd like to now." And with a look to Enderall that could only suggest he evaporate from their presence, Michael said, "Do you mind?"

"Yes, yes . . . of course. I'll, uh . . . a drink of water." Enderall disappeared, leaving them alone.

Michael faced her, his eyes dark with an expression she could not read. "Why?" he asked. "Why didn't you call me?"

"Because, Michael . . . everything had already been said."

"Do you realize I've been crazy thinking about you? My God!" he said, almost violently. "No one would give me your number. I didn't even have your address. Did you read my column?"

"Only today . . ." Jennifer whispered, barely able to keep herself from flying into his arms.

"And?" The one word held a universe of desperation.

"And . . . and I love you, too, Michael."

His eyes fell closed. His chest fell slightly, relaxed, as if after a long strain.

"But," she went on, "loving you can't make up for the fundamental differences—"

He moved so quickly, she didn't have time to back away. His arms went around her and he silenced her with a kiss. "You love me!" He looked at her as if she had just worked a miracle. "I love you!" Laughing, he kissed her again, this time with more urgency.

"Don't," Jennifer said, pushing herself out of his reach and holding up her hand. "Just don't start with all that. Because it's over, Michael."

"Some of it. The bad part." He moved forward and caught her chin, forcing her to look at him. "The good part, the best part, is yet to come." But she wriggled out of his arms.

Michael went after her, capturing her again and saying, "Listen to me . . . your job is yours if you want it back . . . under your terms. And I'm yours, even if you don't want me back."

"I said to cut it out, Michael. You know what I said, and—"

"And you were right."

Jennifer looked at him. "I was right?"

"Absolutely. I wasn't being honest. Not to my readers, not with you, and most important, not with myself." He raised both arms, letting them fall helpless to his sides. "I'm not God."

"No kidding?"

He smiled. "I wanted to be . . . I just didn't have the stuff. Besides which, what the world needed was a good psychologist, not an amateur saint. Jennifer," he said, "I'm not hiding anymore."

"You're not?"

"No."

"You're giving up your column?"

"No."

"Oh, I see, well . . ." Jenny looked up to the ceiling, trying to keep her eyes dry. For a minute she had thought—

"No, you don't see. I'm going to do the column, but not until you introduce me to the world."

"You mean it?"

"There's a condition . . ."

"A condition. I've had enough of conditions, Michael—"

"That you marry me!"

Jennifer forgot what she was about to say as he crossed the distance between them. Forcing her back into his arms, he said, "I absolutely adore you. I love you. I fell in love—hopelessly, irrevocably in love with a beautiful blond lioness the first moment I saw her. She has wide blue eyes and a soft, beautiful body that makes me go crazy whenever I even think of it, let alone touch it." He was kissing her neck, tracing his finger over her closed eyes. Jennifer was finding it difficult to collect her thoughts. There was something she was supposed to be thinking about.

"Will you?" Michael asked.

"What?" she said dreamily.

"Jennifer, I just proposed to you!" He held her away, laughing.

"Yes, oh, yes . . ." she said, and then looking up at him said innocently, "under one condition."

Michael looked down at her, half smiling. "You name it."

Her hand wrapped around his neck, and gently, deliberately, she brought his mouth to hers. He kissed her deeply, his mouth moving hard against her own, as his hands began to roam more freely over her hips, then up to cup the fullness of her breasts.

"What's your condition?" he growled, his tongue flicking her earlobe. "God! I want you, I need you . . . it's been too, too long . . ."

Jennifer nibbled lightly on his lower lip. "Then how about this for a condition?"

He looked at her in surprise, then with feigned and delighted shock. "Here?" Jennifer nodded. "Here?" he asked again, looking around the office.

"Well . . . it's Hollywood," Jennifer said, inching them backward to the door, then felt with her fingers to engage the lock. "And that's a couch. And this is a deal. And . . ." Michael was unbuttoning her blouse. "And . . ." Michael was kissing her breast.

"And?" he said.

"And make love to me . . ."

Behind her, she heard someone try the door knob. "Miss Winters? Oh, Miss Winters?"

"Mr. Enderall, about dinner tonight? Maybe you should go without me. It seems I'm going to be otherwise engaged this evening."

Stealthily, Michael's fingers crept up the slit of her skirt, bunching the material in his fist. "For a long time," he assured her. And from his voice she knew he wasn't joking this time.

Chapter 13

FOR A WEEK THEY KEPT THE TELEPHONE OFF THE HOOK.

They stayed up late, watching old horror movies and eating popcorn in bed, made love and fell asleep twined together. Mornings were spent racing the gulls up and down the beach, falling down on the sand, and becoming lost in each other's arms, in each other's eyes, the laughter turning to a hot passion that would send them home to bed again.

A look from him across a room, and the atmosphere became charged with their mutual desire. Something elemental, deep within her, connected with something in him, her beautiful, tender, ferocious man, who held her captive in his brown velvety gaze. Wherever he was, an invisible string would draw her to him. Sometimes she would have to close her eyes, daring herself to believe that joy he brought to her would last forever. The strength of their love melded her soul to his, and when they joined together at night in the dark, the force of their passion would roar through her body, afterward leaving her trembling from the completeness of the experience they shared.

But it was a serious time for them, too. There were moments when Michael went for walks alone, returning pensive, replying vaguely to her questions of what he was thinking about.

"You're worried," she said, a week before their interview was to take place.

"Yes," he finally admitted.

"What's the worse that can happen?"

"The worst that can happen is that half the world's population will find me a repulsive, phony creep, which will make it slightly difficult for me to hold down any kind of a job that will put food in the mouth of the woman I love and plan to marry."

"I don't care about food. I only care about you."

"Jennifer," Michael said, coming to her, "this is a big risk. Not just for me. For you, too. If you want to back out of it, you—"

She pulled away from him. They were both stunned. But they both understood. "Don't you ever, don't you ever say that to me again. You insult me, you insult us."

And he made love to her then. It was a different kind of lovemaking than ever before, with his fierceness speaking his commitment to their relationship more eloquently than words could ever have done.

His body moved over hers, and he was hot and demanding, slick with moisture. She gasped from the sensation of his strength as he slipped into her, filling her.

"Jenny . . ." he said, holding himself still for a moment. "Jenny . . ." He held her face between his hands and slowly began to move in her again. His tongue probed her mouth, matching the building spirals of her pelvis. The friction of their bodies rubbing together became an almost unbearable ecstasy.

They were lost to their mutual hunger, his mouth on her breasts, taking in her nipples one at a time, while still rocking in her, driving her higher and higher.

"Michael!" she cried out, fighting for air as the familiar waves began deep in her groin. "Michael, don't stop . . . love me . . . oh, oh . . ." The words faded as he moved his mouth onto hers. Like a taut bow, she pulled her body back, then automatically released to let him in, arching again and again, with each of his thrusts. They were both trembling, both rising together.

She was aware of nothing, only of their bodies, the mounting urge within her to unite, to release, to reach somewhere with him . . . and then it spread, radiating through her, a rolling surge, molten liquid . . . the feeling breaking through her like a universe of stars.

She was somewhere. With him. His hardness driving her faster and beyond . . . beyond . . . he cried out . . . her voice with his . . . beyond the edge of the brightest star.

When they awoke, it was dark. There were few stars in the sky, but one in particular winked happily, independently in the heavens. She couldn't be sure, but she liked to think it was Venus watching over them.

Michael lay stretched beside her. His hair was tousled like a child's, his face, so worried recently, peaceful in repose. "I love you," she whispered, and tasted the tear that had trickled down to her lips. She moved closer to him, sliding over and placing her face against his hard belly. "I love you. Body and soul," she said softly.

Michael's fingers twined in her thick hair, lying loose and full over her shoulders. So, he had heard her. She kissed his stomach again, and immediately felt him stir. Touching him, she held and teased his reawakening body. Full again, he moaned. "Love me one more time," he said.

"Always," she replied, and pleasing them both, felt him velvet-smooth against her tongue.

"When are you going to marry me?" she demanded the next morning.

"God, you're pushy, aren't you?"

"Damn right."

Michael grinned. "You look like a tigress." They were in the kitchen, putting away dishes from the dishwasher, and suddenly, he pulled her close to him.

She felt him harden against her, as his hands slid over her breasts. With a laugh, she withdrew from his kiss, and escaped his fondling with the same sleek movement.

"Forget about lions and tigers and the birds and the bees. Think dum-dum-de-dum, dum-dum-de-dum. In case that's not a familiar tune—"

"Not a funeral dirge?"

She threw a pot holder at him. But she laughed, and so did he, until he became suddenly serious.

"We're going to do it right."

"What does that mean?" she asked him.

"I do the interview first."

"Why? I don't want to wait. I told you I don't care if you're a prince or a pauper."

"You've got to wait," he said mysteriously.

"That's still no answer," she complained.

"I've made plans."

"Plans, shmams. Let's just get in the car and take off for Las Vegas! Oh, Michael!" she cried with mock melodrama. "Must I beg?"

Coming to her, he brought her against him again and tenderly this time, kissed her forehead. "Ah, my love, my love . . . things must be perfect. We will wait."

The KZAM interview took place on a Wednesday morning.

Jennifer was too in love to be nervous. Every time she looked into Michael's face, handsome and tanned, she would smile, forgetting the cameras and the network dollars being expended during every bat of her long lashes.

"What do you think?" Michael asked when it was over.

"I think we can get married now."

"About the telecast?" he asked, frowning.

"We'll know soon enough," Jennifer said.

"Yeah," Michael grimaced, "when an angry mob starts pounding on our door."

On Thursday morning Jennifer followed Michael out the front door.

"All's clear," she sang, looking back to Michael. "No lynching mob yet . . ."

"Yet," Michael grumbled. But he winked. He carried the big bags, and she the camera and her overnight case.

"You've got the birth certificates?" he asked, walking ahead.

She was going to say something smart in return, but Morey cut her off. He came chugging around the corner, waving a paper in the air.

"Damn it, Casari! You've always got the damned phone off the hook." He saw the suitcases. "Oh? You going somewhere?" And then his expression changed to one of horrified comprehension. "You aren't. You are."

"Wish us well, Morey," Michael said, and looking at the computer printout being brandished by his agent, said, "and keep the gruesome news until I return."

They continued down the path to the front.

Morey kept pace. "No . . . no, Mike! The figures . . . that's what I'm here to tell you . . . are great! America loves Michael Casari even more than they did Darla Hart! Mikey," Morey wheezed, his breath restricted by his excitement, "don't do this to me—to us," Morey revised. "All over America, female viewers were reputedly swooning over the . . . I quote . . . 'the flashing, lively eyes of Michael Casari. His wit dazzled. His honesty broke through emotional barriers. Michael Casari put his career on the line in the name of truth.' Dammit, Michael, you grabbed the entire female population. You're a superstar sex symbol!"

"I'll drink to that!" Jenny piped up.

Morey threw her a pained look, and groaned.

Michael was smiling, but still walking ahead. Jennifer stopped. So did Morey. They were both staring at the car parked on the side of the road with the "Just Married" slogans painted on the windows.

"Oh, no, oh, no, oh, no . . ." Morey said. He looked to Michael to deny the sight. "You aren't going to really . . . I mean, Mikey, you've got a reputation to uphold now. Your face is known . . . you can't possibly take that . . . thing . . ." Morey's lip curled in disgust.

Jennifer's eyes had filled with tears, but she was smiling from ear to ear and running for Michael who had gone to the MG with the suitcases.

"I love you," she said, kissing his mouth, his eyes, her tears streaking down both their faces. "I love you. You're so crazy. You rescued my wreck!"

"They put it back together, exactly the way it was. I didn't let them do anything to it, except what was absolutely necessary. You will forgive the concession to putting on a top."

"Oh, yes," Jennifer said, taking in the old familiar dents and bangs. "Isn't it beautiful?"

Michael's answer was to throw the bags in the back of the car.

When they were both in, Morey leaned down to the open window. "How far do you think this heap's gonna take you?"

Jennifer and Michael exchanged looks. Then to Morey, Michael said, "All the way . . ."

"To Venus," Jenny finished. She looked up into the blue expanse. It only seemed vacant of stars. It was all in the perspective . . .

"To Venus!" Michael shouted, and the MG lurched forward. It seemed to know the way.

Silhouette
Intimate Moments

more romance, more excitement

—————————— $2.25 each ——————————

Silhouette
Intimate Moments

more romance, more excitement

Silhouette Intimate Moments

Coming Next Month